The Forest Runners

A Story of the Great War Trail in Early Kentucky

Joseph A. Altsheler

The Forest Runners: A Story of the Great War Trail in Early Kentucky

ISBN: 978-1-61895-763-4

CONTENTS

CHAPTER I
PAUL

Paul stopped in a little open space, and looked around all the circle of the forest. Everywhere it was the same—just the curving wall of red and brown, and beyond, the blue sky, flecked with tiny clouds of white. The wilderness was full of beauty, charged with the glory of peace and silence, and there was naught to indicate that man had ever come. The leaves rippled a little in the gentle west wind, and the crisping grass bowed before it; but Paul saw no living being, save himself, in the vast, empty world.

The boy was troubled and, despite his life in the woods, he had full right to be. This was the great haunted forest of Kain-tuck-ee, where the red man made his most desperate stand, and none ever knew when or whence danger would come. Moreover, he was lost, and the forest told him nothing; he was not like his friend, Henry Ware, born to the forest, the heir to all the primeval instincts, alive to every sight and sound, and able to read the slightest warning the wilderness might give. Paul Cotter was a student, a lover of books, and a coming statesman. Fate, it seemed, had chosen that he and Henry Ware should go hand in hand, but for different tasks.

Paul gazed once more around the circle of the glowing forest, and the shadow in his eyes deepened. Henry and the horses, loaded with powder for the needy settlement, must be somewhere near, but whether to right or left he could not tell. He had gone to look for water, and when he undertook to return he merely went deeper and deeper into the forest. Now the boughs, as they nodded before the gentle breeze, seemed to nod to him in derision. He felt shame as well as alarm. Henry would not laugh at him, but the born scholar would be worth, for the time, at least, far less than the born trailer.

Yet no observer, had there been any, would have condemned Paul as he condemned himself. He stood there, a tall, slender boy, with a broad, high brow, white like a girl's above the line of his cap, blue eyes, dark and full, with the width between that indicates the mind behind, and the firm, pointed chin that belongs so often to people of intellect.

Paul and Henry were on their way from Wareville, their home, with horses hearing powder for Marlowe, the nearest settlement, nearly a hundred miles away. The secret of making powder from the nitre dust on the floors of the great caves of Kentucky had been discovered by the people of Wareville, and now they wished to share their unfailing supply with others, in order that the infant colony might be able to withstand Indian attacks. Henry Ware, once a captive in a far Northwestern tribe, and noted for his great strength and skill, had been chosen, with Paul Cotter, his comrade, to carry it. Both rejoiced in the great task, which to them meant the saving of Kentucky.

Paul's eyes were apt at times to have a dreamy look, as if he were thinking of things far away, whether of time or place; but now they were alive to the present, and to the forest about him. He listened intently. At last he lay down and put his ear to the earth, as he had seen Henry do; but he heard nothing save a soft, sighing sound, which he knew to be only the note of the wilderness. He might have fired his rifle. The sharp, lashing report would go far, carried farther by its own echoes; but it was more likely to bring foe than friend, and he refrained.

But he must try, if not one thing, then another. He looked up at the heavens and studied the great, red globe of the sun, now going slowly down the western arch in circles of crimson and orange light, and then he looked hack at the earth. If he had not judged the position of the sun wrong, their little camp lay to the right, and he would choose that course. He turned at once and walked swiftly among the trees.

Paul stopped now and then to listen. He would have uttered the long forest shout, as a signal to his comrade, but even that was forbidden. Henry had seen signs in the forest that indicated more than once to his infallible eye the presence of roving warriors from the north, and no risk must be taken. But, as usual, it was only the note of the wilderness that came to his ears. He stopped also once or twice, not to listen, but to look at the splendid country, and to think what a great land it would surely be.

He walked steadily on for miles, but the region about him remained unfamiliar. No smoke from the little camp-fire rose among the trees, and no welcome sight of Henry or the horses came to his eyes. For all he knew, he might be going farther from the camp at every step. Putting aside caution, he made a trumpet of his two hands, and uttered the long, quavering cry that serves as a signal in the forest. It came back in a somber echo from the darkening wilderness, and Paul saw, with a little shiver, that the sun was now going down behind the trees. The breeze rose, and the leaves rustled together with a soft hiss, like a warning. Chill came into the air. The sensitive mind of the boy, so much alive to abstract impressions, felt the omens of coming danger, and he stopped again, not knowing what to do. He called himself afraid, but he was not. It was the greater tribute to his courage that he remained resolute where another might well have been in despair.

The sun went down behind the black forest like a cannon shot into the sea, and darkness swept over the wilderness. Paul uttered the long cry again and again, but, as before, no answer came back; once he fired his rifle, and the sharp note seemed to run for miles, but still no answer.

Then he decided to take counsel of prudence, and sleep where he was. If he walked on, he might go farther and farther away from the camp, but if he stopped now, while he might not find Henry, Henry would certainly find him. Any wilderness trail was an open road to his comrade.

He hunted a soft place under one of the trees, and, despising the dew, stretched himself between two giant roots, his rifle by his side. He was tired and hungry, and he lay for a while staring at the blank undergrowth, but by and by all his troubles and doubts floated away. The note of the wind was soothing, and the huge roots sheltered him. His eyelids drooped, a singular feeling of peace and ease crept over him, and he was asleep.

It was yet the intense darkness of early night, and the outline of his figure was lost between the giant roots, but after a while a silver moon brought a gray tint to the skies, and the black bank over the forest began to thin and lighten. Then two figures, hideous in paint, crept from the undergrowth, and stared at the sleeping boy with pitiless eyes.

Paul slept on, and mercifully knew nothing of his danger; yet it would have been hard to find in the world two pairs of eyes that contained more savagery than those now gazing upon him. Their owners crept nearer, looking with fierce joy through the darkness at the sleeping boy who was so certainly their prey. Their code contained nothing that taught them to spare a foe, and this youth. In the van of the white invasion, was the worst of foes.

The boy still slept, and his slumber was deep, sweet, and dreamless. No warning came to him while the savage eyes, bright with cruel fire, crept closer and closer, and the merciful darkness, coming again, tried to close down and hide the approaching tragedy of the forest.

Paul returned with a jerk from his peaceful heaven. Hands

and feet were seized suddenly and pinned to the earth so tightly that he could not move, and he gazed up at two hideous, painted faces, very near to his own, and full of menace. The boy's heart turned for a moment to water. He saw at once, through his vivid and powerful imagination, all the terrors of his position, and in the same instant he leaped forward also to the future, and to the agony it had in store for him. But in a moment his courage came back, the strong will once more took command of the body and the spirit, and he looked up with stoical eyes at his captors. He knew that resistance now would be in vain, and, relaxing his muscles, he saved his strength.

The warriors laughed a little, a soundless laugh that was full of menace, and bound him securely with strips of buckskin cut from his own garments. Then they stood up, and Paul, too, rose to a sitting position, gazing intently at his captors. They were powerful men, apparently warriors of middle age, and Paul knew enough of costume and paint to tell that they were of the Shawnee nation, bitterly hostile to him and his kind.

His terrors came back upon him in full sweep. He loved life, and, scholar though he was, he loved his life in the young wilderness of Kentucky, where he was at the beginnings of things. Every detail of what they would do to him, every incident of the torture was already photographed upon his sensitive mind, but again the brave lad called up all his courage, and again he triumphed, keeping his body still and his face without expression. He merely looked up at them, as if placidly waiting their will.

The two warriors talked together a little, and then, seeming to change their minds, they unbound the boy's feet. One touched him on the shoulder, and, pointing to the north, started in that direction. Paul understood, and, rising to his feet, followed. The second warrior came close behind, and Paul was as securely a prisoner as if he were in the midst of a band of a hundred. Once or twice he looked around at the silent woods and thought of running, but it would have been the wildest folly. His hands tied, he could have been quickly overtaken, or, if not that, a bullet. He sternly put down the temptation, and plodded steadily on between the warriors, the broad, brown back of the one in front of him always leading the way.

It seemed to him that they sought the densest part of the undergrowth, where the night shadows lay thickest, and he was wise enough to know that they did it to hide their trail from possible pursuit. Then he thought of Henry, his comrade, the prince of trailers! He might come! He would come! Paul's blood leaped at the thought, and his head lifted with hope.

Clouds swept up, the moon died, and in the darkness Paul had little idea of direction. He only knew that they were still traveling fast amid the thick bushes, and that when he made too much noise in passing one or other of the brown savages would prod him with the muzzle of a gun as a hint to be more careful. His face became bruised and his feet weary, but at last they stopped in an opening among the trees, by the side of a little brook that trickled over shining pebbles.

The warriors wasted little time. They rebound Paul's feet in such tight fashion that he could scarcely move, and then, lying down near him, went to sleep so quickly that it seemed to Paul they accomplished the feat by some sort of a mechanical arrangement. Tired as he was, he could not close his own eyes yet, and he longed for his comrade. Would he come?

Paul's sensitive nerves were again keenly alive to every phase of his cruel situation. The warriors, lying almost at his feet, were monsters, not men, and this wilderness, which in its finer aspects he loved, was bristling in the darkness with terrors known and unknown. Yet his clogged and weary brain slept at last, and when he awoke again it was day—a beautiful day of white and gold light, with the autumnal tints of the forest all about him, and the leaves rustling in a gentle wind.

But his heart sank to the uttermost depths when he looked at the warriors. By day they seemed more brutal and pitiless than at night. From their long, narrow eyes shone no ray of mercy, and the ghastly paint on their high cheek bones deepened their look of ferocity. It was not the appearance of the warriors alone, it was more the deed for which they were preparing that appalled Paul. They were raking dead leaves and fallen brushwood of last year around a small but stout sapling, and they went on with their task in a methodical way.

Paul knew well, too well. Hideous tales of such doings had come now and then to his ears, but he had never dreamed that he, Paul Cotter, in his own person would be such a victim. Even now it seemed incredible in the face of this beautiful young world that stretched away from him, so quiet and so peaceful. He, who already in his boyhood was planning great things for this splendid land, to die such a death!

The warriors did not cease until their task was finished. It was but a brief one after all, for Paul had made no mistake in his guess. There was not time, perhaps, to take a prisoner beyond the Ohio, and they could not forego a savage pleasure. They dragged the hoy to the sapling, stood him erect against the slim trunk, and bound him fast with green withes. Then they piled the dead leaves and brushwood high about him above his knees, and, this done, stood a little way off and looked at their work.

The warriors spoke together for the first time since Paul had awakened, and their black eyes lighted up with a hideous glow of anticipation. Paul saw it, and an icy chill ran through all his veins. Had not the green withes held him, he would have fallen to the ground. Once more his active mind, foreseeing all that would come, had dissolved his strength for the moment; but, as always, his will brought his courage back, and he shut his eyes to put away the hateful sight of the gloating savages.

He had never asked in any way for mercy, he had never uttered a word of protest, and he resolved that he would not cry out if he could help it. They should not rejoice too much at his sufferings; he would die as they were taught to die, and he would show to them that the mind of a white boy could supply the place of a red man's physical fortitude. But Henry might come! Would he come? Oh, would he come? Resigned to death, Paul yet hoped for life.

He opened his eyes, and the warriors were still standing there, looking at him; but in a moment one approached, and, bending down, began to strike flint and steel amid the dry leaves at the boy's feet. Again, despite himself, the shivering chill ran through Paul's veins. Would Henry come? If he came at all, he must now come quickly, as only a few minutes were left.

The leaves were obstinate; sparks flew from the flint and steel, but there was no blaze. Paul looked down at the head of the warrior who worked patiently at his task. The second warrior stood on one side, watching, and when Paul glanced at him he saw the savage move ever so little, but as if driven by a sudden impulse, and then raise his head in the attitude of one who listened intently. Heat replaced the ice in Paul's veins. Had something moved in the forest? Was it Henry? Would he come?

The standing warrior uttered a low sound, and he who knelt with the flint and steel raised his head. Something had moved in the forest! It might be Henry. For Paul, the emotions of a life were concentrated in a single moment. Fear and hope tripped over each other, and the wilderness grew dim to his sight. A myriad of little black specks danced before his eyes, and the blood was beating a quick march in his ears.

The two savages were motionless, as if carved of brown

marble, and over all the wilderness hung silence. Then out of the silence came a sharp report, and the warrior who stood erect, rifle in hand, fell to the earth, stricken by instant death. Henry had come! His faithful comrade had not failed him! Paul shouted aloud in his tremendous relief and joy, forgetful of the second warrior.

The kneeling savage sprang to his feet, but he had made a fatal mistake. To light the fire for the torture, he had left his rifle leaning against the trunk of a tree twenty feet away, and before he could regain it a terrible figure bounded from the bushes, the figure of a great youth, clad in buckskin, his face transformed with anger and his eyes alight. Before the savage could reach his weapon he went down, slain by a single blow of a clubbed rifle, and the next moment Henry was cutting Paul loose with a few swift slashes of his keen hunting knife.

"I knew you would come! I knew it!" exclaimed Paul joyously and wildly, as he stood forth free. "Nobody in the world but you could have done it, Henry!"

"I don't know about that, Paul," said Henry, "but I'd have had you back sooner if it hadn't been for the dark. I followed you all night the best way I could, but I couldn't come up to you until day, and they began work then."

He glanced significantly at the leaves and brushwood, and then, handing Paul's rifle to him, looked at those belonging to the savages.

"We'll take 'em," he said. "It's likely we'll need 'em, and their powder and bullets will be more than welcome, too."

Paul was rubbing his wrists and ankles, where the blood flowed painfully as the circulation was restored, but to him the whole affair was ended. His life had been saved at the last moment, and the world was more brilliant and beautiful than ever. His imagination went quickly to the other extreme. There was no more danger.

But Henry Ware did not lose his eager, wary look. It did not take him more than a minute to transfer the ammunition of the warriors to the pouches and powder-horns of Paul and himself. Then he searched the forest with keen, suspicious glances.

"Come, Paul," he said, "we must run. The woods are full of the savages. I've found out that there's a great war party between us and Marlowe, and I've hid the powder in a cave. I turned the horses loose, hoping that we'll get 'em some time later; but just now you and I have to save ourselves."

Paul came back to earth. Danger still threatened! But he was free for the time, and he was with his comrade!

7

"You lead the way, Henry," he said. "I'll follow, and do whatever you say."

Henry Ware made no reply, but bent his ear again, in the attitude of one who listens. Paul watched his face attentively, seeking to read his knowledge there.

"The big war band is not far away," said Henry, "and it's likely that they've heard my shot. It would carry far on such a still, clear morning as this. I didn't want them to hear it."

"But I'm glad you did shoot," said Paul. "It was a mighty welcome sound to me."

"Yes," said Henry, with grim humor, "it was the right thing at the right time. Hark to that!" A single note, very faint and very far, rose and was quickly gone, like the dying echo of music. Only the trained ranger of the wilderness would have noticed it at all, but Henry Ware knew.

"Yes, they've heard," he said, "and they're telling it to each other. They are also telling it to us. They're between us and Marlowe, and they are between us and Wareville, so we must run to the north, and run as fast as we can."

He led the way with swift, light footsteps through the forest, and Paul followed close behind, each boy carrying on his shoulder two rifles and at his waist a double stock of bullets and powder.

Paul scarcely felt any fear now for the future. The revulsion from the stake and torture was so great that it did not seem to him that he could be taken again. Moreover, they had seized him the first time when he was asleep. They had taken an unfair advantage.

The sun rose higher, gilding the brown forest with fine filmy gold, like a veil, and the boys ran silently on among the trees and the undergrowth. Behind them, and spread out like a fan, came many warriors, fierce for their lives. Amid such scenes was the Great West won.

CHAPTER II
IN THE RIVER

Paul, while not the equal of Henry in the woods, was a strong and enduring youth. His muscles were like wire, and there were few better runners west of the mountains. Although the weight of the second rifle might tell after a while, he did not yet feel it, and with springy step he sped after Henry, leaving the choice of course and all that pertained to it to his comrade. After a while they heard a second cry—a wailing note—and Henry raised his head a little.

"They've come to the two who fell," he said.

But after the single lament, the warriors were silent, and Paul heard nothing more in the woods but their own light footsteps and his own long breathing. Little birds flitted through the boughs of the trees, and now and then a hare hopped up and ran from their path. The silence became terrible, full of omens and presages, like the stillness before coming thunder.

"It means something," said Henry; "I think we've stumbled into a regular nest of those Shawnees, and they're likely to be all about us."

As if confirming his words, the far, faint note came from their right, and then, in reply, from their left. Henry stopped so quickly that Paul almost ran into him.

"I was afraid it would be that way," he said. "They're certainly all around us except in front, and maybe there, too."

Visions of the torture rose before Paul again.

"What are we to do?" he said.

"We must hide."

"Hide I Why, they could find us in the forest, as I would find a man in an open field."

"I don't mean hide here," said Henry; "the river is just ahead, and I think that if we reach it in time we can find a place. Come, Paul, we must run as we never ran before."

The two boys sped with long, swift bounds through the forest as only those who run for their lives can run. Now the voices of the pursuit became frequent, and began to multiply. Henry, with his instinctive skill in the forest, read their meaning. The pursuers were sure of triumph. But Henry shut his lips tightly, and resolved that he and Paul should yet elude them.

"The river is not more than a half mile ahead," he said. "Come, Paul, faster! A little faster, if you can!"

Paul obeyed, and the two, bending their heads lower, sped on with astonishing speed. Trees and bushes slid behind them. Before them appeared a blue streak, that broadened swiftly and became a river.

"We must not let them see us," said Henry. "Bend as low as you can, and be as quiet as you can!"

Paul obeyed, and in a few more minutes they were at the river's edge.

"Fasten your bullets and powder around your neck," said Henry, "and keep the rifle on your shoulder."

Paul did so, following Henry's quick example, and the two stepped into the water, which soon reached to their waists. Henry had been along this river before, and at this crisis in the lives of his comrade and himself he remembered. Dense woods lined both banks of the stream, which was narrow here for miles, and a year or two before a hurricane had cut down the trees as a reaper mows the wheat. The surface of the water was covered with fallen trunks and boughs, and for a half mile at least they had become matted together like a great raft, out of which grass and weeds already were growing. But Paul did not know it, and suddenly he stopped.

"Why, what has become of the river?" he exclaimed, pointing ahead.

The stream seemed to stop against a bank of logs and foliage.

Henry laughed softly.

"It is the great natural raft," he said. "There is where we are to hide."

He hastened his steps, wading as rapidly as he could, and Paul kept by his side. He comprehended Henry's plan, their last and desperate chance. In a few moments more they were at the great raft, and in the bank, amid a dense, almost impenetrable mass of foliage, they hid their rifles and ammunition. Henry uttered a deep sigh as he did it.

"I hate like everything to leave them," he said, "but if we come to close quarters with any of those fellows, we must trust to our knives and hatchets."

Then he turned reluctantly away. It was not a deep river, nowhere above their necks, and he pushed a way amid the trees and foliage that were packed upon the surface, Paul, as usual, following closely. Now and then he dived under a big log, and came up on the other side, his head well hidden among upthrust boughs and among

10

the weeds and grass that had grown in the soil formed by the silt of the river. And Paul always carefully imitated him.

When they were about thirty yards into the mass Paul felt Henry's hand on his shoulder. "Look back, Paul," was whispered in his ear, "but be sure not to move a single bough." Paul slowly and cautiously turned his head, and saw a sight that made him quiver.

Running swiftly, savage warriors were coming into view on either bank of the river—tall men, dark with paint, and, as he well knew, hot with the desire to take life.

"I thank God that this place is here!" breathed Paul.

"Yes, it was just made for us," said Henry, and he laughed ever so little. "Come, Paul, we must get farther into it. But be sure you don't shake any boughs."

They waded on, only their heads above the current, and these always hidden by the interlacing trunks and branches. A great shout, fierce with triumph, rose behind them.

"They've found where our trail entered the water, and they think they've got us," whispered Henry. "Now, be still, Paul; we'll hide here."

They pushed themselves into a mass of debris, where logs and boughs, swept by the current, formed a little arch over the stream. There they stood up to their chins in water, with their heads covered by the arch. Through the slits between the trunks and boughs they could see their pursuers.

It was a numerous band—thirty or forty men—and they divided now into several parties. Some ran along the banks of the stream and others sprang from log to log over the raft, searching everywhere, with keen, black eyes trained to note every movement of the wilderness.

Paul felt Henry's hand again on his shoulder, but neither boy spoke. Both felt as if they were in a little cage, with the fiercest of all wild animals around it and reaching long paws through the bars at them. Each sank a little deeper into the water, barely leaving room to breathe, and watched their enemies still searching, searching everywhere. They heard the patter of moccasins on the logs, and now and then they saw brown, muscular legs passing by. Two warriors stopped within ten feet of them and exchanged comment. Henry, who understood their language, knew that they were puzzled and angry. But Paul, without knowing a word that they said, understood, too. His imagination supplied the place of knowledge. They were full of wrath because they had lost the trail of the two whom they had regarded as certainly theirs, and to seek them in the vast maze of logs and brush was like looking for one dead leaf among the millions.

The two warriors stood still for a full minute, and then moved on out of sight. Paul drew a deep breath of relief, like a sigh, and Henry's hand was pressed once more upon his shoulder.

"Not a sound yet, not a sound, Paul!" he whispered ever so softly. "They will hunt here a long time."

More warriors, treading on the logs, showed that his caution was not misplaced. They poked now and then in the water, amid the great mass of debris, and one stood on a log so near to the two lads that they could have reached out and touched his moccasined feet. But their covert was too close to be suspected, and soon the man passed on.

Presently all of them were out of sight; but Henry, a true son of caution and the wilderness, would not yet let Paul stir.

"They will come back this way," he said. "We risk nothing by waiting, and we may save much."

Paul made no protest, but he was growing cold. The chill from the water of the river was creeping into his veins, and he longed for the dry land and a chance to stir about. Yet he clenched his teeth and resolved to endure. He would not move until Henry gave the word.

He saw what a wise precaution it was, when, a half hour later, seven or eight warriors came walking back on the logs, and thrust with sticks into the little patches of open water between them. Henry and Paul crouched closer in their covert, and the warriors stalked back and forth, still searching.

Henry knew that the Shawnees, failing to find a place beyond the debris where the fugitives had emerged upon the bank, would believe that they might be hidden under the logs, and would not give up the hunt there. If they should happen to find the rifles and ammunition, they would certainly be confirmed in the conclusion, but so far they had not found them. Henry, looking between the logs, saw them pass near the place of concealment, but they did not stop, and were soon near the other bank. It would have bitterly hurt his pride if they had found the rifles, even had he and Paul escaped.

An hour more they waited, and then the last warrior was out of sight, gone up the river.

"I think we may crawl out now," whispered Henry; "but we've still got to be mighty careful about it."

Pad took a step and fell over in the water. His legs were stiff with the wet and cold; but Henry dragged him up, and before trying it again he stretched first one leg and then the other, many times.

"We must make our way back through the logs and brush to the rifles," whispered Henry, "and then take to the woods once more."

"I think I've lived in a river long enough to last me the rest of my life," Paul said.

Henry laughed. He, too, was stiff and cold; but, a born woodsman, he now dismissed their long hiding in the water as only an incident. The two reached the precious rifles and ammunition, drew them forth from concealment, and stepped upon the bank, rivulets pouring from their clothing, and even their hair.

"I think we'd better go back on our own trail now," said Henry. "The war party has passed on, and is still looking for us far ahead."

"We've got to dry ourselves, and somehow or other get that powder to Marlowe," said Paul.

"That's so," said Henry. "We came to do it, and we will do it."

He spoke with quiet emphasis, but Paul knew that he meant to perform what he had set out to do, come what might, and Paul was willing to go with him through anything. Neither would abandon the great task of helping to save Kentucky. But they were still in a most serious position. They had been many hours in water which was not now warmed by summer heat, and they were bound to feel the effect of it soon in every bone. Henry glanced up at the heavens. It was far past noon, and the golden sun was gliding down the western arch.

"I think," said Henry, "that it would be best for us to walk, as fast as we can on the back track, and then try to dry out our clothing a little."

He started at once, and Paul walked swiftly by his side. The rivulets that ran from their clothing decreased to tiny streams, and then only drops fell. The sinking sun shot sheaves of brilliant beams upon them, and soon Paul felt a grateful warmth, driving for the time the chill from his bones. He swung his arms as he walked, as much as the rifles would allow, and nearly every muscle in his frame felt the touch of vigorous exercise. His clothing dried rapidly.

Two hours and three hours passed, and they heard no more the cries of the warriors calling to each other. Silence again hung over the wilderness. Rabbits sprang up from the thickets. A deer, frightened by the sound of the boys' footsteps, held up his head, listened a moment, and then fled away among the trees. Henry took his presence as a sign that no other human being had passed that way in the last hour.

13

The sun sank, the twilight came and died, and darkness clothed the wilderness. Then Henry stopped.

"Paul," he said, "I've got some venison in my knapsack, but you and I ought to have a fire. While our clothes are drying outside they are still wet inside and we can't afford to have a chill, or be so stiff that we can't run. You know we may have another run or two yet."

"But do we dare make a fire?" asked Paul.

"I think so. I can hide the blaze, and the night is so dark that the smoke won't show."

He plunged deeper into the thickets, and came to a rocky place, full of gullies and cavelike hollows. It was so dark that Paul could see only his dim form ahead. Presently their course led downward, and Henry stopped in one of the sheltered depressions.

"Now we'll make our fire," he said.

It was pitchy black where they stood. The walls of the hollow rose far above their heads, and its crest was lined on every side with giant trees and dense undergrowth.

The two boys dragged up dead leaves and brushwood, and Henry patiently ignited the heap with his flint and steel. A tiny blaze arose, but he did not permit it to grow into a flame. Heavier logs were placed upon the top, and the fire only burned beneath, amid the small boughs. Smoke arose, but it was lost in the black heavens. The fire, thus confined, burned fiercely and rapidly within its narrow limits, and a fine bed of coals soon formed. It was time! The night had come on cold, and the chill returned to Paul's veins. Before the fire was lighted he had begun to shiver, but when the deep bed of coals was formed, he sat before it and basked in the grateful and glowing heat.

"I think we'd better take off our clothing and dry it," said Henry, and both promptly did so. They hung part of their garments before the fire, on a stick thrust in the ground, until they were dry, and then, putting them on again, replaced them with the remainder, to dry in their turn. Meanwhile they ate of the venison that Henry carried in his knapsack, and felt very happy. It was a wonderful experience for Paul. This was comfort and safety. They were only a pin point in the wilderness, but for the present the stony hollow fenced them about, and the hidden fire gave forth warmth and pleasure.

"Do you think you could sleep, Paul?" asked Henry, when they had put on again the last of the dried clothing.

Paul laughed.

14

"Could I sleep?" he said. "Would a hungry wolf eat? Will water run down hill? I don't think I could do anything else just now."

"Then try it," said Henry. "After a while I'll wake you up for your watch, and take a turn at it myself."

Paul said not another word, but sank back on the grass and leaves, with his feet to the great bed of coals. He saw their glow for a moment or two, then his eyelids shut down, and he was wafted away on a magic carpet to a dreamless region of happy peace. Henry's eyes, grown used to the dark, looked at him for a moment or two, and then the larger boy smiled. Paul, his faithful comrade, filled a great place in his heart—they liked each other all the better because they were so unlike—and he was silently, but none the less devoutly thankful that he had come.

Henry was warm and dry, and as he tested his muscles he found them supple and strong. Now he took precautions, thinking he had let the fire burn as long as was safe. He scattered the coals with a stick, and then softly crushed out each under the stout heel of his moccasin. With the minute patience that he had learned from his forest life, he persisted in his task until not a single spark was left anywhere. Then he sat down in Turkish fashion, with his rifle lying across his lap and the other rifles near, listening, always listening, with the wonderful ear that noted every sound of the forest, and piercing the thickets with eyes whose keenness those of no savage could surpass. He knew that they were in the danger zone, that the Shawnees were on a great man-hunt, and regarded the two boys as stilt within their net, although they could not yet put their hands upon them. That was why he listened and watched so closely, and that was why he would break his word to Paul and not waken him, keeping the nightlong vigil himself.

The night advanced, the darkness shredded away a little before a half moon, and Henry was very glad that he had put out the last remnant of the fire. Yet the trees still enclosed the hollow like a black wall, and he did not think a foe had one chance in a thousand of finding them there while the night lasted. But he never ceased to watch—a silent, powerful figure, with the rifle lying across his lap, ready to be used at a moment's notice. His stillness was something marvelous. Even had it been light, an ordinary observer would not have seen him move a hair's breadth. He was a part of the silent wilderness.

Midnight, and then the long hours. Faint noises arose in the thickets, bet the ear of the gray statue was alive, and he knew. The rabbits were hopping about, at play, perhaps, in the moonlight; a

15

deer was passing; perhaps a panther stirred somewhere; but these were things that neither he nor Paul feared; it was only man that they dreaded. After a while a faint, clear note rose, far to the east, and to it came three replies like it, and also far away. Henry laughed low. They were the familiar signals, but he and Paul were well hidden, and they would escape through the lines before morning. They might easily go back to Wareville, too, but he was resolved not to abandon either the horses or the powder. The powder was needed at Marlowe, and it would be a bitter humiliation not to take it there.

Two hours more passed, and then Henry heard the signals again, but now closer. By chance, perhaps, the Shawnees had formed their ring about the right place, and it was time to act. Paul had slept well and was rested, so Henry leaned over and shook him. Paul opened his eyes, and any question that he might have wished to ask was cut short at his lips by Henry's low, but commanding,

"Caution! Caution!"

"It is far after midnight, and we must move, Paul," said Henry. "They may have blundered on our trail before it was dark, and they are still looking for us. I think they are coming this way."

Paul understood in a moment, but he asked no question; if Henry said so, it was true, it did not matter how he knew. He rose, imitating Henry, taking his two rifles, and they stole silently away from the little cove that had been so full of comfort for both.

"We'll go toward the south now," said Henry, "and on your life, Paul, don't stumble!"

Paul knew the worth of this advice, and he was woodsman enough to avoid tripping on the vines and bushes, despite the darkness. One mile dropped behind them, then two, then three, and Henry suddenly put his hand upon the shoulder of Paul, who, understanding the signal, sank down at once beside his comrade.

The bushes were thick there, but Paul soon saw the danger, of which Henry's ear had already warned him. A dozen warriors marched in a silent file through the undergrowth. Well for the two that they were some distance away, and that the bushes grew thick and long! And well for them, too, that it was night! The warriors looked keenly on every side as they passed, apparently seeking out the last little leaf and twig; but, acute as were their eyes, they did not see the boys in the bushes. And perhaps it was well for some of them that they did not find what they sought, as the wilderness furnished no more formidable antagonist than Henry Ware, and Paul Cotter, too, was both brave and skillful.

But the warriors passed, and the black wilderness hid them.

Henry watched a little bush that one had brushed against, swinging in the moonlight with short jerks that became shorter until it grew quite still again. But he did not yet go. He and Paul knew that they must not move for many minutes. A warrior might turn on his track, see their risen forms, and with his cry bring the whole band back again. They yet lay motionless and still, while the moonlight filtered through the leaves and the silence of the forest endured. Henry rose at last, and led the way again.

"They are certainly beating up the woods for us," said he, "and I think that party will stumble right upon the little hollow where we rested. It was well we moved."

They increased their southward pace, and when it was scarcely two hours to the dawn Henry said:

"I know of a good place in which to rest, and a still better place in which to fight if they should find us."

"Where?"

"Holt's lone cabin. It's less than half a mile from here. I've had it in mind."

Paul did not know what he meant by Holt's lone cabin, but he was always willing to trust Henry without questions. His imagination, flowering at once into splendor, depicted it as some kind of an impregnable fortress.

"Come, we mustn't lose time!" said Henry, and he suddenly increased his speed, running so fast that Paul had much to do to keep pace with him. Paul looked up, and he saw why Henry hastened. The black curtain was rolled back a little in the east, and a splendid bar of gray appeared just at the horizon's edge. As Paul looked, it broadened and turned to silver, and then gold. Paul thought it a very phantasy of fate that the coming of day, which is like life, should bring such terrors.

They reached a clearing—a high, stony piece of ground—and in its center Paul saw a little old log cabin, with a heavy open door that sagged on rude wooden hinges.

"Come," said Henry, and they crossed the clearing to the cabin, pushing open the door. Paul looked around at the narrow place, and the protecting walls gave him much comfort. Evidently it had been abandoned in great haste. In one corner lay a tiny moccasin that had been a baby's shoe, and no one had disturbed it. On a hook on the wall hung a woman's apron, and two or three rude domestic utensils lay on the floor. The sight had Its pathos for Paul, but he was glad that the Holts had gone in time. He was glad, too, that they had left their house behind that he and Henry might use it

17

when they needed it most, because he began to be conscious now of a great weakness, both of body and spirit.

Hooks and a stout wooden bar still remained, and as Henry closed the door and dropped the bar into place, he exclaimed exultantly:

"They may get us, Paul, but they'll pay a full price before they do it."

"I'd rather they wouldn't get us at all," said Paul.

Nevertheless his imagination, leaping back to the other extreme, made the lone cabin the great fortress that he wished. And a fortress it was in more senses than one. Built of heavy logs, securely chinked, the single window and the single door closed with heavy oaken shutters, no bullet could reach them there. Paul sat down on a puncheon bench, and breathed laboriously, but joyously. Then he looked with inquiry at Henry.

"It was built by a man named Holt," said Henry. "He was either a great fool or a very brave man to come out here and settle alone. But a month ago, after the Indian wars began, he either became wiser or less brave, and he went into Marlowe with his family, leaving the place just as it is."

"He left in time," said Paul.

CHAPTER III
THE LONE CABIN

Henry was deeply thankful for this shelter because he knew how badly it was needed. He went to the single little window, which sagged half open on hinges made of the skin of the buffalo. He pushed it back in place, and fastened it, too, with a smaller bar, which he was lucky enough to find lying on the floor.

"Well, Paul, we are here," he said.

As he spoke he looked keenly and anxiously at his comrade.

"Yes, Henry," Paul replied. "Here we are, and mighty glad am I. It's good to be in a house again after that river."

Henry noticed at once that his voice was thinner and weaker than usual, and he saw also that the color on Paul's face was high— the rest and the little fire in the forest had not been enough. Again he was deeply grateful for the presence of the cabin. He looked around, with inquiring eyes that could see everything. It was dusky in the cabin with both door and window closed, but he observed with especial pleasure, among the abandoned articles, a small iron pot, suitable for cooking purposes, and a large water bowl. When he summed up all, it seemed to this resourceful son of the wilderness that Fortune had been very kind to them. Then he looked at Paul and distinctly saw a tremor pass over his frame.

"Paul," he said, "are you cold?"

"A little," replied Paul reluctantly. It hurt his pride to confess that he felt on the verge of physical collapse.

"Then we must have a fire, and I'm going to build it now."

"Won't it be dangerous?" asked Paul. "Won't it be seen?"

"Oh, no," replied Henry lightly. "We are alone in the forest now."

His tone was convincing to Paul, but Henry himself was aware that they were taking great risks. Yet they must be taken.

"Now, Paul," he said cheerfully, "you keep a good watch while I bring in deadwood. But first we will rake clean the welcoming hearth of our good friends who departed so quickly."

Ashes and dead coals were lying in the fireplace, and he raked them carefully to one side. Then he unbarred the door. The crisp October air rushed into the close, confined space, and it felt very welcome to Henry, but Paul shivered again.

"Sit down in one of those chairs and rest, Paul," he said, as he pointed to two homemade chairs that stood by the wall. "I'll be back in a minute or two."

Then he shut the door behind him.

"I must take the risk," he murmured. It was characteristic of Henry Ware, that in this emergency not even a vague thought of deserting his comrade entered his mind. And faithful as he was to Paul, Paul would have been as faithful to him. Both meant to finish together their great errand.

Henry looked around. The settler had made but little impression upon the surrounding forest. The trees had been cut away for a distance of fifteen or twenty paces on every side, but the wilderness still curved in solid array about the lone cabin, as if it would soon reclaim its own and blot out the sole sign of man's intrusion. Everywhere the foliage glowed with the deep reds and yellows and browns of October, and afar hung a faint bluish haze, like an early sign of Indian summer. The slight wind among the leaves had a soothing note, and breathed of nothing but peace. Peace Henry Ware devoutly hoped that it would be.

His task was easy. The forest all about was littered with the fallen and dead wood of preceding years, and in a few moments he gathered up an armful, with which he returned to the house. Then he brought in dry leaves, and heaped leaves and wood together in the chimney-place. He glanced at Paul and saw him trembling. As if by chance he touched his comrade's hand, and it felt ice-cold. But he did not depart one jot from his cheerful manner, all his words showing confidence.

"Now, Paul," he said, "In less than a minute you'll see burning before you the finest, warmest, glowingest and most comfortable fire in all the West."

Paul's eyes glistened.

Henry drew forth flint and steel, and with a few strokes sent out the vivifying spark. The dry leaves caught, a light flame formed, the wood caught in its turn, and then the blaze, leaping high, roared up the chimney. In a moment the hearth was glowing, and presently a bed of deep red coals began to grow.

Paul uttered a low laugh of joy, and spread out his hands to the flames. The red light glowed across the delicately cut but strong face of the boy, and Henry noticed now that all his color was gone, leaving his features white and drawn.

"Sit a little closer, Paul, a little closer," he said, still in tones of high, good cheer. "Isn't it the most beautiful fire you ever saw?"

"Yes," said Paul, "it is. It looks mighty good, but it's curious that it doesn't warm me more."

Henry had closed the door, and it was already very hot in the cabin; but he decided now on another step—one that would take more time, but it must be taken.

"Paul," he said, "I'm going out in the woods to look for something, and I may be gone at least half an hour. Take good care of our house while I'm away."

"All right," said Paul. But as he spoke his teeth struck together.

Henry closed the door once more, with himself on the outside. Then he walked to the edge of the clearing, and looked back at the cabin. He had been careful to choose the kind of wood that would give out the least smoke, and only a thin column rose from the chimney. The wind caught it before it rose far, and it was lost among the great trees of the wilderness. It seemed again to Henry Ware that Fortune was kind to them.

The single look sufficed, and then, drawing his long-bladed hunting knife from its sheath, he began to search the forest. Henry Ware had been long a captive among the Northwestern Indians, and he had learned their lore. He had gained from the medicine men and old squaws a knowledge of herbs, and now he was to put it to use. He sought first for the bitter root called Indian turnip, and after looking more than twenty minutes found it. He dug it up with his sharp knife, and then, with another search of a quarter of an hour, he found the leaves of wild sage, already dried in the autumn air. A third quarter of an hour and he added to his collection two more herbs, only the Indian names of which were known to him. Then he returned to the house, to find that the icy torrent in Paul's blood had now become hot.

"I can't stand this, Henry," he said. "We've got the door and window closed and a big fire burning, and I'm just roasting hot."

"Only a little while longer," said Henry. "The truth is, Paul, you've had a big chill, and now the fever's come on you. But I'm Dr. Ware, and I'm going to cure you. When I was up there among the Indians, I learned their herb remedies, and mighty good some of 'em are, too. They're particularly strong with chills and fever, and I'm going to make you a tea that'll just lay hold of you and drive all the fever out of your veins. What you want to do, Paul, is to sweat, and to sweat gallons."

He spoke in rapid, cheerful tones, wishing to keep up Paul's spirits, in which effort he succeeded, as Paul's eyes sparkled, and a gleam of humor lighted up his face.

21

"Well, Dr. Ware," he said, "I'm mighty glad to know what's the matter with me. Somehow you always feel better when you know, and I'll trust to your tea."

He meant what he said. He knew Henry too well to doubt him. Any assertion of his inspired him with supreme confidence.

"Now, Paul," Henry resumed, "you keep house again, and I'll find where our unknown friend got his drinking water."

He took the iron pot that he had noticed and went forth into the forest. It was an instinctive matter with one bred in the wilderness like Henry Ware to go straight to the spring. The slope of the land led him, and he found it under the lee of a little hill, near the base of a great oak. Here a stream, six inches broad, an inch deep, but as clear as burnished silver, flowed from beneath a stony outcrop in the soil, and then trickled away, in a baby stream, down a little ravine. There was a strain of primitive poetry, the love of the wild, in Henry's nature, and he paused to admire.

He saw that human hands had scraped out at the source a little fountain, where one might dip up pails of water, and looking down into the clear depths he beheld his own face reflected back in every detail. It seemed to Henry Ware, who knew and loved only the wilderness, that the cabin, with its spring and game at its very doors, would have made a wonderfully snug home in the forest. Had it been his own, he certainly would have undertaken to defend it against any foe who might come.

But all these thoughts passed in a second, treading upon one another's heels. Henry was at the fountain scarcely a moment before he had filled the pot and was on the way back to the cabin. Then he cast in the herbs, put it upon a bed of red coals, and soon a steam arose. He found an old, broken-sided gourd among the abandoned utensils, and was able to dip up with it a half dozen drinks of the powerful decoction. He induced his comrade to swallow these one after another, although they were very bitter, and Paul made a wry face. Then he drew from the corner the rude bedstead of the departed settler, and made Paul lie upon it beside the fire.

"Now go to sleep," he said, "while I watch here."

Paul was a boy of great sense, and he obeyed without question, although it was very hot before the fire. But it was not a dry, burning heat that seemed to be in the blood; it was a moist, heavy heat that filled the pores. He began to feel languid and drowsy, and a singular peace stole over him. It did not matter to him what happened. He was at rest, and there was his faithful comrade on guard, the comrade who never failed. The coals glowed deep red, and the sportive flames danced before him. Happy visions passed through his brain, and then his eyes closed. The red coals passed away and the sportive flames ceased to dance. Paul was asleep.

Henry Ware sat in silence on one of the chairs at the corner of the hearth, and when Paul's breathing became long, deep, and regular, he saw that he had achieved the happy result. He rose soundlessly, and put his hand upon Paul's forehead. It came back damp. Paul was in a profuse perspiration, and his fever was sinking rapidly. Henry knew now that it was only a matter of time, but he knew equally well that in the Indian-haunted wilderness time was perhaps the most difficult of all things to obtain.

No uneasiness showed in his manner. Now the lad, born to be a king of the wilderness, endowed with all the physical qualities, all the acute senses of a great, primitive age, was seen at his best. He was of one type and his comrade of another, but they were knitted together with threads of steel. It had fallen to his lot to do a duty in which he could excel, and he would shirk no detail of it.

He brought in fresh wood and piled it on the hearth. At a corner of the cabin stood an old rain barrel half full of water. He emptied the barrel and brought it inside. Then, by means of many trips to the little spring with the iron pot, he filled it with fresh water. All the while he moved soundlessly, and Paul's deep, peaceful slumber was not disturbed. He took on for the time many of the qualities that he had learned from his Indian captors. Every sense was alert, attuned to hear the slightest sound that might come from the forest, to feel, in fact, any alien presence as it drew near.

When the store of water was secure he looked at their provisions. They had enough venison in their knapsacks to last a day or two, but he believed that Paul would need better and tenderer food. The question, however, must wait a while.

The day was now almost gone. Great shadows hovered over the eastern forest, and in the west the sun glowed in its deepest red as it prepared to go. Henry put his hand upon Paul's forehead again. The perspiration was still coming, but the fever was now wholly gone. Then he took his rifle and went to the door. He stood there a moment, a black figure in the red light of the setting sun. Then he slid noiselessly into the forest. The twilight had deepened, the red sun had set, and only a red cloud in the sky marked its going. But Henry Ware's eyes pierced the shadows, and none in the forest could have keener ears than his. He made a wide circle around the cabin, and found only silence and peace. Here and there were tracks and traces of wild animals, but they would not disturb; it was for something else that he looked, and he rejoiced that he could not find it. When he returned to the cabin the last fringe of the red cloud was gone from the sky, and black darkness was sweeping down over the earth. He secured the door, looked again to the fastenings of the window, and then sat down before the fire, his rifle between his knees.

Paul's slumber and exhaustion alike were so deep that he would not be likely to waken before morning, so Henry judged, and presently he took out a little of the dried venison and ate it. He would boil some of it in the pot in the morning for Paul's breakfast, but for himself it was good enough as it now was. His strong white teeth closed down upon it, and a deep feeling of satisfaction came over him. He, too, was resting from great labors, and from a task well done. He realized now, for the first time, how great a strain had been put upon him, both mind and body.

The night was sharp and chill, but it was very warm and comfortable in the little cabin. Paul slept on, his breathing as regular as the ticking of a clock, healthy color coming back into his pale face as he slept. Henry's own eyes began to waver. A deep sense of peace and rest soothed him, heart and brain. He had meant to watch the night through, but even he had reached the limit of endurance. The faint moaning of the wind outside, like the soft, sweet note of a violin, came to his ears, and lulled him to slumber. The fire floated far away, and, still sitting in his chair with his rifle between his knees, he slept.

Outside the darkness thickened and deepened. The forest was a solid black, circling wall, and the cabin itself stood in deepest shadow. Inside a fresh piece of wood caught, and the blaze burned brighter and higher. It threw a glow across the faces of the two boys, who slept, the one lying upon the bed and the other sitting in the chair, with the rifle between his knees. It was a scene possible only in the great wilderness of Kain-tuck-ee.

Meanwhile word was sent by unknown code through the surrounding forest to all its inhabitants that a great and portentous event had occurred. Not long before they had welcomed the departure of the strange intruder, who had come and cut down the forest and built the house. Then, with the instinct that leaped into the future, they saw the forest and themselves claiming their own again; the clearing would soon be choked with weeds and bushes, the trees would grow up once more, the cabin would rot and its roof fall, and perhaps the bear or the panther would find a cozy lair among its timbers.

Now the strange intruders had come again. The fox, creeping to the edge of the clearing, saw with his needlelike eyes a red gleam through the chinks of the cabin. The red gleam smote him with terror, and he slunk away. The wolf, the rabbit, and the deer came; they, too, saw the red gleam, and fled, with the same terror striking at their hearts. All, after the single look, sank back into the shadows, and the forest was silent and deserted. Paul and Henry, as they slept, were guarded by a single gleam of fire from all enemies save human kind.

But as the night thickened there had been a whirring in the air not far away. An hour earlier the twilight had been deepened by something that looked like a great cloud coming before the sun. It was a cloud that moved swiftly, and it was made of a myriad of motes, closely blended. It resolved itself soon into a vast flock of wild pigeons, millions and millions flying southward to escape the coming winter.

Presently they settled down upon the forest for the night, and all the trees were filled with the chattering multitude. Often the bough bent almost to the ground beneath the weight of birds, clustered so thick that they could scarcely find a footing. The fox and the wolf that had looked at the lone cabin came back now to seek, an easier prey.

Henry Ware slept until far after midnight, and then he awoke easily, without jerk or start. The fire had burned down, and a deep bed of coals lay on the hearth. Paul still slept, and when Henry touched him he found that he had ceased to perspire. No trace of the fever was left. Yet he would be very weak when he awoke, and he would need nourishing food. It was his comrade's task to get it. Henry took his rifle and went outside. The moon was shining now, and threw a dusky silver light over all the forest. He might find game, and, if so, he resolved to risk a shot. The chances were that no human being save himself would hear it. He felt rather than saw that nothing had happened while he slept. No enemy to be feared had come, while all his own strength and elasticity had returned to him. Never had he felt stronger or more perfectly attuned in body and mind.

He moved again in a circuit about the cabin, watching carefully, and now and then looking up among the trees. Perhaps an opossum might be hanging from a bough! But he saw nothing until he widened his circuit, and then he ran directly into the myriads of wild pigeons. Here was food for an army, and he quickly secured plenty of it. The danger of the rifle report was gone, as he had

25

nothing to do but take a stick and knock off a bough as many of the pigeons as he wished. Then he hastened back to the cabin with his welcome burden. Paul still slept, and it pleased Henry to give him a surprise. He kindled the fire afresh, cleaned two of the youngest, fattest, and tenderest of the pigeons, and began to boil them in the pot.

When the water simmered and pleasant odors arose, he was afraid that Paul would awake, as he turned once or twice on his bed and spoke a few incoherent words. But he continued to sleep, nevertheless, and at last the pigeon stew was ready, throwing out a savory odor.

The day was now coming, and Henry opened the window. The forest, wet with morning dew, was rising up into the light, and afar in the east shone the golden glory of the sun. He drew a deep breath of the fresh, good air, and decided to leave the window open. Then he filled the broken gourd with the grateful stew, and, holding it in his right hand, shook Paul violently with his left. Paul, who had now slept his fill, sat up suddenly and opened his eyes.

"Here, Paul, open your mouth," said Henry commandingly, "and take this fine stew. Dr. Ware has prepared it for you specially, and it is sure to bring hack your strength and spirits. And there's plenty more of it."

Paul sniffed hungrily, and his eyes opened wider and wider.

"Why—why, Henry!" he exclaimed. "How long have I slept, and where did you get this?"

"You've slept about twenty hours, more or less," replied Henry, laughing with satisfaction, "and this is wild pigeon stew. Fifteen or twenty millions roosted out there in the forest last night, and they won't miss the dozen or so that I've taken. Here, hurry up; I'm hungry, and it's my turn next."

Paul said no more, but, thankful enough, took the stew and ate it. Then, by turns, they used the broken gourd and ate prodigiously, varied by drinks from the water barrel. They had fasted long, they had undergone great exertions, and it took much to remove the sharp edge from their appetites. But it was done at last, and they rested content.

"Henry," said Paul, upon whose mind the fortunate advent of the wild pigeons made a deep impression, "while we have had great mischances, it seems to me also that we have been much favored by Providence. Our finding of this cabin was just in time, and then came the pigeons as if specially for us. You remember in the Bible how the Lord sent the manna in the wilderness for the Israelites; it seems to me that He's doing the same thing for us."

26

"It looks so," replied Henry reverently. "The Indians with whom I once lived think that the Great Spirit often helps us when we need it most, and I suppose that their Great Spirit—or Manitou, as they call Him—is just the same as our God."

Both boys were now silent for a while. They had been reared by devout parents. Life in the forest deepens religious belief, and it seemed to them that there had been a special interposition in their favor.

"What are we going to do now?" asked Paul at length.

"We can't take up our journey again for a day or two," replied Henry. "We've got to get that powder to Marlowe some time or other. Wareville sent us to do the job, and we'll do it; but you are yet too weak, Paul, to start again. You don't know how really weak you are. Just you get up and walk about a little."

Paul rose and walked back and forth across the room, but in a few moments he became dizzy and had to sit down. Then he uttered an impatient little cry.

"You're right, Henry," he said, "and I can't help it. Find the horses and take the powder to Marlowe by yourself. I guess I can get back to Wareville, or come on later to Marlowe."

Henry laughed.

"You know I wouldn't dream of doing such a thing, Paul," he said. "Besides, I don't think they need to be in any hurry at Marlowe for that powder. We'll rest here two or three days, and then take a fresh start."

Paul said no more. It would have been a terrible blow to him to have no further share in the enterprise, but he had forced himself nevertheless to make the offer. Now he leaned back luxuriously, and was content to wait.

"Of course," said Henry judicially, "we run risks here. You know that, Paul"

"Everybody who lives in Kentucky runs risks, and big ones," said Paul.

"Then we'll sit here for the present and watch the forest. I don't like to keep still, but it's a fine country to look at, isn't it, Paul?"

The love of the wilderness was upon Henry, and his eyes glowed as he looked at the vast surrounding forest, the circling wall of deep-toned, vivid colors. For him, danger, if absent, did not exist, and there was inspiration in the crisp breeze that came over a thousand miles of untenanted woods. He sat in the doorway, the door now open, and stretched his long legs luxuriously. He was

27

happy; while he might be anxious to go on with the powder, he pined for neither Wareville nor Marlowe for their own sakes.

Paul looked at his comrade with understanding and sympathy. The forest made its appeal to him also, but in another way; and since Henry was content, he would be content, too. Used as he was to hardships and narrow quarters, the little cabin would not be a bad place in which to pass two or three days. He turned back to the fire and held out his hands before the mellow blaze.

Henry examined the forest again, widening his circle, and saw no traces of an enemy. He judged that they had passed either to east or west, and that he and Paul would not be molested just yet, although he had no confidence in their permanent security. He saw a deer, but in view of their bountiful supply of pigeons he did not risk a shot, and returned before noon, to find Paul rapidly regaining his strength. He cooked two more of the pigeons in their precious iron pot, and then they rested.

They left both door and window open now, and they could see forest and sky. Henry called attention to a slight paleness in the western heavens, and then noted that the air felt damp.

"It will rain to-night, Paul," he said, "and it is a good thing for you, in your weakened condition, that we have a roof."

They ate pigeon again for supper, and their wilderness appetites were too sharp to complain of sameness. They had barred window and door, and let the fire die down to a bed of glowing coals, and while they ate, Paul heard the first big drops of rain strike on the board roof. Other drops came down the chimney, fell in the coals, and hissed as they died. Paul shivered, and then felt very good indeed in the dry little cabin.

"You were a real prophet, Henry," he said. "Here's your storm."

"Not a storm," said Henry, "but a long, cold, steady rain. Even an Indian would not want to be out in it, and bear and panther will hunt their holes."

The drops came faster, and then settled into a continuous pour. Paul, after a while, opened the window and looked out. Cold, wet air struck his face, and darkness, almost pitchy, enveloped the cabin. Moon and stars were gone, and could not see the circling wail of the forest. The rain beat with a low, throbbing sound on the board roof, and, with a kind of long sigh, on the ground outside. It seemed to Paul a very cold and a very wet rain indeed, one that would be too much for any sort of human beings, white or red.

"I think, we're safe to-night, Henry," he said, as he closed and fastened the window.

"Yes, to-night," replied Henry.

Paul slept a dreamless sleep, lulled by the steady pour of the rain on the roof, and when he awoke in the morning the sun was shining brightly, without a cloud in the sky. But the forest dripped with rain. He was strong enough now to help in preparing the breakfast, and Henry spoke with confidence of their departure the next morning.

The hours passed without event, but when Henry went as usual through the forest that afternoon, he came upon a footprint. He followed it and found two or three more, and then they were lost on rocky ground. The discovery was full of significance to him, and he thought once of hurrying back to the cabin, and of leaving with Paul at once. But he quickly changed his mind. In the forest they would be without defense save their own strong arms, while the cabin was made of stout logs. And perhaps the danger would pass after all. Already the twilight was coming, and in the darkness his own footprints would not be seen.

Paul was at the door when Henry returned, and he did not notice anything unusual in his comrade's face, but Henry advised that they stay inside now. Then he looked very carefully to the bars of the door and the window, and Paul understood. The danger flashed instantly on his mind, but his strong will prepared him to meet it.

"You think we are likely to be besieged?" he said.

"Yes," replied Henry.

Paul did not ask why Henry knew. It was sufficient that he did know, and he examined his arms carefully. Then began that long period of waiting so terrible to a lad of his type. It seemed that the hours would never pass. The coals on the hearth were dead now, and there was no light at all in the cabin. But his eyes grew used to the dusk, and he saw his comrade sitting on one of the benches, one rifle across his lap and the other near, always listening.

Paul listened, too. The night before the rain had fallen on the board roof with a soothing sound, but now he could hear nothing, not even the wind among the trees. He began to long for something that would break this ominous, deadly silence, be it ever so slight— the sound of a falling nut from a tree, or of a wild animal stirring in the undergrowth—but nothing came. The same stillness, heavy with omens and presages, reigned in all the forest.

CHAPTER IV
THE SIEGE

The whole night passed without event and the day came. Paul saw the light grow deeper and deeper, but nothing stirred in the forest. It stretched before him, a living curve of glowing red and yellow and brown, but it was now like a sea of dangerous depths, and the little cabin was their sole island of safety.

"It's a good thing we brought the extra rifles with us," said Henry. "They look like good weapons, and they may save us in case of a rush. Ah, there they come!"

Paul had noticed nothing, but Henry had seen the bushes at the edge of the forest quiver, and then move contrary to the wind. His eye did not rest upon any brown body, but he knew as well as if they had cried out that the warriors were there. How many? That was the question that concerned him most. If a great war party, they might hang on a long time; but if only a small one, he and Paul might beat them off as often as they came. They had four rifles, plenty of ammunition, enough food to last several days, and he thanked God for the providential presence of the rain barrel.

These were but brief passing thoughts, and he never ceased to watch the forest. Still no sign of a face, but now and then the unnatural quiver of the bushes, and above them the sun spinning a fine golden, veil over all the great wilderness.

"Our guests have come, Paul," said he, "but from safe cover they are inspecting our front yard."

"And they don't know yet whether or not they would like to disport themselves on our lawn."

"That is just it. They have doubts about their welcome."

"That being so," said Paul, in the light, jesting spirit that he loved, "I'll just wait until they knock at our door. Meanwhile I'll take a drink from that lucky cistern of ours."

He bent his head into the barrel, and as he drank he felt fresh strength and courage rushing into his veins.

"It was great luck, wasn't it, to find this barrel?" he said.

"It certainly was," replied Henry, and his words came from the bottom of his heart. "Now you watch while I take a drink."

Paul did so, but he noticed nothing unusual in the woods. The faint signs that Henry read with such an unerring eye were hidden from him. But his skill was sufficient to cover all the cleared space. No warrior could pass there unseen by him. Henry rejoined him.

"You watch from one side and I'll take the other," he said.

They did so, but the single room of the cabin was so small that they were only a few feet from each other, and could talk together in low tones.

"It will be a trial of patience," said Henry. "The Indian always has more time than anybody else in the world, and he is willing to make the most of it."

Paul, too, knew that Shawnees, no matter what their numbers, would not yet risk a headlong attack on the cabin, and now his curiosity as to what they would do was aroused. It was surprise that Henry and he must guard against. What was to be expected? His sense of curiosity was as keenly aroused as his sense of danger.

Over an hour dragged slowly by, minute by minute. The sun blazed brilliantly over the wilderness, and the shut little cabin grew close and hot. No fresh air came except by the loopholes, and it was not enough for coolness. Paul's forehead grew damp, and his eyes ached from continual watching at the loophole. Curiosity now began to give way to anger. If they were going to do anything, why didn't they do it? He watched the forest so much and so intently that he began to create images there for himself. A tall stump was distorted into the figure of an Indian warrior, a clump of bushes took the shape of an entire group of Shawnees, and many savage, black eyes looked from the leaves. Paul's reason told him that he beheld nothing, but his fancy put them there, nevertheless. He saw presently a little jet of smoke, rising like a white feather; he heard a report, and then the sound of a bullet burying itself with a soft sigh in a log of the cabin. He laughed at the futility of it, but Henry said:

"They're just trying us a little—skirmishing, so to speak. Be careful there, Paul! A chance bullet might catch you in the eye at the loophole."

More lead came from the forest, and there was a sharp crackle of rifle fire. Bullets thudded into the stout walls of the cabin, and Paul's soul swelled with derision. His vivid mind pictured himself as safe from the warriors as if they were a thousand miles away. He was attracted suddenly by a slight, gurgling sound, and then a cry of dismay from Henry. He wheeled in alarm. Henry had sprung to the water barrel, the precious contents of which were oozing from a little round hole in the side, about two thirds of the way up. A bullet had entered one of the loopholes and struck the barrel. It was an unfortunate chance, one in a thousand, and had not Henry's acute

31

ear detected at once the sound of flowing water, it might have proved a terrible loss.

But Henry was rapidly stuffing a piece of buckskin, torn from his hunting shirt, into the little round hole, and he waved Paul back to the wall.

"You stay there and watch, Paul," he said. "I'll fix this."

The buckskin stopped all the flow but a slight drip. Then, with his strong hunting knife, he cut a piece of wood from the bench, whittled it into shape, and drove it tightly into the bullet hole.

"That's all secure," he said, with a sigh of relief. "Now I must get it out of range."

He wheeled it to a point in the cabin at which no chance bullet could reach it, and then resumed the watch with Paul.

"Aren't you glad, Paul," said Henry, "that you were not in the place of the water barrel?"

"Yes," replied Paul lightly, "because a piece of buckskin and a round stick wouldn't have healed the damage so quickly."

He spoke lightly because he was still full of confidence. The little cabin was yet an impregnable castle to him. The crackle of rifle fire died, the last plume of white smoke rose over the forest, drifted away, and was lost in the brilliant sunshine. Silence and desolation again held the wilderness.

"Nothing will happen for some hours now," said Henry cheerfully, "so the best thing that we can do, Paul, is to have dinner."

"Yes," said Paul, with his quick fancy. "We can dine sumptuously—venison and pigeon and spring water."

"And lucky we are to have them," said Henry.

They ate of the venison and pigeon, and they drank from the barrel. They were not creatures of luxury and ease, and they had no complaint to make. When they finished, Henry said:

"Paul, you ought to take a nap, and then you'll be fresh for to-night, when things will be happening."

Paul at first was indignant at the idea that he should go to sleep with the enemy all about them, but Henry soon persuaded him what a wise thing it would be. Besides, the air was all the time growing closer and warmer in the little cabin, and he certainly needed sleep. His head grew heavy and his eyelids drooped. He lay down on the bed, and in a surprisingly quick time was slumbering soundly.

Henry looked at the sleeping lad, and his look was a compound of great friendship and admiration. He knew that Paul was not, like himself, born to the wilderness, and he respected the courage and skill that could triumph nevertheless. But it was only a fleeting look. His eyes turned back to the forest, where he watched lazily; lazily, because he knew with the certainty of divination that they would not attempt anything until dark, and he knew with equal certainty that they would attempt something then.

He awakened Paul in two hours, and took his place on the bench. He had not slept at all the night before, when they were expecting a foe who had not yet come, and he, too, must be fresh when the conflict was at hand.

"When you see shadows in the clearing, wake me, without fail, Paul," he said.

Then he closed his eyes, and like Paul slept almost at once. Neither the weary waiting nor the danger could upset his nerves so much that sleep would not come, and his slumber was dreamless.

The afternoon waned. Paul, peeping from the loophole, saw the sun, red like fire, seeking its bed in the west, but the shadows were not yet over the clearing. Refreshed by his sleep, and his nerves steadied, he no longer saw imaginary figures in the wilderness. It was just a wall of red and yellow and brown, and it was hard to believe that men seeking his life lay there. By and by the east began to turn gray, and over the clearing fell the long shadows of coming twilight. Then Paul awakened Henry, and the two watched together.

The shadows lengthened and deepened, a light wind arose and moaned among the oaks and beeches, a heavy, dark veil was drawn across the sky, and the forest melted into a black blur. Now Henry looked with all his eyes and listened with all his ears, because he knew that what the warriors wanted, the covering veil of the night, had come.

It was a very thick and black night, too, and that was against him and Paul, as the objects in the clearing were hidden almost as well now as anything in the forest. Hence he trusted more to ear than to eye. But he could yet hear nothing, save the wind stirring the leaves and the grass. Inside the little cabin it grew dark, too, but their trained eyes, becoming used to the gloom, were able to see each other well enough for all the needs of the defense.

Time passed slowly on, and to Paul every moment was tense and vivid. The darkness was far more suggestive of danger than the day had been. He took his eyes now and then from the loophole, for a moment, to glance at Henry's face, and about the third or fourth time he saw a sudden light leap into the eyes of his comrade. The

33

next instant Henry thrust his rifle into the loophole and, taking quick aim, fired.

A long, quavering cry arose, and after that came a silence that lay very still and deadly upon Paul's soul. Henry had seen in the shadow a deeper shadow quiver, and he had fired instantly but with deadly aim. Paul, looking through the loophole on his own side of the cabin, could see nothing for a little space, but presently arose a patter of feet, and many forms darted through the dusk toward the cabin. He quickly fired one rifle, and then the other, but whether his bullets hit he could not tell. Then heavy forms thudded against the log walls of the hut, and through the loophole he heard deep breathing.

"They've gained the side of the cabin," said Henry, "and we can't reach 'em with our rifles now."

"I did my best, Henry," said Paul ruefully. Conflict did not appeal to him, but the wilderness left no choice.

"Of course, Paul," said Henry, with every appearance of cheerfulness, "it's not your fault. In such darkness as this they were bound to get there. But they are not inside yet by a long sight. Be sure you don't get in front of any of the loopholes."

There came a heavy push at the door, but neither it nor the bar showed the slightest sign of giving way. Henry laughed low.

"They can't get enough warriors against that door to push it in," he said.

The two boys rapidly reloaded the empty rifles, and now each crouched against the wall, where no chance bullet through a loophole could reach him. An eye unused to the darkness could have seen nothing there. Their figures were blended against the logs, and they did not speak, but each, listening intently, could hear what was going on outside. Paul's fancy, as usual, added to the reality. He heard men moving cautiously, soft footfalls going pit-a-pat, pit-a-pat around the cabin, and it seemed to him a stray word of advice or caution now and then.

The silence was broken suddenly by a blaze of fire that seemed to come through the wall, a report that roared like a cannon in the cabin. A spurt of smoke entered at one of the holes, and a bullet burled itself in the opposite wall. A savage had boldly thrust the muzzle of his rifle into a loophole and fired.

"Be still, Paul," whispered Henry. "They can't hit us, and they are wasting their ammunition."

A second shot was tried by the besiegers, but the result was only the roaring, echoing report, the smoke and the flame, and the bullet that found a vain target of wood. But to Paul, with an imagination fed by stories of mighty battles, it was like a cannonade. Great guns were trained upon Henry and himself. A thin, fine smoke from the two shots had entered the cabin, and it floated about, tickling his nostrils, and adding, with its savor, to the fever that began to rise in his blood. He dropped to his knees, and was creeping, rifle ready, toward one of the loopholes, eager with the desire to fire back, when Henry's strong hand fell upon his shoulder.

"I understand what you want, Paul," he whispered. "I, too, feel it, but it pays us to wait. Let 'em waste their lead."

Paul stopped, ashamed of himself, and his blood grew cooler. He was not one to wish anybody's life, and again his mind rebelled at the necessity of conflict.

"Thank you, Henry," he said, and resumed his place by the wall.

No more shots were fired. The warriors could not know whether or not their bullets had hit a human mark, and Henry inferred that they would wait a while, crouched against the cabin. He reckoned that when they did move they would attack the door, and he noiselessly made an additional prop for it with the heavy wooden bench. But the faint sound of footsteps suddenly ceased, and Henry, listening intently, could hear nothing save the rising wind. He looked through one of the loopholes, but he could not see anything of the savages. Either they were still crouching against the wall, or had slipped back to the forest. But he saw enough to tell him that the night was growing cloudy, and that the air was damp.

Presently rain fell in a slow drizzle, but Henry still watched at the loophole, and soon he caught a glimpse of two parallel rows of men bearing something heavy, and approaching the cabin. They had secured a tree trunk, and would batter down the door; but they must come within range, and Henry smiled to himself. Then he beckoned to Paul to come to his side.

"Bring me your two rifles," he whispered. "This is the only place from which we can reach them now, and I want you to pass me the loaded guns as fast as I can fire them."

Paul came and stood ready, although his mind rebelled once more at the need to shoot. Henry looked again, and saw the brown files approaching. He thrust the muzzle of the rifle through the hole and fired at a row of brown legs, and then, with only a second between, he discharged another bullet at the same target. Cries of pain and rage arose, there was a thud as the heavy log was dropped to the ground, and Henry had time to send a third shot after the fleeing warriors as they ran for the forest.

35

"They won't try that again," said Henry. "They cannot approach the door without coming within range of the loophole, and they'll rest a while now to think up some new trick."

"What will be the end of it?" asked Paul.

"Nobody can say," replied the great youth calmly. "Indians don't stick to a thing as white men do; they may get tired and go away after a while, but not yet, and it's for you and me, Paul, to watch and fight."

A certain fierce resolve showed in his tone, and Paul knew that Henry felt himself a match for anything.

"Better eat and drink a little more, Paul," said Henry. "Take the half of a pigeon. We'll need all our strength."

Paul thought the advice good, and followed it. Then came another period of that terrible waiting.

CHAPTER V
THE FLIGHT

Paul was half reclining against the wall, when he suddenly saw Henry look up. Paul's eyes followed his comrade's, and then he heard a soft, faint sound over their heads. He understood at once. Danger had come from a new quarter. The Shawnees were upon the board roof, through which a rifle bullet could easily pass. The menace was serious, but the men up there could not see their targets below, and they themselves were in a precarious position.

Henry once pointed his rifle toward a portion of the roof from which a slight sound came, but for a reason that he did not give he withheld his fire. Then came a dead stillness, to be broken a few moments later by fierce war cries all around the cabin and a crash of rapid shots. It seemed to Paul that an attack in great force was being made from every side, and, thrusting his rifle through the loophole, he fired quickly at what he took to be the flitting form of a foe. The next moment he became aware of a terrible struggle in the cabin itself. He heard a thud, the roar of a rifle shot within the confined space, a fall, and then, in the half darkness, he saw two powerful figures writhing to and fro. One was Henry and the other a mighty Shawnee warrior, naked to the waist, and striving to use a tomahawk that he held in a hand whose wrist was clenched in the iron grasp of his foe. Lying almost at their feet was the body of another warrior, stark and dead.

Paul sprang forward, his second and loaded rifle in his hand.

"No, no, Paul!" cried Henry. "The chimney! Look to the chimney!"

Paul whirled about, and he was just in time. A savage warrior dropped down the great wide chimney that all the log cabins had, and fell lightly on his feet among the dead embers of a month ago. His face was distorted horribly with ferocity, and Paul, all the rage of battle upon him now that battle had come, fired squarely at the red forehead, the rifle muzzle only three feet away. The savage fell back and lay still among the cinders. The next instant the deep, long-drawn sigh of a life departing came from behind, and Paul whirled about again, his heart full of sickening fear.

But it was Henry who stood erect. He had wrenched the warrior's own tomahawk from him, and had slain him with it. His

37

face was flushed with a victorious glow, but he stood there only a moment. Then he seized his own second and loaded rifle, and ran to the chimney. But nothing more came down it, and there were no more sounds of warriors walking on the roof. The three who had come had been daring men, but they had paid the price. The shots and shouts around continued for a little space, forms dashed heavily against the door, and then, as suddenly as it began, the tumult ceased.

Paul felt a chill of horror creeping through his bones. It was all so ghastly. The dead warriors lay, each upon his back, one among the dead coals, and Paul could hear nothing but his own and Henry's heavy breathing.

"It was a daring thing to do," said Henry at last, "to come down the chimney that way; but it has been done before in Kentucky."

Then they reloaded their rifles, but Paul was like one in a dream. It seemed to him now that he could not endure the long hours in the cabin with those dead faces on the floor staring at him with their dead eyes.

"Henry," he said, "we can't keep them here."

"No," replied Henry, "we can't; but we must wait a little."

Paul sat down on the bench. He felt for a moment faint and sick. The little cabin was full of rifle smoke, and it lay heavy in his nostrils and upon his lungs. He felt as if he were breathing poisoned air. But the smoke gradually drifted away up the chimney, and the thick, clogging feeling departed from his lungs and nostrils. Strength and spirit came back.

"How are we to get rid of them?" he asked, nodding toward the dead warriors.

"Let's wait an hour at least, and I'll show you," replied Henry.

The hour passed, but to Paul it seemed two. Then Henry took the largest of the warriors and dragged him to the wall just beneath the window. The second and third he did the same way.

"Now, Paul," he said, "you must take down the bar and open the window. Then I'll pitch them out. The besiegers will be surprised, and they won't have time to get at us."

Paul accepted his part of the task eagerly. There might be danger, but better that than having the dead men lying on the floor and staring at him with dead eyes. He took down the bar and quickly held the window open. Henry heaved up the bodies of the warriors and cast them out, one by one, each falling with a dull, heavy sound to the ground below. Then Paul slammed back the window and shot the bar into place. As he did so three or four rifles flashed from the forest, and the bullets pattered upon the heavy oaken shutter.

"Too late," said Henry, "We took 'em by surprise, as I thought we should."

Paul drew a long and deep breath. The cabin had taken on a brighter aspect.

"I'm mighty glad that's done," he said.

"If you'll listen carefully, I think you'll hear something later," said Henry.

Henry was right. In about half an hour they heard soft, shuffling noises beside the cabin, just under the window.

"They're taking away the dead warriors," said Henry.

"I don't want to fire on them while they're doing it," said Paul.

"Nor I," said Henry. "We might reach 'em, but I'm glad they're doing what they are."

The slight, sliding noises continued for a little while, and then they heard only the light sweep of the rain. On the roof it became a patter, and here and there a drop made its way between the boards and fell on the floor. It was soothing to Paul after the excitement of those terrible moments, and he felt a queer, pleasant languor. His eyes half closed, but his vague look fell on somber, dark spots on the floor, and the sight was repellent to him. He went to the hearth, heaped up the whole of the embers and ashes, and sprinkled them carefully over the spots, which would have been red in the light, but which were black in the night and gloom of the cabin. Henry watched him do it, but said nothing. He understood Paul, and gave him his sympathy.

Paul sat down again on the floor, and leaned against the wall. The pleasant, languorous feeling came once more, but he was roused suddenly by scattered rifle shots, and sprang up. Henry laughed.

"They're not attacking," he said. "It was only a volley, fired from the wood, to show how angry they are. I don't think we need expect anything more to-night. You might really go to sleep, Paul, if you feel like it."

"No, I will not!" exclaimed Paul with energy. "I won't do all the sleeping, and let you do all the watching. Besides, I couldn't sleep, anyhow; my nerves wouldn't let me. I looked sleepy just because I was tired, it's your time."

"All right," said Henry. "Now, you watch good, Paul."

Then Henry lay down upon the floor and closed his eyes. He

might not have done so, but he felt sure that nothing more would be attempted that night; and if, by any chance, they should attack again, Paul would be sure to waken him in time. The rain grew harder on the roof, and its steady patter was like the rocking of a cradle to a child. His nerves were of steel, and the mechanism of his body and brain were not upset at all. The half-dropped lids dropped down entirely, and he slept, breathing peacefully.

Paul watched, his brief lethargy gone; but his accustomed eyes could see little now through the loopholes, only the dim forest and the rain, falling slowly but steadily. He and Henry seemed to be alone in the world. Outside all the wilderness was in gloom, but in the little cabin it was dry and warm. The few drops that came through the boards now and then, and fell with a little pat on the floor, were nothing. He and Henry were dry and safe, and it seemed to him that so far, at least, they had all the better of the battle. The glow of triumph came again.

Paul watched until dawn, and saw the sun spring up over the eastern forests. Then he awakened Henry, and the great youth, stretching himself, uttered a long sigh.

"That was fine, Paul!" he said, "fine! Now, what are our friends outside doing?"

"Nothing that I can see. There are only stumps in the clearing, and trees and hushes in the forest. I see no warrior."

Henry laughed, and his laugh had a most cheerful tone.

"They are not far away," he said. "It is likely they'll try to starve us out, or rather conquer us with thirst. They don't know anything about our barrel of water."

"Blessed barrel!" ejaculated Paul.

It seemed that Henry was right in his prediction. As long hours passed, the sun rose higher and higher, and it grew very close in the little cabin. Paul thought the warriors must have gone away, disgusted with their losses, but Henry cautioned him against savage patience. Toward noon they ate a little more of their pigeon and dried venison, and Paul looked with some dismay at the small portions that were left.

"Henry," he exclaimed, "there is enough for supper, and no more."

"Just so," said Henry, "and our enemies remain on guard. They'll wait for us."

He thought it best to put the case plainly and in all its hideous phases to Paul. While savages sometimes abandoned a siege very soon, they did not show signs of ceasing now. Perhaps they relied on starving out the besieged, and if they only knew the state of affairs within the cabin theirs was a good reliance.

Their brief dinner over, the two boys sat down on the floor, and from the loopholes on either side watched the forest. To Paul the whole air and atmosphere of the cabin had now become intolerably oppressive. At first it had been such a strong, snug place of refuge that he rejoiced, but at last his sensitive spirit was weighed down by the long delay, the gloom, and the silence. The sight of their limited rations brought to him all the future—the vigilant enemy on guard, the last little piece of food gone, then slow starvation, or a rush on the savage bullets and sure death. As usual, his uncommon imagination was depicting everything in vivid colors, far in advance.

But he said nothing, nor did Henry. They had already exhausted all subjects for talk, and they waited—Henry with real, and Paul with assumed patience. Fully two hours passed in silence, but after that time it was naturally Paul who spoke first.

"Henry," he said in a tone that indicated unbelief in his own words, "don't you think that they must have got tired and gone away?"

"No, they are surely in the forest about us; but since they won't go, Paul, you and I must leave to-night."

"What do you mean?" Paul's words expressed the greatest surprise.

Henry stood up, and figure, face, and words alike showed the greatest decision.

"Paul," he said, "our last piece of venison will soon be gone, and the Shawnees, I think, will stay, expecting to starve us out, which they can do; but the night shows all the signs of being very dark, and you and I must slip through their lines some way or other. Are you ready to try it?"

It was like a signal to Paul, those words, "Are you ready to try it?" He was ready to try anything now, as a release from the cabin, and a fine flare of color mounted to his cheeks as he replied:

"I'll follow you anywhere, Henry."

Henry said nothing more; Paul's reply was sufficient; but he resumed his position at the loophole, and attentively watched the heavens. Somber clouds were rolling up from the southwest and the air was growing cooler, but heavy with damp. Already the sun, so bright and pitiless in the morning, was obscured, and mists and vapors hung over the forest. He judged that it would be a dark night, with flurries of mist and rain, just suited to his purpose, and he felt a sensation of relief.

41

"Paul," he said, after a while, "I think we'd better take the two captured rifles with us again. If we come face to face with 'em, a couple of extra shots might save us."

"Whatever you say, Henry," replied Paul.

The afternoon passed slowly away, and the night came on thick and dark, as Henry had hoped. The rain fell again in intermittent showers, and it was carried in gusts by the wind. The two boys drank deeply from the barrel, and ate what was left of the venison.

"Be sure your powder horns are stopped up tight, Paul," said Henry. "We've got to keep our powder dry. The sooner we go the better, because the Shawnees won't be expecting us to come out so soon."

The darkness was now rolling up so thick and black that to Paul it seemed like a great sable curtain dropping its folds over them. It enveloped the forest, then the clearing, then the hut, and those within it. The inky sky was without a star. The puffs of rain rattled dismally on the roof of the old cabin. But all this somberness of nature brought comfort and lightness of heart to the besieged. Paul's spirits rose with the blackness of the night and the wildness of the rain.

"Are you all ready, Paul?" asked Henry.

"Yes," replied Paul cheerfully.

Accustomed as they were to the darkness of the cabin, they could not see each other's faces now, only the merest outlines of their figures.

"We must keep close together," said Henry. "It won't do to lose sight of each other."

He slipped to the door, lifted the bar and put it soundlessly on one side, and he and Paul stood together in the open space, just a moment, waiting and listening.

The rush of air and raindrops on Paul's face felt wonderfully cool and invigorating. His chest expanded and his spirits rose to the top. It was like leaving a prison behind.

"Step more lightly than you ever did before in your life," said Henry, and he and Paul put foot together on mother earth. The very pressure of the damp earth felt good to Paul all the way through his moccasins. A step or two from the door they paused again, waiting and listening. The forest was invisible, and so were the stumps in the clearing. But nothing stirred. Henry's acute ear told him that.

"We'll follow the wall around to the other side of the cabin," he whispered to Paul. "They don't know yet that we've come out,

42

and naturally they'll watch the door closest. Be careful where you put your feet."

But the very dampness prevented any rustle in the weeds and grass, and they passed to the other side of the cabin without an alarm coming from the forest. There they paused again, and once more Henry whispered his instructions.

"I think we'd better get down and crawl," he said. "It's a hard thing to do with two rifles each, but we must do it until we get to the woods."

It was difficult, as Henry had said, and Paul felt, too, a sense of humiliation; but then one's life was at stake, and without hesitation he dropped to his knees, crawling slowly after the dark figure of his comrade. Henry made no sound and Paul but a little, not enough to be heard ten feet away. Henry stopped now and then, as if he would listen intently a moment or two, and Paul, of course, stopped just behind him. Fortune seemed to favor their daring. The great silence lasted, broken only by puffs of wind and rain, and the wet leaves of the forest rubbing softly against each other. Paul looked back once. The cabin was already melting into a blur, although not twenty yards distant, and in as many yards more it would be lost completely in the surrounding darkness.

Now the forest was only a few yards away, but to Paul it seemed very far. His knees and wrists began to ache, and the two rifles became awkward for him to carry. He wondered how Henry could go forward with so much ease, but he resolved to persist as long as his comrade led the way.

The dark outline of the wood slowly came nearer, then nearer yet, and then they entered it, pressing silently among the hushes and the black shadows of the lofty trees. Here Henry rose to his feet and Paul imitated him, thankful to rest his aching knees and wrists, and to stand up in the form and spirit of a man.

"We may slip through unseen and unheard," whispered Henry, "and then again we may not. Come on; we'll need all our caution now."

But as they took the first step erect, a cry arose behind them, a cry so full of ferocity and chagrin that Paul absolutely shuddered from head to foot. It came from the clearing, near the hut, and Paul, without the telling of it, knew what had happened.

"They've tried the door of the cabin, only to find it open and the place empty," whispered Henry. "Now, we must not go too fast, Paul. In this pitchy darkness not even a Shawnee could see us ten feet away, but he could hear us. No noise, Paul!"

They stole forward, one close behind the other, going but slowly, seeking with sedulous care to avoid any noise that would bring the savages upon them. The rain, which had grown steadier, was a Godsend. It and the wind together kept up a low, moaning sound that hid the faint pressure of Paul's footsteps. The cry behind them at the cabin was repeated once, echoing away through the black and dripping forest. After that Paul heard nothing, but to the keener ears of Henry came now and then the soft, sliding sound of rapid footsteps, a word or two uttered low, and the faint swish of bushes, swinging back into place after a body passed. He knew that the warriors were now seeking eagerly for them, but with the aid of the intense darkness he hoped that he and Paul would steal safely through their lines. They went slowly forward for perhaps half an hour, stopping often and listening. Once Henry's hand on Paul's shoulder, they sank a little lower in the bushes, and Henry, but not Paul, saw the shadowy outline of a figure passing near.

Fortunately the forest was very dense, but unfortunately the clouds began to thicken, and a rumble dull and low came from the far horizon. Then the clouds parted, cut squarely down the middle by a flash of lightning, and for a moment a dazzling glow of light played over the dripping forest. Everything was revealed by it, every twig and leaf stood out in startling distinctness, and Paul, by impulse, sank lower to hide himself among the bushes.

The glow vanished and Henry had seen nothing; he was sure, too, that no one had seen them, but he knew that it was only luck; another flash might reveal them, and he and Paul must now hasten, taking the chances of discovery by noise. He spoke a word to his comrade, and they plunged more rapidly through the undergrowth. The thunder kept up an unceasing and threatening murmur on the far horizon, and the lightning flared fitfully now and then, but they were still unseen, and Henry hoped that they had now passed the ring of savages in the forest and the dusk.

Paul had dropped back from Henry's side, but was following closely behind him. He was deeply impressed by a situation so extraordinary for one of his type. The thunder, the lightning, the darkness and the danger contained for him all the elements of awe and mystery.

"I think we've shaken them off," said Henry presently, "and unless the lightning shows us to some stray member of the band they can't pick up our trail again before morning."

Paul was grateful for the assurance, and he noticed, too, that the danger of the lightning's revelation was decreasing, as the flashes were becoming less frequent and vivid. His breathing now grew easier and his spirits rose. Much of the gloom departed from the forest. The thunder that had kept up a continuous low rolling, like a dirge, died away, and the lightning, after a few more weak and ineffectual flashes, ceased.

"We won't have any further trouble to-night, that's sure," said Henry. "They could not possibly find our trail before day, and I think we'd better push on, as nearly as we can, in the direction of our hidden powder. You know we still mean to do what we started out to do."

They traveled all night, with brief periods of rest, through rough and densely wooded country. Toward morning the rain ceased, and the clouds all floated away. The stars came out in a clear sky, and a warm wind blew over the wet forest. Henry looked more than once at Paul, and his look was always full of sympathy. Paul's face was pale, but his expression was set in firm resolve, and Henry knew that he would never yield.

After a while the dark began to lighten, and Henry stopped short in surprise. Paul was walking in such automatic fashion that he almost ran against him before he stopped. Henry pointed with a long forefinger to a red spot deep in the forest.

"See that?" he said.

"Yes, I guess it's the sun rising," said Paul, who was staggering a little, and who saw through a cloud, as it were.

Henry looked at him and laughed.

"The sun!" he said. "Well, Paul, it's the first time I ever knew the sun to rise in the west."

"The sun's likely to do anything out here where we are," rejoined Paul.

"That's a fire, a camp fire, Paul," said Henry, "and I'm thinking it must be made by white men."

"White men! Friends!" exclaimed Paul. He stood up straight, and his eyes grew brighter. An hour or two ago it had scarcely seemed possible to him that they should ever see white faces again.

"It's only my belief," said Henry. "We've got to make sure. Now, you wait here, Paul, and I'll do a little bit of scouting. Sit down among those bushes there and I'll be back soon."

Paul was fully content to do what Henry said. He found a good place in a thick clump of underbrush, and sank down easily. He would have been quite willing to lie down, because he was terribly tired and sleepy, but with an effort he held himself to a sitting posture and watched Henry. He was conscious of a vague

45

admiration as the tall form of his comrade went forward swiftly, making no noise and hiding itself so quickly in the forest that he could not tell where it had gone.

Then Paul was conscious of a great peace, and a heavy tugging at his eyelids. Never in his life before was he so tired and sleepy. The last raindrop was gone, and the bushes and grass were drying in the gentle wind. A fine golden sun was bringing with it a silver dawn, and a pleasant warmth stole all through him. His head sank back a little more and his elbow found a soft place in the turf.

The boy, with his half-closed eyes and pale face, was not alone as he lay among the bushes. Little neighbors came and looked at the newcomer. A hare gazed solemnly at him for a moment or two, and then hopped solemnly away. A bluebird flew down to the very tip of a bough, surveyed him at leisure, and then flew off in search of food. Neither hare nor bird was scared. Tiny creeping things scuttled through the grass, but the boy did not move, and they scuttled on undisturbed.

Paul was just sinking away into a pleasant unknown land when a shout brought him back to earth. He sprang to his feet, and there was Henry returning through the forest.

"Friends, Paul! Old friends!" he cried. "Up with you and we'll pay 'em a surprise visit!"

Paul shook his head to clear his thoughts, and followed Henry. Henry walked swiftly now, not seeming to care whether or not he made noise, and Paul followed him toward the fire, which now rapidly grew larger.

CHAPTER VI
THE BATTLE ON THE HILL

Six men were sitting around a camp fire, and they showed every sign of comfort and cheerfulness. It was a big fire, a glowing fire, a warm fire, and it took all trace of damp from the rain or cold of the autumn morning. They were just having breakfast, and their food was buffalo hump, very tender as it came from beneath a huge bed of red-hot embers.

The men seemed to have no fear of an enemy, perhaps because their fire was in an open space, too far from the forest for the rifle shot of an ambushed foe to reach them. Perhaps, too, they felt security in their numbers and valor, because they were certainly a formidable-looking party. All were stalwart, dressed in wilderness fashion—that is, in tanned deerskin—and every one carried the long, slender-barreled Kentucky rifle, with knife and hatchet at his belt. There was Tom Ross, the guide, of middle years, with a powerful figure and stern, quiet face, and near him lounged a younger man in an attitude of the most luxurious and indolent ease, Shif'less Sol Hyde, who had attained a great reputation for laziness by incessantly claiming it for himself, but who was nevertheless a hunter and scout of extraordinary skill. Jim Hart, a man of singular height and thinness, whom Sol disrespectfully called the "Saplin'"—that is, the sapling, a slim young tree—was doing the cooking. The others were typical frontiersmen—lean, big of build, and strong.

The shiftless one curled himself into an easier position against a log, and regarded with interest a particularly juicy piece of the buffalo hump that lay on the grass some distance from him.

"Say, Saplin'," he drawled, "I wish you'd bring me that piece o' hump. I think it would just suit my teeth."

"Git it yourself," replied Saplin' indignantly. "Do you think I'm goin' to cook for a lazy bag o' bones like you, an' then wait on you, too?"

"Well, I think you might," said Shif'less Sol sorrowfully. "I'm pow'ful tired."

"If I wuz to wait on you when you wuz tired, I'd wait on you all my life."

"Which 'ud he puttin' yourself to a mighty good use," said Sol tolerantly. "But if you won't bring it to me, I reckon I'll have to go after it."

47

He rose, with every appearance of reluctance, and secured the buffalo meat. But he stood with it in his hand and regarded the forest to the east, from which two figures were coming. Ross had already seen them, but he had said nothing. The keen eyes of the shiftless one were not at fault for a moment.

"Paul Cotter an' Henry Ware," he said.

"Yes," said Tom Ross.

"And Paul's just about done up."

"Yes," said Tom Ross.

"Looks like they've had a big fight or a big run, one or t'other or both."

"Yes," said Tom Ross.

Then all went forward to meet the two boys, so well known to them. Paul was staggering a little, and there was a high color, as of fever, in his face, but Henry showed signs of neither fatigue nor excitement.

"We're glad to find you," said Henry briefly.

"We're glad, awful glad!" began Paul, with more fervor; but he suddenly reeled, and everything grew dim about him. Shif'less Sol caught him.

"Here, Paul," he said, "stand up. You're a heavy weight for a tired man to hold."

His words were rough, but his tone was kindly. Paul, all his pride aroused, made a great effort and stood straight again. Slowly the world about him swam back, into its proper position.

"Who said I wasn't standing up?" he asked.

"Nobody," replied Shif'less Sol; "but if I'd been through what I reckon you've been through, I'd fall flop on the ground, an' Jim Hart would have to come an' feed me or I'd starve to death right before his eyes."

Paul laughed, and then he felt more like himself. Ross, too, had been regarding him with sympathy, but he glanced inquiringly at Henry.

"You've had it hot an' hard?" he said.

"Yes," replied the boy laconically; "we've run against Shawnees, and about everything that could has happened to us."

"Then it's fire, warmth, meat, rest, an' sleep for Paul right away," said Ross.

Henry nodded.

Paul was looking at the fire, which seemed to him the most glorious one ever built, and he did not notice anything more until he was lying beside it, stretched on a blanket, and eating the very piece

48

of tender buffalo meat that Shif'less Sol had coveted for himself. Despite his relaxed and half-dreamy condition, his imagination leaped up at once to magnificent heights. All danger and hardship were gone. He was surrounded by a ring of dauntless friends, and the fire glowed splendidly.

Shif'less Sol sat down near him, and regarded him with the deepest sympathy, mingled with a certain amount of envy.

"Paul," he said, "I wish I wuz in your place for an hour or two. They've jest got to wait on you. Nobody ever believes me when I say I'm sick, though I'm took pow'ful bad sometimes, an' they don't care whether I'm tired or not. Now, Paul, take all the advantages o' your position. Don't you reach your hand for a thing. Make 'em bring it to you. Ef I can't get waited on myself, I like to see another fellow waited on. Here, Saplin', some more o' that buffalo steak for Paul, who is mighty hungry."

Saplin' cast a look of scorn upon Shif'less Sol, but he brought the steak, and Paul ate again, for he was voraciously hungry. But one cannot eat always, and by and by he had enough. Then his restful, dreamy feeling grew. He saw Henry and the men talking, but he either did not hear what they said or he was not interested. Soon the whole world faded out, and he slept soundly. And as he slept the touch of fever left him. Shif'less Sol looked down at him kindly.

"I'm tired, too," he said, "but I suppose if I wuz to go to sleep some o' you 'ud be mean enough to shove me in the side with his foot."

"I'd try to be the first," said Jim Hart, "an' I'd shove pow'ful hard."

"It 'ud be jest like you," said Shif'less Sol, "but I suppose you can't any more help bein' mean, Jim, than I can help bein' tired."

Jim shrugged his shoulders and returned to his cooking, his tall, lean form bent over like a hoop. Paul slept peacefully on the blanket, but the others talked much and earnestly. Henry, as he ate of the buffalo meat, told them all that had happened to him and Paul in that brief period which yet looked so long. That the band would pick up the trail, daylight now come, and follow on, he did not doubt. There he stopped, and left the conclusion to the others. Shif'less Sol was the first to speak.

"This gang," he said, "come out to hunt buffalo, an', accordin' to what Henry says, a war party—he don't know how big—is comin' this way huntin' him an' Paul. Well, ef it keeps on huntin' him an' Paul, it's bound to run up agin us, because Paul an' Henry are now a part o' our gang. Ez fur me, I've done a lot o' trampin' after buffalo, an' I feel too tired to run, I jest do."

"I ain't seen no better place for cookin' than this," said Jim Hart, undoubling himself, "an' I like the looks o' the country round here pow'ful well. I'd hate to leave it before I got ready,"

"'Tain't healthy to run afore you're ready," said Ike Stebbins, a short, extremely thick man. "It ain't good for the stomach. Pumps the blood right up to the heart, an' I ain't feelin' very good just now, noway. Can't afford to take no more risks to my health."

A slight smile passed over the stern, bronzed face of Tom Ross.

"I expected to hear you talk that way, boys," he said, "it's in your blood; but thar's a better reason still for our not goin'. If this war band stays around here, it'll be pickin' off settlers, an' it's fur us to stop it. Now, them Shawnees are comin' a-huntin' us. I jest wish to say that we don't mean to be the hunted; we're to be the hunters ourselves."

Sharp exclamations of approval broke from all these fierce spirits of the border. But the deepest and most dangerous gleam of all was in the eyes of Henry Ware. All his primeval instincts were alive, and foremost among them was the desire to fight. He was tired of running, of seeking to escape, and his warlike blood was up and leaping. Two more men who had been out ranging the woods for buffalo, or any other worthy game that might happen in their way, came in presently, and the little army, with the addition of the two boys, was now raised to the number of ten. And a real little army it was, fortified with indomitable hearts and all the skill and knowledge of the wilderness.

When Paul awoke beneath the pressure of Henry's hand on his shoulder, the sun was much higher, and the forest swam in limpid light. He noticed at once that the fire was out, trampled under strong heels, and that all the men looked as if ready for instant conflict. He rubbed his eyes and sprang to his feet, half in shame that he should have slept while others watched. It was Shif'less Sol who came to his rescue.

"It's all right, Paul," he drawled. "We all know you were pow'ful tired, an' I'd have slept, too, ef them fellows hadn't been mean enough to keep me from it. You wuz just nacherally overpowered, an' you had to do it."

Paul looked around at the little group, and he read the meaning in the eye of every man.

"You are going to fight that war band?" he said.

50

"It 'pears to me that it's a sight less tirin' than runnin' away," replied Shif'less Sol, "though we hate to drag you, Paul, into such a fracas."

The blood flushed into Paul's face.

"I'm ready for it!" he exclaimed. "I'm as ready as any of you! Do you think I want to run away?"

"We know, Paul, that you've got ez much grit ez anybody in the world," said Tom Ross kindly; "but Sol maybe didn't think a boy that's a big scholar, an' that kin read an' understand anything, would he as much interested in a real hair-raisin' fight as the rest o' us."

Paul was mollified. He knew their minds now, and in a way it was an unconscious tribute that these wild borderers paid to him.

"I'm with you to the end of it," he said. And they, too, were satisfied. Then the entire party moved forward into the deep woods, watching and listening for the slightest sign of the Shawnee advance. Tom Ross naturally took command, but Henry Ware, as always, was first scout. No other eye was so keen as his, nor any other ear. All knew it, and all admitted it willingly. His form expanded again, and fierce joy surged up in his heart. As Ross truly said, the hunted had turned into the hunter.

It was the purpose of the men to circle to the east, and to strike the war party on the Hank. They knew that the Shawnees had already discovered the junction of the fugitives with a larger force, but the warriors could not yet know that the new party intended to stand and fight. Ross, therefore, like the general of a great army going into battle, intended to seek the best possible position for his force.

They traveled in a half circle for perhaps two hours, and then Henry struck a trail, calling at once to Ross. They examined it carefully, and judged that it had been made by a force of about twenty warriors, undoubtedly the band that was following Henry and Paul.

"We're behind 'em now," said Henry.

"But they'll soon be coming back on our trail," said Ross. "They know that they are more than two to one, and they will follow hard."

"I'm gittin' mighty tired ag'in," said Shif'less Sol. "It 'pears to me thar's a pow'ful good place fur us to rest over thar among all them big trees on that little hill."

Ross and Henry examined the hill, which was not very high, but small, and crowned with mighty beeches. The great tree-trunks would offer admirable cover for the wilderness fighter.

"It does kinder invite us," said Ross meaningly, "so we'll jest go over thar, Sol, an' set a while longer."

A few minutes later they were on the hill, each man lying behind a tree of his own selection. Shif'less Sol had chosen a particularly large one, and luckily there was some soft turf growing over its roots. He stretched himself out luxuriously.

"Now, this jest suits an easy-goin' man like me," he said. "I could lay here all day jest a-dreamin', never disturbin' nobody, an' nobody disturbin' me. Paul, you and me ain't got no business here. We wuz cut out fur scholars, we wuz."

Nevertheless, lazy and luxurious as he looked, Shif'less Sol watched the forest with eyes that missed nothing. His rifle lay in such a position that he could take aim almost instantly.

There was a long and tense silence, full of strangeness to Paul. He could never get used to these extraordinary situations. When preparing for combat, as well as in it, the world seemed unreal to him. He did not see why men should fly at each other's throats; but the fact was before him, and he could not escape it.

The little hill was so situated that they could see to a considerable distance at all points of the compass, but they yet saw nothing. Shif'less Sol stretched himself in a new position and grumbled.

"The wust thing about this bed o' mine here," he said to Paul, "is that sooner or later I'll be disturbed in it. A fellow never kin make people let him alone. It's the way here, an' it's the way back in the East, too, I reckon. Now, I'm only occupyin' a place six feet by two, with the land rollin' away thousands o' miles on every side; but it's this very spot, six feet by two, that the Shawnees are a-lookin' fur."

Paul laughed at the shiftless one's complaint, and the laugh greatly relieved his tension. Fortunately his tree was very close to Sol's, and they could carry on a whispered conversation.

"Do you think the Shawnees will really come?" asked Paul, who was always incredulous when the forest was so silent.

"Come! Of course they will!" replied Shif'less Sol. "If for no other reason, they'll do it jest to make me trouble. I ought to be back thar in the East, teachin' school or makin' laws fur somebody."

Paul's eyes wandered from Sol to his comrade, and he saw Henry suddenly move, ever so little, then fix his gaze on a point in the forest, three or four hundred yards away. Paul looked, too, and saw nothing, but he knew well enough that Henry's keener gaze had detected an alien presence in the bushes.

52

Henry whispered something to Ross, who followed his glance and then nodded in assent. The others, too, soon looked at the same point, Jim Hart craning his long neck until it arched like a bow. Presently from a dense clump of bushes came a little puff of white smoke, and then the stillness was broken by the report of a rifle. A bullet buried itself in one of the trees on the hill, and Shif'less Sol turned over with a sniff of contempt.

"If they don't shoot better'n that," he said, "I might ez well go to sleep."

But the forest duel had begun, and it was a contest of skill against skill, of craft against craft. Every device of wilderness warfare known to the red men was practiced, too, by the white men who confronted them.

Paul at first felt an intense excitement, but it was soothed by the calm words of Shif'less Sol.

"I'd be easy about it, Paul," said the shiftless one. "That wuz jest a feeler. They've found out that we're ready for 'em. There ain't no chance of a surprise, an' they shot that bullet merely as a sort o' way o' tellin' us that they had come. Things won't be movin' fur some time yet."

Paul found that Shif'less Sol was right. The long waiting customary in such forest combats endured, but he was now becoming more of a stoic, and he used the time, at least in part, for rest, although every nerve and muscle was keyed to attention. It was fully an hour later when a shot came from behind a tree much nearer to them, and a bullet cut a fragment of bark from the gigantic beech that sheltered Shif'less Sol. There was a second report before the sound of the first had died away, and a Shawnee, uttering a smothered cry, fell forward from his shelter, and lay upon the ground, quite still. Paul could see the brown figure, and he knew that the man was dead.

"It was Tom Ross who did that," said Shif'less Sol. "The savage leaned too fur forward when he fired at me, an' exposed hisself. Served him right fur tryin' to hurt me."

Then Sol, who had raised himself up a little, lay down again in his comfortable position. He did not seem disturbed at all, but Paul kept gazing at the figure of the dead warrior. Once more his spirit recoiled at the need of taking life. Presently came a spatter of rifle fire—a dozen shots, perhaps—and bullets clipped turf and trees. The Shawnees had crept much nearer, and were in a wide semicircle, hoping thus to uncover their foes, at least in part, and they had a little success, as one man, named Brewer, was hit in the fleshy part of the arm.

53

Paul saw nothing but the smoke and the flashes of fire, and he was wise enough to save his own ammunition—he had long since learned the border maxim, never to shoot until you saw something to shoot at.

But the enemy was creeping closer, hiding among rocks and bushes, and a second and longer spatter of rifle fire began. One man was hit badly, and then the borderers began to seek targets of their own. Their long, slender-barreled rifles flashed again and again, and more than one bullet went straight to the mark. The plumes of white smoke grew more numerous, united sometimes, and floated away in little clouds among the trees.

Paul saw that his comrades were firing slowly, but with terrible effect, as five or six still, brown figures now lay in the open. Shif'less Sol, at the next tree, only four feet away, was stretched almost perfectly flat on his face on the ground, and every movement he made seemed to be slow and deliberate. Yet no one was firing faster or with surer aim than he, and faint gleams of satisfaction showed now and then in his eyes. Paul could not restrain speech.

"It seems to me, Sol, that you are not tired as you said you were," he said.

"Perhaps not," replied Sol slowly, "but I will be."

The savages suddenly began to shout, and kept up a ferocious yelling, as if they would confuse and terrify their opponents. The woods echoed with the din, the long-drawn, whining cry, like that of a wolf, and despite all the efforts of a strong will, Paul shuddered as he had not shuddered at the sound of the rifle fire.

"'Tain't no singin' school," said Shif'less Sol, in a clear voice that Paul could hear above the uproar, "but, then, yellin' don't hurt nobody, either. I'd be pow'ful tired ef I used my mouth that way. But jest you remember, Paul, that noise ain't bullets."

It seemed to Paul that the Shawnees had come to the same conclusion, because all the yelling suddenly ceased, and with it the firing. Brown forms that had been flitting about disappeared, too, and all at once there was silence in the wilderness, and nothing to be seen save the hunters and the still, brown figures among the rocks and bushes. To Paul it was wonderful, this melting away of the battle, and this disappearance of the foe, all in a flash. He rubbed his eyes, and could scarcely believe that it was real. But there were the still, brown figures, and by a tree near him lay another still figure, in hunting shirt and leggings, with his face upturned to the sky. One of the hunters had been shot through the heart, and had died instantly and without noise. Three others had been wounded, but they were not complaining.

54

Presently a little hum of talk arose, and Shif'less Sol once more moved comfortably.

"Bit off more'n they could chaw," he said reflectively. "Will wait a while before takin' another bite. Guess I'll rest now."

He stretched himself luxuriously, took out a piece of venison and began to eat it, at the same time handing a piece to Paul.

"Atween fights I allus eat," he said. "Better do the same, Paul."

But Paul had no appetite. He crawled over to Henry, and asked him what he expected to happen next.

"They won't give up," replied Henry, "that is sure. They know that they outnumber us two or three to one, and I've an idea that this is a band of picked warriors."

"You think, too, they'll want to revenge their losses?"

"Of course. And they're likely to attack again before night. It's not noon yet, and they have lots of time."

Paul crawled back to his tree, and, knowing that he would have to wait again, forced himself to eat the venison that Shif'less Sol had given to him.

The Shawnees remained silent and hidden in the forest, and the white men, voiceless, too, lay waiting behind the trees. Between them stretched the fallen, their brown faces upturned to the red sun, which sailed peacefully on in a sky of cloudless blue.

CHAPTER VII
WHAT HAPPENED IN THE DARK

Shif'less Sol rose to a sitting position, and carefully cracked his joints, one by one.

"I wuz a bit afeard, Paul," he said, "that I had jest petrified, layin' thar so long. A tired man likes to rest, but thar ain't no sense in turnin' hisself into a stone image."

Sol seemed so careless and easy that Paul drew an inference from his manner.

"You are not expecting anything more from them just now, Sol?"

His nod toward the forest indicated the "them."

"No, not yet a while," replied Shif'less Sol. "I guess they'll lay by until night."

His face showed some apprehension as he spoke of night, but it was gone quickly. Shif'less Sol was not a man who took troubles to heart, else he never would have earned his name.

"We'll jest chaw a little more venison, Paul," he said. "I know you think a drink o' water would go pow'ful well with it, an' so do I; but since it ain't to be had, we'll jest do without it and say no more."

The remainder of the day passed undisturbed, but as the first wan shade of twilight appeared the men began to look closely to their arms. Horns were held up to the light in order that the powder line might show, bullets were counted, and flints examined. Paul knew what it all meant. The Shawnees would attack in the darkness, and there would be all the confusion of a midnight battle, when one might not be able to tell friend from friend nor foe from foe. The sense of weirdness and awe overcame him again. They were but the tiniest of atoms in that vast wilderness, which would be just the same to-morrow and the next day, no matter who won.

But Paul had in him the stuff of which heroes are made, and his strong will brought his mind back to present needs. He, too, measured his powder and counted his bullets, while he strove also to forget the hot thirst that tormented him.

The sun sank in the forest, the wan twilight deepened into shadow, and the shadow darkened into night. The trees where the Shawnees lay hidden were gone in the dusk, which hung so close that Paul could see but the nearest of his comrades. Only the murmur of night insects and the faint rustle of leaves came to his

56

ears. The feeling of awe returned, and his blood grew chill. Then it was a relief to him to know that he had a comrade in this sensation.

"Ef an owl would only hoot once or twice now," whispered Shif'less Sol, "I think I'd jump right out o' my huntin' shirt."

Paul laughed and felt better.

"Now, Paul," continued Shif'less Sol, very gravely this time, "lemme give you a piece o' mighty good advice. When the muss comes on, don't move about much. Lay close. Stick to me an' Henry, an' then thar ain't so much chance to git mixed up with them that's lookin' fur you here."

"I'll remember what you say, Sol," replied Paul earnestly, as he girded his spirit for action. He knew that the attack would come very soon, as the Indians would choose the darkest period before the moon rose. Nor was he wrong. The battle in the night began only a half hour later.

Paul first saw a pink point appear in the darkness, but he knew that it was the flame from a rifle shot. It came from a place not far away, to which some Shawnee had crawled; but the hunters paid no attention to it, nor to a second, nor to a third, as all the bullets flew wild. Paul, forgetting for the moment that those bullets were sent to kill, became engrossed in the spectacle of the fireworks. He was always wondering where the next spurt of blue or pink flame would break through the darkness, and the popping of the shots formed a not unpleasant sound in the night.

"Comin' closer, comin' closer, Paul!" whispered Shif'less Sol. "One o' them bullets flyin' in the dark may hit somethin' putty soon."

Sol was a prophet. A hunter not far away uttered a low cry. He was struck in the shoulder, but after the single cry he was silent. Henry was the first to see one of the creeping brown bodies and fired, and after that the shots on either side increased fast. It was all confused and terrible to Paul. The darkness, instead of thinning to accustomed eyes, seemed to him to grow heavier. The pin points of light from the rifle fire multiplied themselves into hundreds, and the front of the foe shifted about, as if they were trying to curve around the defenders.

Paul could not definitely say that he saw a single savage, but he fired now and then at the flashes of light, and also tried to obey Sol's injunction about sticking close to him and Henry. But he was not always sure that the figures near him were theirs, the darkness remaining so intense. He heard occasional low cries, the light impact of bullets, and the shuffling sound of feet, but he was fast losing any ordered view of the battle. He knew now that the savages were very close, that the combat was almost hand to hand, but he knew little else. The night enclosed all the furious border conflict, and hid the loss or gain of either side from all but the keenest eyes.

Paul could never tell how long this lasted, but he felt confident that the area of conflict was shifting. Having first faced one side, they were now facing another, as the savages wheeled about them. He rose to his feet in order to keep with his friends. He had been loading and firing more rapidly than he knew, and the barrel of his rifle was hot to his touch. He stood a moment listening for the savages, and then turned to two indistinct figures near him.

"Sol," he said, "can you and Henry see them?"

The two indistinct figures suddenly became distinct, and sprang upon him. He was seized in a powerful grasp and hurled down so violently that he became unconscious for a little while. Why he was not killed he did not know that night, nor ever after—probably they wished to show a trophy. When he gathered his scattered senses he was being dragged away, and his hands were bound. He was too dazed to cry aloud for rescue, but he remembered afterwards that the battle behind him was waning at the time.

He was dragged deeper into the forest, and the shots on the hill became fainter and fewer. His sight cleared, but the darkness was so great that he could yet see little except the warrior who pulled him along. Paul made an effort and gained a better footing. It hurt his pride to be dragged, and now he walked on in the path that the warrior indicated.

They stopped after a while in an open space in the forest. The moon was clearing a little, and Paul saw other warriors standing about. Nearly all were wounded. Hideous and painted they were, with savage eyes filled with rage and disappointment, and the looks they gave Paul made him consider himself as one dead.

As the moon cleared, more warriors drifted back into the glade. Some of these, too, bore wounds, and Paul's heart leaped up with fierce joy as he saw that they had been defeated. The firing had ceased and the wilderness was returning to silence, broken only by the low words of the savages and the soft sound of their moccasins on the earth.

Paul was still in a sort of daze. The warriors were grouped about him, their sole visible trophy of the battle, and they regarded him with vengeful eyes. But he had passed through so much that he was not afraid. His only feeling was that of dull stupefaction, and mingled with it a sort of lingering pride that his comrades had been the victors, although he himself was a prisoner. He did not know whether they would kill him or take him with them, and at that moment his mind was so dulled that he felt little curiosity about the question.

A thin, sharp-faced warrior of middle years seemed to be the leader of the band, and he talked briefly to the others. They nodded toward Paul, and then, with a warrior on each side of the prisoner, they started northward. Paul, his brain clearing, judged that they were taking him as a trophy, as a prize to show in their village before putting him to death.

They marched silently through the forest, curving far to the left of the battlefield. The warriors were about a score in number, and Paul thought they must have lost at least half as many in battle. Their hideous paint and their savage faces filled him with repulsion. Their wild life and the mystery of wild nature did not appeal to him as they had once appealed to Henry in a similar position. To Paul, the chief thing about the wilderness was the magnificent home it would make in the future for a great white race. Spared for the present, he expected to live. Henry had saved him once, and he and his comrades would come again to the rescue.

He stumbled at first in their rapid flight from weakness, and the warrior next to him struck him a blow as a reminder. Paul would have struck back, but his hands were tied, and he could only guard himself against another stumble. Pride sustained him.

They did not stop until nearly dawn, when they camped by the bank of a creek and ate. Paul's arms were unbound, and the hatchet-faced chief tossed him a piece of venison, which he ate greedily because he was very hungry. Then, as the warriors seemed in no hurry to move, he sagged slowly over on his side and went to sleep. Despite his terrible situation, he was so thoroughly worn out that he could not hold up his head any longer.

When Paul awoke the sun was high, and he was lying where he had sunk down. The warriors were about him, some sitting on the grass or lying full length, but the party seemed more numerous than it was the night before. He looked again. It was certainly more numerous, and there, too, sitting near him, was a white youth of nearly his own age. Paul rose up, inspired with a feeling of sympathy, and perhaps of comradeship, and then, to his utter amazement, he saw that the youth was Braxton Wyatt, one of the boys who had come over the mountains with the group that had settled Wareville.

Braxton Wyatt, a year or two older than Paul, had always been disliked at Wareville. Of a sarcastic, sneering, unpleasant temperament, he habitually made enemies, and did not seem to care. Paul disliked him heartily, but in this moment of sudden meeting he felt only sympathy and fellowship. They were captives together, and all feeling of hostility was swept from his mind.

"Braxton!" he exclaimed. "Have they got you, too?"

59

Wyatt rose up, came to Paul, and took his hand in the friendliest manner.

"Yes, Paul," he said. "I was out hunting, thinking that there were no savages south of the Ohio, and I was taken last night by a band which joined yours this morning while you slept."

"Why haven't they killed us?" asked Paul.

"I suppose they'd rather show us to the tribe first, or maybe they think they can adopt us, as Henry Ware was once. They haven't treated me badly."

"That may be because you were taken without any loss to them," said Paul. "We've had a big fight, and I'm the only one they got. Henry Ware, Tom Ross, Shif'less Sol, and the others beat them off."

"That was grand fighting!" said Braxton. "Tell me about it."

Wyatt's fellowship and sympathy greatly cheered Paul, and he told in detail about the battle with the band, and all that preceded it. Braxton Wyatt listened with attention, but more than once expressed surprise.

"How many did you say were left back there on the hill?" he asked at last.

"We were ten when we began the fighting," replied Paul. "One that I know of was killed, and it is likely that one or two more were. Then I'm gone. Not more than six or seven can be left, but they are the best men in all these woods. Twice their number of Indians cannot whip them."

Paul said the last words proudly, and then he added:

"Henry and Ross and Shif'less Sol will come for me. They'll be sure to do it. And they'll rescue you, too."

Braxton Wyatt looked thoughtful.

"I think you're right," he said; "but it'll be a very risky thing for them, especially if the Shawnees expect it. Be sure you don't let the Indians think you are dreaming of such a thing."

"Of course not," said Paul.

The sharp-faced chief now came up, and said something to Wyatt. Braxton replied in the Indian tongue.

"I didn't know that you understood any Shawnee," said Paul in surprise, as the chief turned away.

"I've picked it up, a word here and a word there," replied Wyatt, "and I find it very useful now. The Chief—Red Eagle is his name—says that if you'll give 'em no trouble, he won't bind your hands again, for the present, anyway. I've followed that plan, and I've found it a heap easier for myself."

Paul pondered a little. Braxton Wyatt's advice certainly

60

seemed good, and he did not wish to be bound again. It would be better to go along in docile fashion.

"All right, Braxton," he said, "I'll do as you suggest. We won't make them any trouble now, but after a while we'll escape."

"That's the best way," said Wyatt.

Red Eagle and another warrior, who seemed to be his lieutenant, were talking earnestly. The chief presently beckoned to Wyatt, who went over to him and replied to several questions. But Wyatt came back in a few moments, and took his seat again beside Paul.

A half hour later they resumed the march, and Paul knew by the sun that they were going northward. Hence he inferred that they would make no further attack upon the white hunters, and were bound for what they called home. Refreshed by his rest and sleep, and relieved by the removal of the bandages from his wrists, he walked beside Wyatt with a springy step, and his outlook upon life was fairly cheerful. It was wonderful what the comradeship of one of his own kind did for him! After all, he had probably been deceived about Braxton Wyatt. Merely because his ways were not the ways of Henry and Paul was not proof that he was not the right kind of fellow. Now he was sympathetic and helpful enough, when sympathy and help were needed.

The march northward was leisurely. The Shawnees seemed to have no further expectation of meeting a foe, and they were not so vigilant. Paul and Braxton Wyatt were kept in the center of the group, but they were permitted to talk as much as they pleased, and Paul was not annoyed by any blow or kick.

"Have you any idea how far it is to their village, Braxton?" Paul asked.

"A long distance," replied Wyatt. "We shall not be there under two weeks, and as the party may turn aside for hunting or something else, it may be much longer."

"It will give Henry and Ross and the others more time to rescue us," said Paul.

Braxton Wyatt shrugged his shoulders.

"I wouldn't put much hope in that if I were you, Paul," he said. "This band is very strong. Since the two parties joined it numbers forty warriors, and our friends could do nothing. We must pretend to like them, to fall in with their ways, and to behave as if we liked the wild life as well as that back in the settlements, and in time would like it better."

"I could never do that," said Paul. "All kinds of savages repel me."

Braxton Wyatt shrugged his shoulders again.

"One must do the best he can," he said briefly.

The leisurely march proceeded, and they camped the next afternoon in the midst of a magnificent forest of beech, oak, and hickory, building a great fire, and lounging about it in apparently careless fashion. But Paul was enough of a woodsman to know that some of the warriors were on watch, and he and Braxton, as usual, were compelled to sit in the center of the group, where there was no shadow of a chance to escape.

Hunters whom they had sent out presently brought in the bodies of two deer, and then they had a great feast. The venison was half cooked in strips and chunks over the coals, and the warriors ate it voraciously, chattering to each other, meanwhile, as Paul did not know that Indians ever talked.

"What are they saying, Braxton?" he asked.

"I can't catch it very well," replied Wyatt, "but I think they are talking about a stay near the Ohio—for hunting, I suppose. That ought to be a good thing for us, because they certainly will not decide about our fate until we get back to their village, and the more they are used to us the less likely they are to put us to death."

Paul watched the warriors eating, and they were more repellent to him than ever. Savages they were, and nothing could make them anything else. His ways could never become their ways. But the fresh deer meat looked very good, and the pleasant aroma filled his nostrils. Braxton Wyatt noticed his face.

"Are you hungry, Paul?" he asked.

"No, not hungry; merely starving to death."

Wyatt laughed.

"I'm in the same condition," he said, "but I can soon change it."

He spoke to Red Eagle, and the thin-faced chief nodded. Then Braxton picked up two sharpened sticks that the savages had used, and also two large pieces of venison. One stick and one piece he handed to Paul.

"Now we also will cook and dine," he said.

Paul's heart warmed toward Braxton Wyatt. Certainly he had done him wrong in his thoughts when they lived at Wareville. But he was thinking the next moment about the pleasant odor of the deer meat as he fried it over the coals. Then he ate hungrily, and with a full stomach came peace for the present, and confidence in the future. He slept heavily that night, stretched on the ground before the fire, near Braxton Wyatt, and he did not awaken until late the next morning.

The Indians were very slow and leisurely about departing, and Paul realized now that, vigilant and wonderful as they were in

62

action, they were slothful and careless when not on the war path, or busy with the chase. He saw, also, that the band was entirely too strong to be attacked by Henry and his friends.

They marched northward several days more, at the same dawdling pace, and then they stopped a week at one place for the hunting. Half the warriors would go into the forest, and the next day the other half would go, the first remaining. They brought in an abundance of game, and Paul never before saw men eat as they ate. It seemed to him that they must be trying to atone for a fast of at least six months, and those who were not hunting that day would lie around the fire for hours like animals digesting their food. He and Braxton Wyatt were still treated well, and their hands remained unbound, although they were never allowed to leave the group of warriors.

Paul was glad enough of the rest and delay, but the life of the Shawnees did not please him. He was too fastidious by nature to like their alternate fits of laziness and energy, their gluttony and lethargy afterwards, but he took care not to show his repulsion. He acted upon Wyatt's advice, and behaved in the friendliest manner that he could assume toward his captors. Wyatt once spoke his approval. "The Chief, Red Eagle, thinks of adopting you, if you should fall into their ways," said Wyatt.

"He may adopt me, but I'll never adopt him," replied Paul sturdily.

But Wyatt only laughed and shrugged his shoulders, after his fashion.

A few days later they reached the Ohio. It was running bankful, and where Paul saw it the stream was a mile wide, a magnificent river, cutting off the unknown south from the unknown north, and bearing on its yellow bosom silt from lands hundreds of miles away. The warriors took hidden canoes from the forest at the shore, and Paul thought they would cross at once and continue their journey northward, but they did not do so. Instead, they dawdled about in the thick forest that clothed the southern bank, and ate more venison and buffalo meat, although they did not kindle any fire. A day or two passed thus amid glorious sunshine, and Paul still could not understand why they waited.

Meanwhile he still clung tenaciously to his great hope. He might escape, he might be rescued, and then Henry and he would resume their task which would help so much to save Kentucky. No matter what happened, Paul would never lose sight of this end.

CHAPTER VIII
AT THE RIVER BANK

The days dragged into a week, and the Shawnees still clung to the banks of the great river, occasionally hunting, but more often idling away their time in the deep woods near the shore. Paul's wonder at their actions increased. He could not see any purpose in it, and he spoke several times to Braxton Wyatt about it. But Wyatt always shrugged his shoulders.

"I do not know," he said. "It is true they build no camp fires, at least no big ones, and they do not seem to be much interested in hunting; but I cannot guess what they are about, and I should not dare to ask Red Eagle."

Paul noticed that Red Eagle himself often went down to the bank of the river, and would watch its surface with the keenest attention. But Paul observed also that he always looked eastward— that is, up the stream—and never down it.

Paul and Wyatt were allowed an increasing amount of liberty, but they were held nevertheless within a ring through which they could not break; Paul was shrewd enough to perceive it, and for the present he made no effort, thinking it a wise thing to appear contented with his situation, or at least to be making the best of it. Braxton Wyatt commended his policy more than once.

On the morning of the seventh day the chief went down to the bank of the river once more, and began to watch its surface attentively and long, always looking up the stream. Paul and Braxton Wyatt and some of the warriors stood among the trees, not fifty feet away. They also could see the surface of the river for a long distance, and Paul's eyes followed those of the chief, Red Eagle.

The Ohio was a great yellow river, flowing slowly on in its wide channel, the surface breaking into little waves, that crumpled and broke and rose again. Paul could see the stream for miles, apparently becoming narrower and narrower, until it ended in a yellow thread under the horizon. Either shore was overhung with heavy forest red with autumn's touch. Wild fowl occasionally flew over the current. It was inexpressibly weird and lonely to Paul, seemingly a silent river flowing on forever through silent shades.

He saw nothing on the stream, and his eyes came back to the thin, hatchet-faced chief, who stood upon the bank looking so intently. Red Eagle had begun to interest him greatly. He impressed Paul as being a thorough savage of savages, fairly breathing cruelty and cunning, and Paul saw now a note of expectation, of cruel expectation, in the fierce black eyes of the Shawnee. And as he looked, a sudden change came over the face of the chief. A gleam appeared in the black eyes, and the tall, thin figure seemed to raise itself a little higher. Paul again looked up the stream, and lo! a tiny dark spot appeared upon its surface. He watched it as the chief watched it, and it grew, coming steadily down the river. But he did not yet know what it was.

Now the spirit of action descended quickly upon the whole band. The chief left the shore and gave quick, low orders to the men, who sank back into the forest, taking Paul and Braxton Wyatt with them. Two warriors, having Paul between them, crouched in a dense thicket, and one of them tapped the unarmed boy meaningly with his tomahawk. Paul did not see Braxton Wyatt, but he supposed that he was held similarly by other warriors, somewhere near. In truth, he did not see any of the savages except the two who were with him. All the rest had melted away with the extraordinary facility that they had for hiding themselves, but Paul knew that they were about him, pressed close to the earth, blurred with the foliage or sheltered by tree trunks.

The boy's eyes turned back to the river, and the black blot floating on its surface. That blot, he knew, had caused this sudden disappearance of a whole band of Shawnees, and he wanted to know more. The black blot came down the stream and grew into shape and outline, and the shape and outline were those of a boat. An Indian canoe? No; it rapidly grew beyond the size of any canoe used by the savages, and began to stand up from the water in broad and stiff fashion. Then Paul's heart thumped, because all at once he knew. It was a flatboat, and it was certainly loaded with emigrants coming down the Ohio, women and children as well as men, and the Shawnees had laid an ambush. This was what the crafty Red Eagle had been waiting for so long.

It was the final touch of savagery, and the boy's generous and noble heart rebelled within him. He started up, propelled by the impulse to warn; but the two warriors pulled him violently back, one of them again touching him significantly with his tomahawk. Paul knew that it was useless. Any movement or cry of his would cause his own death, and would not be sufficient to warn those on the boat. He sank back again, trembling in every nerve, not for himself but for the unsuspecting travelers on the river.

The boat came steadily on, Paul saw a number of men, some

65

walking about and others at the huge sweeps with which it was controlled. And—yes, there was a woman and a child, too; a little girl with long, yellow curls, who played on the rude deck. Paul put his hand to his face, and it came back wet.

Then he remembered, and his heart leaped up. The river was a mile wide, and the boat was keeping near the middle of the stream. No bullet from the savages could reach it. Then what was the use of this ambush? It had merely been a chance hope of the savages that the boat would come near enough for them to fire into it, but instead it would go steadily on! Paul looked exultantly at the two warriors beside him, but they were intently watching the boat, which would soon be opposite them.

Then a ghastly and horrible thing occurred. A white face suddenly appeared upon the shore in front of Paul—the face of a white youth whom he knew. The figure was in rags, the clothing torn and tattered by thorns and bushes, and the hair hung in wild locks about the white face. Face and figure alike were the picture of desolation and despair.

The white youth staggered to the very edge of the water, and, lifting up a tremulous, weeping voice, cried out to those on the boat:

"Save me! Save me! In God's name, save me! Don't leave me here to starve in these dark woods!"

It was a sight to move all on the boat who saw and heard—this spectacle of the worn wanderer, alone in that vast wilderness, appealing to unexpected rescue. Fear, agony, and despair alike were expressed in the tones of Braxton Wyatt's voice, which carried far over the yellow stream and was heard distinctly by the emigrants. To hear was also to heed, and the great flatboat, coming about awkwardly and sluggishly, turned her square prow toward the southern shore, where the refugee stood.

Braxton Wyatt never ceased to cry out for help. His voice now ran the gamut of entreaty, hope, despair, and then hope again. He called upon them by all sacred names to help him, and he also called down blessings upon them as the big boat bore steadily toward the land where two score fierce savages lay among the bushes, ready to slay the moment they came within reach.

Paul was dazed at first by what he saw and heard. He could not believe that it was Braxton Wyatt who was doing this terrible and treacherous thing. He rubbed away what he thought might be a deceptive film before his eyes, but it was still Braxton Wyatt. It was the face of the youth whom he had known so long, and it was his voice that begged and blessed. And there, too, came the boat, not thirty yards from the land now! In two more minutes it would be at

66

the bank, and its decks were crowded now with men, women, and children, regarding with curiosity and pity alike this lone wanderer in the wilderness whom they had found in such a terrible case. Paul heard around him a rustling like that of coiled snakes, the slight movement of the savages preparing to spring. The boat was only ten yards from the shore! Now the film passed away from his eyes, and his dazed brain cleared. He sprang up to his full height, reckless of his own life, and shouted in a voice that was heard far over the yellow waters:

"Keep off! Keep off, for your lives! It is a renegade who is calling you into an ambush! Keep off! Keep off!"

Paul saw a sudden confusion on the boat, a running to and fro of people, and a bucking of the sweeps. Then he heard a spatter of rifle shots, all this passing in an instant, and the next moment he felt a heavy concussion. Fire flashed before his eyes, and he sank away into a darkness that quickly engulfed him.

When Paul came back to himself he was lying among the trees where he had fallen, and his head ached violently. He started to put up his hand to soothe it, but the hand would not move, and then he realized that both hands were bound to his side. His whole memory came back in a flash, and he looked toward the river. Far down the stream, and near the middle of it, was a black dot that, even as he looked, became smaller, and disappeared. It was the flatboat with its living freight, and Paul's heart, despite his own desperate position, leaped up with joy.

From the river he glanced back at the Indian faces near him, and so far as he could tell they bore no signs of triumph. Nor could he see any of those hideous trophies they would have been sure to carry in case the ambush had been a success. No! the triumph had been his, not theirs. He rolled into an easier position, shut his eyes again to relieve his head, and when he opened them once more, Braxton Wyatt stood beside him. At the sight, all the wrath and indignation in Paul's indomitable nature flared up.

"You scoundrel! you awful scoundrel! You renegade!" he cried. "Don't you ever speak to me again! Don't you come near me!"

Braxton Wyatt did not turn back when those words, surcharged with passion, met him full in the face, but wore a sad and downcast look.

"I don't blame you, Paul," he said gently, "for speaking that way when you don't understand. I'm not a renegade, Paul. I did what I did to save our lives—yours as well as mine, Paul. The chief, Red Eagle, threatened to put us both to the most awful tortures at once if I didn't do it."

"Liar, as well as scoundrel and renegade!" exclaimed Paul fiercely.

But Braxton Wyatt went on in his gentle, persuading, unabashed manner:

"It is as true as I stand here. I could not take you, too, Paul, to torture and death, and all the while I was hoping that the people on the boat would see, or suspect, and that they would turn back in time. If you had not cried out—and it was a wonderfully brave thing to do!—I think that at the last moment I myself should have done so."

"Liar!" said Paul again, and he turned his back to Braxton Wyatt.

Wyatt looked fixedly at the bound boy, shrugged his shoulders a little, and said:

"I never took you for a fool before, Paul."

But Paul was silent, and Braxton Wyatt went away. An hour or two later Red Eagle came to Paul, unbound his arms, and gave him something to eat. As Paul ate the venison, Braxton Wyatt returned to him and said:

"It is my influence with the chief, Paul, that has secured you this good treatment in spite of their rage against you. It is better to pretend to fall in with their ways, if we are to retain life, and ever to secure freedom."

But Paul only turned his back again and remained silent. Yet with the food and rest the ache died out of his head, and he was permitted to wash off the blood caused by the heavy blow from the flat of a tomahawk. Then he crossed the Ohio with the band.

Paul was in a canoe with Red Eagle and two other warriors, and Braxton Wyatt was in another canoe not far away. But Paul resolutely ignored him, and looked only at the great river, and the thick forest on either shore. He was now more lonely than ever, and the Ohio that he was crossing seemed to him to be the boundary between the known and the unknown. Below it was Wareville and Marlowe, tiny settlements in the vast surrounding wilderness, it was true, but the abodes of white people, nevertheless. North of it, and he was going northward, stretched the forest that savages alone haunted. The crossing of the river was to Paul like passing over a great wall that would divide him forever from his own. All his vivid imagination was alive, and it painted the picture in its darkest and most somber colors.

They reached the northern shore without difficulty, hid the canoes for future use, and resumed their leisurely journey northward. Braxton Wyatt, who seemed to Paul to have much freedom, resumed his advances toward a renewal of the old friendship, but Paul was resolute. He could not overcome his repulsion, Braxton Wyatt might plead, and make excuses, and talk about the terror of torture and death, but Paul remained unconvinced. He himself had not flinched at the crucial moment to undo what Wyatt was doing, and in his heart he could find no forgiveness for the one whom he called a renegade.

Wyatt refused to take offense. He said, and Paul could not but hear, that Paul some day would be grateful for what he was doing, and that it was necessary in the forest to meet craft with craft, guile with guile.

The days passed in hunting, eating, resting, and marching, and Paul lost count of time, distance, and direction. He had not Henry's wonderful instinct in the wilderness, and he could not now tell at what point of the compass Wareville lay. But he kept a brave heart and a brave face, and if at times he felt despair, he did not let anyone see it.

They came at last to a place where the forest thinned out, and then broke away, leaving a little prairie. The warriors, who had previously been painting themselves in more hideous colors than ever, broke into a long, loud, wailing chant. It was answered in similar fashion from a point beyond a swell in the prairie, and Paul knew that they had come to the Indian village. The wailing chant was a sign that they had returned after disaster, and now all the old squaws were taking it up in reply. Paul was filled with curiosity, and he watched everything.

The warriors emerged from the last fringe of the forest, their faces blackened, the hideous chant for their lost rising and falling, but never ceasing. Forward to meet them poured a mongrel throng—old men, old squaws, children, mangy curs, and a few warriors. Paul was with Red Eagle, and when the old squaws saw him, they stopped their plaintive howl and sent up a sudden shrill note of triumph. In a moment Paul was in a ring of ghastly old faces, in every one of which snapped a pair of cruel black eyes. Then the old women began to push him about, to pinch him, and to strike him, and they showed incredible activity.

Thoroughly angry and in much pain, Paul struck at the hideous hags; but they leaped away, jabbered and laughed, and returned to the attack. While he was occupied with those in front of him, others slipped up behind him, jabbed him in the back, or violently twitched the hair on his neck. Tears of pain and rage stood in Paul's eyes, and he wheeled about, only to have the jeering throng wheel with him and continue their torture. At last he caught one of them a half blow, and she reeled and fell. The others shouted uproariously, and the warriors standing by joined in their mirth.

One of the hags finally struck Paul a resounding smack in the face, and as he turned to pursue her another from behind seized a wisp of hair and tried to tear it out by the roots. Paul whirled in a frenzy, and so quickly that she could not escape him. He seized her withered old throat in both his hands, and then and there he would have choked her to death, but the warriors interfered, and pulled his hands loose. But they also drove the old women away, and Paul was let alone for the time. As he stood on one side, gasping as much with anger as with pain, Braxton Wyatt, who had not been persecuted at all, came to him again with ironic words and derisive gesture.

"It was just as I told you, Paul," he said. "I gave you good advice. If you had taken it, they would have spared you. What you have just got is only a taste to what you may suffer."

Paul felt a dreadful inclination to shudder, but he managed to control himself.

"I'd rather die under the torture than do what you have done, you renegade!" he said.

This was the first time since they crossed the Ohio that he had replied to Braxton, but even now he would say no more, and Wyatt, following his custom, shrugged his shoulders and walked away. Then all, mingled in one great throng, went forward to the village. Paul saw an irregular collection of buffalo-skin and deer-skin tepees, and a few pole wigwams, with some rudely cultivated fields of maize about them. A fine brook flowed through the village, and the site, on the whole, was well chosen, well watered, and sheltered by the little hills from cold winds. It was too far away from those hills to be reached by a marksman in ambush, and all about hung signs of plenty—drying venison and buffalo meat, and skins of many kinds.

When they came within the circle of huts and tents, Paul was again regarded by many curious eyes, and there might have been more attempts to persecute him, but the chief, Red Eagle, kept them off. Red Eagle was able to speak a little English, but Paul was too proud to ask him about his own fate. Not a stoic by nature, the boy nevertheless had a will that could control his impulses.

He was thrust into a small pole hut, and when the door was tightly fastened he was left alone there. The place was not more than six feet square, and only a little higher than Paul's head when he stood erect. In one corner was a couch of skins, but that was its whole equipment. Some of the poles did not fit closely together, leaving cracks of a quarter of an inch or so, through which came welcome fresh air, and also the subdued hum of the village noises. He heard indistinctly the barking of dogs, and the chatter of old squaws scolding, but he paid little heed to them because he felt now the sudden rush of a terrible despair.

The Ohio had been the great wall between Paul and his kind, and with the steady march northward, through the forests and over the little prairies, still another wall, equally great, had been reared. It seemed to Paul that Henry and Shif'less Sol and his other friends could never reach him here, and whatever fate the Shawnees had in store for him, it would be a hard one. Wild life he liked in its due proportion, but he had no wish to become a wild man all his days. He wanted to see the settlements grow and prosper, and become the basis of a mighty civilization. This was what appealed to him most. His great task of helping to save Kentucky continually appealed to him, and now his chance of sharing in it seemed slender and remote—too slender and remote to be considered.

The boy lay long on his couch of skins. The hum of the village life still came to his ears, but he paid little heed to it. Gradually his courage came back, or rather his will brought it back, and he became conscious that the day was waning, also that he was growing hungry. Then the door was opened, and Red Eagle entered. Behind him came a weazened old warrior and a weazened old squaw, hideous to behold. Red Eagle stepped to one side, and the old squaw fell on Paul's neck, murmuring words of endearment. Paul, startled and horrified, pushed her off, but she returned to the charge. Then Paul pushed her back again with more force. Red Eagle stepped forward, and lifted a restraining hand.

"They would adopt you in place of the son they have lost," he said in his scant and broken English.

Paul looked at Red Eagle. It seemed to him that he saw on the face of the chief the trace of a sardonic grin. Then he looked at the weazened and repulsive old pair.

"Put me to the torture," he said.

Now the sardonic grin was unmistakable on die face of the chief.

"Not yet," he said, "but maybe later."

Then he and the old pair left the hut, and presently food was brought to Paul, who, worn out by his trials, ceased to think about his future. When he had finished eating he threw himself on the couch again, and slept heavily until the next day.

CHAPTER IX
A CHANGE OF PLACES

Now came a time which Paul did not wholly understand, but which seemed to him a period of test. The repulse of the old couple was not permanent. They came back again and again, inviting him to be their son, and patiently endured all his rebuffs until he began to feel a kind of pity for them. After that he was always gentle to them, but he remained firm in his resolve that he would not become a savage, either in reality or pretense.

After a week he was allowed to walk in the village and to look upon barbaric life, but he saw not the remotest chance of escape. The place contained perhaps five hundred souls—men, women, children, and papooses—and at least fifty mangy curs, every one of whom, including the papooses and curs, seemed to Paul to be watching him. Black eyes followed him everywhere. Nothing that he did escaped their attention. Every step was noted, and he knew that if he went a yard beyond the village he would bring a throng of warriors, squaws, and dogs upon him. But he was grateful for this bit of freedom, the escape from the confinement of close walls, and the forest about them, glowing with autumnal foliage, looked cool and inviting. He saw nothing of Braxton Wyatt, but Red Eagle told him one day that he had gone northward with a band, hunting. "He good boy," said Red Eagle. Paul shuddered with disgust.

More than two weeks passed thus, and it seemed to Paul that he was not only lost to his own world, but forgotten by it. Kentucky and all his friends had dipped down under the horizon, and would never reappear. Henry and Ross and Shif'less Sol would certainly have come for him if they could, but perhaps they had fallen, slain in the night battle. His heart stood still at the thought, but he resolutely put it away. It did not seem to him that one of such strength and skill as Henry Ware could be killed.

Paul sat on a rock about the twilight hour one day, and watched the sun sinking into the dark forest. He was inexpressibly lonely, as if forsaken of men. Savage life still left him untouched. It made no appeal to him anywhere, and he longed for Wareville, and his kind, which he was now sure he would never see again. Behind him rose the usual hum of the village—the barking of dogs, the chatter of squaws, and the occasional grunt of a warrior. In their way, these people were cheerful. Unlike Paul, they were living the only life they knew and liked, and had no thoughts of a better.

The lonely boy rose from the rock and walked back toward the pole hut, in which they fastened him every night. It had become a habit with him now, and he knew that it saved useless resistance and a lot of trouble. Had he taken a single step toward the forest instead of his own prison hut, a score of watchful eyes would have been upon him.

The twilight melted into the dark, and fires gleamed here and there in the village. Dusky figures passed before and behind the fires—those of squaws cooking the suppers. Paul's eyes wandered, idle and unobserving, over the savage scene, and then he uttered a little cry of impatience as a hulking warrior lurched against him. The man seemed to have tripped upon a root, an unusual thing for these sure-footed sons of the forest, and Paul drew back from him. But the savage recovered himself, and in a low voice said:

"Paul!"

Paul Cotter started violently. It was the first word in good English that he had heard in a time that seemed to be eternity—save those of Braxton Wyatt, whom he hated—and the effect upon him was overpowering. It was like a voice of hope coming suddenly from another world.

"Paul," continued the voice, now warningly, "don't speak. Go on to your hut. Friends are by."

Then the hulking and savage figure walked away, and Paul knew enough to take no apparent notice, but to continue on as if that welcome voice Had not come out of the darkness. Yet a thousand little pulses within him were throbbing, throbbing with joy and hope.

But whose was the voice? In his excitement he had not noticed the tone except to note that it was a white man's. He glanced back and saw the hulking form near the outskirts of the village, but the light was too dim to disclose anything. Henry? No, it was not Henry's figure. Then who was it? A friend, that was certain, and he had said that other friends were by.

Paul walked with a light step to his prison hut, sedulously seeking to hide the exultation in his face. He was not forgotten in his world! His friends were ready to risk their lives for him! His heart was leaping as he looked through the dusk at the smoking camp fires, the dim huts and tepees, and the shadowy figures that passed and repassed. He would soon be leaving all that savage life. He never doubted it.

He came to his prison hut, went calmly inside, and a few minutes later, the regular time being at hand, the door was fastened on the outside by Red Eagle or some of his people. He might perhaps have forced the door in the night, but he had not considered himself a skillful enough woodsman to slip from the village unobserved, and accordingly he had waited. Now he was very glad of his restraint.

Paul lay down on the couch of skins, but he was not seeking sleep. Instead he was waiting patiently, with something of Indian stoicism. He saw through the cracks in his hut the Indian fires, yet burning and smoking, and the dim figures still passing and repassing. There was also the faint hum to tell him that savage life did not yet sleep, and now and then a mongrel cur barked. But all things end in time, and after a while these noises ceased; even the cure barked no more, and the smoking fires sank low.

The Indian village lay at peace, but Paul's heart throbbed with expectation. Nor did it throb in vain. A muffled sound appeared in time at his door. It was some one at work on the fastenings, and Paul listened with every nerve a-quiver. Presently the noise ceased, a shaft of pale night light showed, and then was gone. But the door had been opened, and then closed, and some one was inside.

Paul waited without fear. He could barely see a dark, shapeless outline within the dimness of his hut, but he was sure it was the figure of the slouching warrior who had bumped against him. The man stood a moment or two, seeking to pierce the dusk with his own eyes, and then he said in a low voice:

"Paul! Paul! Is it you?"

"Yes," replied Paul, in the same guarded tone, "but I don't know who you are."

The figure swayed a little and laughed low, but with much amusement.

"It 'pears to me that we are forgot purty soon," it said. "An' I've worked hard fur a tired man."

Then Paul knew the familiar, whimsical tone. The light had burst upon him all at once.

"Shif'less Sol!" he exclaimed.

"Jest me," said Sol; "an' ain't I about the purtiest Shawnee warrior you ever saw? Why, Paul, I'm so good at playin' a loafin' savage from some other village that nary a Shawnee o' them all has dreamed that I am what I ain't. If ever I go back thar in the East, I'm goin' to be a play-actor, Paul."

"You can be anything on earth you want to be, Sol!" said Paul jubilantly. "It was mighty good of you to come."

"You'd a-thought Henry would a-come," whispered Sol; "but we decided that he was too tall an' somehow too strikin'-lookin' to come in here ez a common, everyday Injun, so it fell to me to loaf in, me bein' a tired-lookin' sort o' feller, anyway. But they're out thar in the woods a-waitin', Henry an' Tom Ross an' that ornery cuss, Jim Hart."

"I knew that you fellows would never desert me!" exclaimed Paul.

"Why, o' course not!" said Sol. "We never dreamed o' leavin' you. Now, Paul, we've got to git through this village somehow or other. Lucky it's purty dark, an' you'll have to do your best to walk an' look like a Red. Maybe we kin git fur enough to make a good run fur it, and then, with the woods an' the night helpin' us, we may give them the slip. Here, take this."

He pressed something cold and hard into Paul's hand, and Paul slipped the pistol into his belt, standing erect and feeling himself much of a man.

"It's time to be goin'," said Shif'less Sol.

"I'm ready," said Paul.

But neither took more than a single step forward, stopping together as they heard a light noise at the door.

"Thunder an' lightnin'!" said Shif'less Sol, under his breath. "Somebody's suspectin'."

"It looks like it," breathed Paul.

"Lay down on the skins and pretend to be asleep," said Shif'less Sol.

Paul lay down on the couch at once, in the attitude of one who slumbers, and closed his eyes—all but a little. Shif'less Sol shoved himself into the corner, and blotted out his figure against the wall.

The door opened and Braxton Wyatt stepped in. What decree of fate had caused him to be spying about that night, and what had caused him to find the door of Paul's prison hut unfastened? He stood a few moments, trying to accustom his eyes to the dark, and he plainly heard the regular breathing of Paul on the bed of skins. Presently he saw the dim, recumbent figure also. But he was still suspicious, and he took a step nearer. Then a big form, projected somewhere from the dark, hurled itself upon him, and he was thrown headlong to the earthen floor. Strong fingers compressed his throat, and he gasped for breath.

"Here, Paul," said Sol, "tear off a piece o' that skin an' stuff it into his mouth."

Paul, who had leaped to his feet, obeyed at once.

75

"An' cut off some stout strips o' the same with this knife o' mine," said Shif'less Sol.

Paul again obeyed at once, and in three minutes Braxton Wyatt lay bound and gagged on the earthen floor. Shif'less Sol Hyde and Paul Cotter stood over him, and looked down at him, and even in the dark they saw the terror of all things in his eyes.

"The Lord has been good to us to-night, Paul," said Shif'less Sol, with a certain solemnity, "an' He wuz best o' all when He sent this hound here a-spyin'."

"You know what he is?" said Paul.

"Ef I don't know, I've guessed."

Then the two stood silent for a little space, still gazing down at Braxton Wyatt, bound and gagged. Paul had never before seen such stark dread in the eyes of any one, and he shuddered. Despite himself, he felt a certain amount of pity.

"He would have lured a boat-load of our people into the hands of the savages," he said.

"I'll put this knife in his foul heart, Paul," said Shif'less Sol.

The bound figure quivered in its bonds, and the eyes became wild and appealing.

"No, not that," replied Paul; "I couldn't bear to see anyone helpless put to death."

"It was just the thought uv a moment," said Shif'less Sol. "We've got a better use fur him. It's the one that the Lord sent him here fur. Now, Paul, help me strip off his huntin' shirt."

They took off Braxton Wyatt's hunting shirt, leggins, and cap, and Paul put them on, his own taking their place on the form of the gagged youth.

"Now, Paul," said Shif'less Sol, "you're Braxton Wyatt—for a little while, at least, you've got to stand it—an' he's you. Help me roll him up thar on your bed o' skins, an' he kin sleep in calm an' peace until they bring him his breakfast in the mornin'."

They put Wyatt on the couch, and his eyes glared fiercely at them. He struggled to speak, but they did not care to hear him. Sol took the weapons from his belt and gave them to Paul.

"Good-night, Braxton," said Shif'less Sol pleasantly. "Fine dreams to you. We're glad you came. You happened in jest in time."

Wyatt quivered convulsively on his bed of skins. Paul was filled with repugnance, but he would not exult. His nature would not permit him. Shif'less Sol opened the door, and the two stepped out into the open air and a dark night. No one was about, and the shiftless one deliberately fastened the doors on the outside in the usual manner. Then he and Paul strolled away through the village.

"Remember that you are Braxton Wyatt," whispered Shif'less Sol. "Walk ez near like him ez you kin. You've seen him often enough to know."

The two sauntered lazily forward. An old squaw, crouched by a low and smoking fire, gave one glance at them, but no more. She went on dreaming of the days when she was young, and when the braves fought for her. A mangy cur barked once, and then lay down again at the foot of a deer-skin lodge. A warrior, smoking a pipe in his own doorway, looked up, but saw nothing unusual, and then looked down again.

The coolness of Shif'less Sol was something wonderful to see. He merely loafed along, as if he had no object in the world but to pass away the time, and there was nothing in the course he chose to indicate that he meant to reach the forest. Now and then he spoke apparently casual words to Paul, and the boy, in the faint light, wearing Braxton Wyatt's clothes, might easily pass for Braxton Wyatt himself, even to the keen eyes of the Shawnees.

Presently they reached the northern end of the village, the one nearest to the forest, and it was here that Shif'less Sol intended to make the escape. Paul kept close to him, and he noticed with joy that all the time the light, already faint, was growing fainter. The friendly forest seemed to curve very near. Paul's heart throbbed with painful violence.

Shif'less Sol passed the last wigwam, and he took a step into the open space that divided them from the forest. Paul stepped with him, but a gaunt and weazened figure rose up in their path. It was that of the old squaw who wished a new son, and she stared for a few moments at the clothes of Braxton Wyatt, and the figure within them. Then she knew, and she uttered a shrill cry that was at once a lament and a warning. At the same time she flung her arms around Paul in a gesture that was intended alike for affection and detention.

"Run, Paul, run!" exclaimed Shif'less Sol.

Paul attempted to throw off the old woman, but she clung to him like a wild cat, showing marvelous strength and tenacity for one so little and weazened and old. Shif'less Sol saw the difficulty and, seizing her in his powerful grasp, tore her loose.

"Don't hurt her, Sol!" cried Paul.

Shif'less Sol understood, and he cast her from them, but not with violence. Then the two ran with utmost speed and desperate need toward the forest, because the village behind them was up and alive. Lights flared, dogs barked, men shouted, and before the friendly trees were reached rifles began to crack.

"Jumpin' Jehoshaphat!" cried Shif'less Sol, as a bullet whistled past his ear. "Ef that don't put life into a tired man, I don't know what will."

He ran with amazing swiftness, and Paul, light-footed, kept beside him. But the alert Shawnee warriors, ever quick to answer an alarm, were already in fleet pursuit, and only the darkness kept their bullets from striking true. Paul looked back once—even in the moment of haste and danger he could not help it—and he saw three warriors in advance of the others, coming so fast that they must overtake them. He and Sol might beat them off, but one cannot fight well and at the same time escape from a multitude. His heart sank. He would be recaptured, and with him the gallant Shif'less Sol.

Flashes of fire suddenly appeared in the forest toward which they ran, and death cries came from the two warriors who pursued. Shif'less Sol uttered an exultant gasp.

"The boys!" he said. "They're thar in the woods, a-helpin'."

Daunted by the sudden covering fire, the pursuing mob fell back for a few moments, and the two fugitives plunged into the deep and friendly shadows of the woods. Three figures, all carrying smoking rifles, rose up to meet them. The figures were those of Henry Ware, Tom Ross, and Jim Hart. Henry reached out his hand and gave Paul's a strong and joyous grasp.

"Well, Sol has brought you!" he said.

"But Sol's not goin' to stop runnin' yet for a long time, tired ez he is," gasped the shiftless one.

"Good advice," said Henry, laughing low, and without another word the five ran swiftly and steadily northward through the deep woods. Henry had on his shoulder an extra rifle, which he had brought for Paul, so confident was he that Sol would save him; but he said nothing about it for the present, preferring to carry the added weight himself. They heard behind them two or three times the long-drawn, terrible cry with which Paul was so familiar, but it did not now send any quiver through him. He was with the ever-gallant comrades who had come for him, and he was ready to defy any danger.

Henry Ware, after a while, stopped very suddenly, and the others stopped with him.

"I think we'd better turn here," he said, unconsciously assuming his natural position of leader. "It's not worth while to run ourselves to death. What we've got to do is to hide."

"Them's blessed words!" gasped Shif'less Sol. "I wuz never so tired in all my born days. Seems to me I've been chased by Shawnees all over this here continent of North Ameriky!"

78

Paul laughed low, from pure pleasure—pleasure at his escape and pleasure in the courage, loyalty, and skill of his comrades.

"You may be tired, Sol," he said, "but there was never a braver man than you."

"It ain't bravery," protested the shiftless one. "I get into these things afore I know it, an' then I've got to kick like a mule to get out o' 'em."

But Paul merely laughed low again.

Henry turned from the north to the west, and led now at a pace that was little more than a walk. Paul and Sol drew deep breaths, as they felt the heavenly air flowing back into their lungs and the spring returning to their muscles. They went in Indian file, five dusky figures in the shadow, a faint moonlight touching them but wanly, and all silent. Thus they marched until past midnight, and they heard nothing behind them. Then their leader stopped, and the others, without a word, stopped with him.

"I think we've shaken 'em off," said Henry, "and we'd better rest and sleep. Then we can make up our plans."

"Good enough," said Shif'less Sol. "An' ef any man wakes me up afore next week, I'll hev his scalp."

He sank down at once in his buckskins on a particularly soft piece of turf, and in an incredibly brief space of time he was sound asleep. Jim Hart, doubling up his long, thin figure like a jackknife, imitated him, and Paul was not long in following them to slumberland. Only Henry and Ross remained awake and watchful, and by and by the moonlight came out and silvered their keen and anxious faces.

CHAPTER X
THE ISLAND IN THE LAKE

When Paul awoke the others were munching the usual breakfast of dried venison, and Henry handed him a piece, which he ate voraciously. Henry was sitting on the ground, with his back against a fallen log, and he regarded Paul contemplatively.

"Paul," he said, in the dryest possible tones, "I don't see how you could have been so hard-hearted."

Paul looked at him, startled. "Why, what do you mean?"

"To tear yourself away, as you did, from a loving father and mother. Why, Sol, here, tells me that you actually threw your mother from you."

"Truth, Gospel truth," put in Shif'less Sol. "I never seen sech a cruel, keerless person. He gives her jest one fling into the south, an' then he bolts off into the north, like an arrow out o' the bow. I follows him lickety-split to bring him back, but he runs so fast I can't ketch him."

Paul smiled.

"I've one father and mother already," he said, "and so I have no use for two. Rather than cause embarrassment, I came away as quickly as I could."

"You did come fast," said Henry dryly.

"It was mighty fine of all of you to come after me," said Paul earnestly, "and to risk your lives to save me from the Shawnees. But I knew you'd do it."

"Uv course," said Tom Ross simply. "The rest uv our party would hev come, too, but they were needed back thar in Kentucky. Besides, we could spare 'em, ez it took cunnin' an' not numbers to do what we had to do."

"What's our next step?" asked Paul, who was in the highest of spirits—his imagination, with its usual vivid rebound, now painted everything in glowing colors.

"We are going northward," said Henry.

"Northward?"

"Yes, it's necessary. There's some great movement on foot among the tribes. It's not the Shawnees alone, but the Miamis and Wyandots and others as well, though the Shawnees are leaders. War belts are passing between all the tribes, and we think they are joining together to destroy all the white settlements in Kentucky."

"An' some renegades are helpin' 'em," said Tom Ross. "They may hev better luck than they did when they attacked Wareville."

"Yes, an' there's Braxton Wyatt," said Shif'less Sol sorrowfully, "He's cunnin' an' revengeful, an' he'll do us a power o' harm. Paul, you ought to a-let me put a knife in atween his ribs when I had the chance. I might a-saved some good lives an' a power o' sufferin'."

Paul did not reply, but he was not sorry that he had interfered. He could not see a bound youth killed.

"I think we'd better be goin' now," said Tom Ross. "We've got to keep to the north, to throw the Shawnees off the track, an' then we'll come back an' spy on 'em."

"An' me with only ten hours o' rest got to git up an' start to runnin' ag'in," said Shif'less Sol plaintively.

"Wa'al, no, you needn't run," said Tom Ross, grinning. "You can jest walk for about forty hours without stoppin'!"

Shif'less Sol heaved a deep sigh, but made ready. Jim Hart undoubled himself, cracked his joints, and said deliberately:

"Ef I wuz ez lazy ez Shif'less Sol Hyde, I'd a-stayed back thar in the East, whar a feller might jest sleep hisself to death, an' no Injuns to torment him."

"Ef I wuz es mean an' onchristian ez Jim Hart, I'd go an' join Braxton Wyatt an' become a renegade myself," rejoined Shif'less Sol.

Paul smiled. He enjoyed the little spats of Sol and Jim, but he knew that the two were as true as steel, and the best of friends to each other. Moreover, he was about to take up again the mission which Fate seemed so constantly to interrupt. The scene of action had been shifted to the great northern woods, and it now seemed to Paul that perhaps Fortune had been kind in bringing him there. If a league of the tribes were being attempted for a new attack upon the settlements, the powder for Marlowe might well rest, for the present, in its hiding-place in the woods, while his comrades and he undertook more important action elsewhere.

Before they started, Henry and Ross took stock of their ammunition, of which they had a plentiful supply, replenished more than once from their enemies, and also gave an abundance to Paul. The extra rifle given to him, one of those taken from the two warriors that Henry had slain, was a fine weapon, carrying far and true, and he was perfectly satisfied with it.

Then they started, and they traveled all day northward, through a fine rolling country, with little prairies and great quantities of game. It was fully equal to Kentucky, but Paul knew they were in the heart of the chosen home of the northern Indians, and it behooved them to be cautious. But there were no signs of pursuit, and they went on all day undisturbed.

Late in the afternoon they entered a dense forest, and walked through it about two hours, when Paul saw an opening among the trees. It was a great flash of silver that all at once greeted his eyes. But as he looked it turned to gold under the late sun.

"Another of those little prairies," he said.

Henry laughed.

"No, Paul," he said, "that's not a prairie. The sun and the sky together have fooled you. It's a lake, and we're going to live in it for a little while."

"A lake," echoed Paul, "and we're going to live in it? Come on, I want to see it!"

Kentucky was not a country of lakes, and Paul did not know much about them. Hence, as he hastened forward, he was thinking more of the lake itself than of Henry's somewhat enigmatic words, "We're going to live in it."

They soon reached its margin, and Paul uttered a little cry of delight. It was a splendid sheet of water, shaped like a half moon, seven miles long, perhaps, and two miles across at the center. But at the widest part stood a gem of a wooded island, covered with giant trees. High hills, clothed with magnificent forest, rose all around the lake.

The beauty of the scene penetrated the souls of all. Uneducated men like Shif'less Sol and Jim Hart felt it as well as Paul. The five stood in silence, gazing at the lake and the gem of a wooded island. The light from the sinking sun gleamed in red and gold flame across the silver waters, and on the wooded island the boughs of the trees seemed to be touched with fire.

"That's where we are to stay," said Henry, pointing to the little island. "No Indian will ever trouble us there."

"Why?" asked Paul, looking at him questioningly.

"Wait and you'll see," replied Henry.

Henry led the way along the shore, and from a dense thicket at the water's edge he took a light canoe.

"I captured this once," he said; "brought it across the woods and hid it here, thinking it might be useful some day, and now you see I am right. Get in! Light as it is, it will hold us all."

Henry and Ross took the paddles, and they pushed out into the lake. Shif'less Sol uttered a long and deep sigh of satisfaction.

"Now, this jest suits a tired man," he said. "Henry, you an'

Tom can paddle jest ez long ez you please. I'd like to do all my travelin' this way."

"An' you'd get so lazy you'd want somebody to come an' feed you with a spoon," said Jim Hart.

"An' it would jest suit me to have you do it. That's jest the kind uv a job you're fit fur, Jim Hart."

"Shet up, you two," said Ross. "You hurt my ears, a-buzzin' an' a-buzzin'."

Shif'less Sol sank back a little and closed his eyes. An expression of heavenly luxury and ease came over his face, but it could not last long because in a few minutes the boat reached the wooded island. Shif'less Sol opened his eyes, to find that the sun was almost gone, and that the shadows had come among the great trees.

"Cur'us kind o' place," he said. "Gives me a sort o' shiver."

Paul had felt the same sensation, but he said nothing. Before them lay the little island, a solid, black blot, its trees blended together, and behind them the lake shone somberly in the growing darkness.

"All out!" said Henry cheerfully. "This is home for a while, and we need rest."

They sprang upon the narrow beach, and Henry and Ross dragged the canoe into some thick bushes, where they hid it artfully. Paul meanwhile was looking about him, and trying to keep down the ghostly feeling that would assail him at times. The island, so far as he could judge, was perhaps two hundred yards long, half as broad, and thickly covered with forest. But he could see nothing of the interior.

"Come," said Henry Ware, in the same tone of cheerful confidence, as he led the way.

The others followed, stepping lightly among the great tree trunks, and Henry did not stop until he came to a small, open space in the very center of the island, where a spring bubbled up among some rocks, and flowed away in a tiny brook in a narrow channel to the lake. The open space was almost circular, and the great trees grew so thickly around that they looked like a wall.

"Here is the place to rest," said Henry. "There is no need for anybody to watch."

They lay down upon the ground, disposing themselves on the softest spots that they could find. Paul stared up for a few moments at the great circular wall of trees, and the weird, chilly sensation came again, but he was too tired and sleepy to think about it long. In fifteen minutes he slumbered soundly, and so did all the others. They lay with their faces showing but faintly in the dusk, and as they lay in the sheltered cove a soft wind breathed gently over them.

All were up early in the morning, and Paul was surprised to see Henry lighting a fire with flint and steel.

"Why do you do that, Henry?" he said. "Will not the smoke give warning to our enemies that we are here?"

"We shall send up but little smoke," replied Henry; "but if they should see it, they will not come."

He went on with the fire, and Paul, although mystified, would not ask anything more, too proud to show ignorance, and confident that anyhow he would soon learn the cause of these strange proceedings. The fire was lighted, and burned brightly, but cast off little smoke. Then Henry turned to Paul.

"Let's go up to the north end of the island," he said.

It was a walk of but a few minutes, and Henry, stopping before they reached the margin of the lake, said:

"Look up, Paul!"

Paul did so, and saw many dark objects in the forks of trees about him, or tied to the boughs. They looked like shapeless bundles, and he did not know what they were.

"A burying ground," said Henry, in answer to his inquiring look.

Paul felt the same weird little shiver that had assailed him the night before.

"A burying ground!"

"Yes, but by some old, old tribe before the Shawnees or Miamis. What you see are only bundles of sticks and skeletons. No bodies have been left here in a long time, and the Indians think the island is haunted by the ghosts of those who died and were left here long, long ago. That is why we needed to keep no watch last night. I discovered this place on a hunting trip, and I've always kept it in mind.

"Let's go back," said Paul, who did not like to look at this burying ground in the air.

Henry laughed a little, but he did willingly as Paul requested, and when they returned to the fire they found that Jim Hart, falling easily into his natural position, had already cooked the venison. Paul's spirits at once went up with a bound. The bright fire, the pleasant odor of the venison, the cheerful faces of his comrades, and assured safety appealed to his vivid imagination, and made the blood leap in a sparkling torrent through his veins.

"Graveyard or no graveyard, I'm glad I'm here," he said energetically.

They laughed, and Shif'less Sol, who, as usual, had found the softest place and had stretched himself upon it, said, with drawling emphasis:

"You're mighty right, Paul, an' I'm a'gin' movin' from here afore cold weather comes. I'm pow'ful comf'table."

"If you don't git up an' stir aroun', how do you expect to eat?" said Jim Hart indignantly. "We ain't got venison enough for more'n ten more meals."

"Henry an' Tom will shoot it, an' you'll cook it fur me," said Sol complacently.

Jim Hart growled, but Henry and Ross were already discussing this question of a food supply, and Paul listened.

"The Indians don't come about the lake much," said Henry, "and it will be easy enough to find deer, but we must hunt at night. We mustn't let the savages see us, as it might break the island's spell."

"We'll take the canoe and go out to-night," said Ross.

"And this lake ought to be full of fish," said Paul. "We might draw on it, too, for a food supply."

"Looks likely," said Ross. "But we'd best not try that, either, till dusk."

But they worked in the course of the day at the manufacture of their rude fishing tackle, constructed chiefly of their clothing, the hooks being nothing more than a rough sort of pin bent to the right shape. This done, they spent the rest of the day in loafing and lolling about, although Paul took a half hour for the thorough exploration of the island, which presented no unusual features beyond those that he had already seen. After that he came back to the little cove and luxuriated, as the others were doing. It was the keenest sort of joy now just to rest, to lie at one's ease, and to feel the freedom from danger. The old burying ground was a better guard about them than a thousand men.

But when night came, Henry and Ross took out the canoe again, and Paul asked to go with them.

"All right," said Henry, "you come with us, and Sol, you and Jim Hart can do the fishing and the quarreling, with nobody to bother you."

"Jest my luck," said Shif'less Sol, "to be left on a desert island with an ornery cuss like Jim Hart."

Henry, setting the paddle against the bank, gave the canoe a great shove, and it shot far out into the lake. Paul looked back. Already their island was the solid dark blot it had been the night before, while the waters moved darkly under a light, northern wind.

"Sit very quiet, Paul," said Henry. "Tom and I will do the paddling."

Paul was more than content to obey, and he remained very still while the other two, with long, sweeping strokes, sent the canoe toward a point where the enclosing bank was lowest.

"Don't you think we'd better stay in the boat, Henry?" said Ross.

"Yes; game must be thick hereabouts, and if we wait long enough we're sure to find a deer coming down to drink."

They cruised for a while along the shore, keeping well in the darkest shadow until they reached a point where the keen eyes of Henry Ware saw, despite the darkness, that many hoofs had trampled.

"This is a favorite drinking place," he said. "Back us into those bushes, Tom, and we'll wait."

Ross pushed the canoe into some bushes until it was hidden, though the occupants could see through the leaves whatever might come to the water to drink, and they took up their rifles. They lay a little to the north of the drinking place, and the wind blew from the south.

"I don't think we'll have to wait long," said Henry.

Then they remained absolutely silent, but within fifteen minutes they heard a heavy trampling in the woods. It steadily grew louder, and was mingled with snortings and puffings. Whatever animal made it—and it was undoubtedly a big one—was coming toward them. Paul was filled with curiosity, but he knew too much to do more just now than breathe.

A huge bull buffalo stumbled from the trees to the edge of the lake, where the moonlight had just begun to come. He was a monstrous fellow, and Paul knew by his snapping red eyes that he was in no good humor. Henry shook his head to indicate that he was no game for them, and Paul understood. Whatever they killed they intended to put in the canoe, and then clean and dress it on the island. The angry monster, an outcast from some herd, was safe.

The buffalo drank, puffing and snorting between drinks, and then stamped his way back into the forest. Still the hunters waited in ambush. Some other animal, with a long, sinuous body, crept down to the margin and lapped the water. Paul did not know what it was, and he could not break the silence to ask the others; but after drinking for a few minutes it drew its long, lithe body back through the undergrowth, and passed out of sight. Then nothing came for a while, because this was a ferocious beast of prey, and to the harmless creatures of the wilderness the air about the drinking place was filled for a space with poison.

But as the wind continued to blow lightly from the south, the dread odor passed away and the air became pure and fresh again. Back in the deeps of the forest the timid creatures found courage once more, and they crept down to the water's edge to slake their thirst. But they were small, and the ambushed marksmen in the boat still waited, silent and motionless. Paul saw them sometimes, and sometimes he did not. Then his eyes would wander to the surface of the lake, now pale, heaving silver in the moonlight, and to the wall of black forest that circled it round.

A heavier step came again, and a light puff! puff! Paul knew now that a great animal was approaching, and that the timid little ones would give it room. He looked with all his eyes, and a magnificent stag stepped into the moonlight, antlers erect, waiting and listening for a moment before he bowed his head to drink. Paul almost leaped up in the boat as a rifle cracked beside him, and he saw the stag spring into the air and fall dead, with his feet in the water.

Henry and Ross promptly shoved the boat from the bushes, and the three of them lifted the body into it, disposing it in the center with infinite care. Then, with food enough to last for days, they rowed back across the lake to the haunted island. Shif'less Sol and Jim Hart, with their rude tackle, had succeeded in catching four fish, of a species unknown to Paul, but large and to all appearances succulent.

"We'll eat the fish to-morrow, because they won't keep," said Sol, "but Jim Hart here kin jerk the venison. It will give him somethin' to do, an' Jim is a sight better off when he has to work. He ain't got no time fur foolishness."

"An' you can tan its hide," growled Jim Hart, "although your own needs tannin' most."

A few minutes later the two were amicably dressing the body of the stag, but Paul was already asleep. He assisted the next morning at a conference, and then he learned what Henry and Ross intended to do. The powder for Marlowe, as Paul had surmised, must be left for the present in its hidden place while they spied upon the great northern confederacy, now being formed for the destruction of the white settlements, and they would do what they could to impede it. Henry, Ross, and Sol would leave that night on an expedition of discovery, while Paul and Jim Hart held the haunted island. Paul, in this case, did not object to being left behind, because he had, for the present at least, enough of danger, and he knew that he was better suited to other tasks than the one on which the three great woodsmen were now departing.

Jim Hart was to row them over to the mainland, and they were to signal their return with three plaintive, long-drawn cries of the whip-poor-will. They departed at the first coming of the dusk with short good-bys, leaving Paul alone on the island. He stood near the margin under the foliage of a great beech and watched them go. The boat, as it left a trailing wake of melting silver, became a small black dot at the farther shore, and then vanished.

Paul turned back toward the center of his island, inexpressibly lonely for the while. Again he was a solitary being in the vast, encircling wilderness, and, in feeling at least, no one was nearer than a thousand miles away. He walked as swiftly as he could to the cove, where the supper fire still smoldered, and he sought companionship in the light and warmth that came from the bed of coals. No amount of hardship, no amount of experience could change Paul's vivid temperament, so responsive to the influences of time and place. He sat there, his knees drawn up to his chin, and the ring of darkness came closer and closer; but out of it presently arose the tread of footsteps, and all the brightness and cheeriness returned at once to the boy's face.

Jim Hart walked into the rim of the firelight, and his long, thin, saplinglike figure looked very consoling to Paul. He doubled into his usual jackknife formation and, sitting down by the fire, looked into the coals.

"Well, Paul," he said, "I've seen 'em off, an' a-tween you and me, I'd rather be right here on this here haunted islan', a-hobnobbin' with Injun ghosts an' havin' a good, comfortable, easy time, than be dodgin' braves, an' feelin' every minute to see ef my scalp is on out thar among the Injun villages."

"You don't think they'll be taken?" asked Paul, in some alarm.

Long Jim Hart laughed scornfully.

"Them fellers be took?" he said. "Why, they are the best three woodsmen in North Ameriky, an', fur that, in the hull world. Nobody can take 'em, an' if they wuz took, nobody could hold 'em. You could have Henry Ware tied to the stake, with fifty Shawnees holdin' him an' a thousand more standin' aroun', an' he'd get away, certain sure."

Paul smiled. It was an extravagant statement, but it restored his confidence.

"And meanwhile we are safe here, protected by ghosts," he said. "Do you believe in ghosts, Jim?"

Jim Hart looked up at the black rim of the forest, and then edged a little closer to the fire.

"No, I don't," he said, "but sometimes I'm afeard of 'em, jest the same."

Paul laughed.

"That's about the way I feel, too," he said, "but they're mighty handy just now, Jim. They're keeping us safe on this island. You won't deny that?"

"No, I won't," said Jim; "but at night time I'm goin' to leave 'em all by themselves in the trees over at their end uv of the island."

"So am I," said Paul; and ten minutes later both were sound asleep.

CHAPTER XI
A SUDDEN MEETING

Paul and queer, long Jim Hart spent a week together on the island, and they were pleasant days to the boy. He was sure that Henry, Ross, and Sol could take care of themselves, and he felt little anxiety about them. He and Hart stayed well in the woods in the day, and they fished and hunted at night. Hart killed another deer, this time swimming in the water, but they easily made salvage of the body and took it to land. They also shot a bear in the edge of the woods, near the south end of the lake, and Hart quickly tanned both deerskins and the bearskin in a rude fashion. He said they would need them as covers at night, and as the weather turned a little colder, Paul found that he could use one of the skins quite comfortably.

They built of sticks and brushwood a crude sort of lean-to against one of the stony sides that enclosed the cove, and when a rain came they were able to keep quite dry within its shelter. They also found rabbits on the island, some of which they killed, and thus added further to their larder. These labors of house-building and housekeeping kept them busy, and Paul was surprised to find how well content he had become. Hart did all the cooking, but Paul made amends in other directions, and at night, when they were not fishing or hunting, they would sit by the little fire and talk. Once about the noon hour they saw a smoke far to the south, and both regarded it speculatively.

"Think likely it's an Injun huntin' party," said Jim Hart, "an' they don't dream o' any white men bein' about. That's why they are so careless about their fire, because the different tribes o' these parts are all at peace with one another."

"How far away would you say that smoke is?" asked Paul.

"Three or four miles, anyway, an' I'm pow'ful glad this is a haunted islan', so they won't come over here."

"So am I," said Paul devoutly.

He lay on his back on the soft turf, and watched the smoke rising away in a thin spire into the heavens. He could picture to himself the savage party as it sat about the fire, and it gave him a remarkable feeling of comfort and safety to know that he was so well protected by the ghosts that haunted the little island.

The smoke rose there all the morning, but Paul ceased by and by to pay any attention to it, although he and Jim Hart kept well within the cove, busying themselves with additions to their lean-to. Paul had found great strips of bark shed by the trees, and he used these to patch the roof. More pieces were used for the floor, and, with the bearskin spread over them, it was quite dry and snug. Then he stood off and regarded it with a critical and approving eye.

"You haven't seen a better house than that lately, have you, Jim?" he said, in a tone of pride.

"Considerin' the fact that I ain't seen any other uv any kind in a long time, I kin truthfully say I haven't," replied Jim Hart sardonically.

"You lack appreciation, Jim," said Paul. "Besides, your imagination is deficient. Why don't you look at this hut of ours and imagine that it is a magnificent stone castle?"

Jim Hart gazed wonderingly at the boy.

"Paul," he said, "you always wuz a puzzle to me. I can't see no magnificent stone castle—jest a bark an' brush hut."

Paul shook his head reprovingly.

"I am sorry for you, Jim," he said. "I not only see a magnificent stone castle, but I see a splendid town over there on the mainland."

"You talk plumb foolish, Paul," said Jim Hart.

"They are all coming," said Paul.

But Jim Hart continued to see only the bark and brush hut on the island, and the vast and unbroken wilderness on the mainland. His eyes roved back, from the mainland to the hut.

"Now, ef I had an ax an' a saw," he said regretfully, "I could make that look like somethin'. I'm a good cook, ef I do say it, Paul, but I'd like to be a fust-class carpenter. Thar ain't no chance, though, out here, whar thar ain't nothin' much but cabins, an' every man builds his own hisself."

"Never mind, Jim," said Paul, "your time will come; and if it doesn't come to you, it will come to your sons."

"Paul, you're talkin' foolisher than ever," said Jim indignantly. "You know that I ain't a married man, an' that I ain't got no sons."

Paul only smiled. Again he was dreaming, looking far into the future.

The spire of smoke was still on the horizon line when the twilight came, but the next morning it was gone, and they did not see it again. Several days more passed in peace and contentment, and, desiring to secure more game, Paul and Hart took out the canoe one evening and rowed to the mainland.

They watched a while about the mouth of the brook, the favorite drinking place of the wild animals, but they saw nothing. It seemed likely to Paul that a warning had been sent to all the tenants of the forest not to drink there any more, as it was a dangerous place, and he expressed a desire to go farther into the forest.

"All right, Paul," said Jim Hart, "but you kain't be too keerful. Don't git lost out thar in the woods, an' don't furgit your way back to this spot. I'll wait right here in the boat and watch fur a deer. One may come yet."

Paul took his rifle and entered the woods. It was his idea that he might find game farther up the little stream, and he followed its course, taking care to make no noise. It was a fine moonlight night, and, keeping well within the shadow of the trees, he carefully watched the brook. He was so much absorbed in his task that he forgot the passage of time, and did not notice how far he had gone.

Paul had acquired much skill as a hunter, and he was learning to observe the signs of the forest; but he did not hear a light step behind him, although he did feel himself seized in a powerful grasp. This particular warrior was a Miami, and he may have been impelled by pride—that is, a desire to take a white youth alive, or at least hold him until his comrades, who were near, could come and secure him. To this circumstance, and to a fortunate slip of the savage, the boy undoubtedly owed his life.

Paul was strong, and the grasp of the Indian was like the touch of fire to him. He made a sudden convulsive effort, far greater than his natural physical powers, and the arms of the warrior were torn loose. Both staggered, each away from the other, and while they were yet too close for Paul to use his rifle, he did, under impulse, what the white man often does, the red man never. His clenched fist shot out like lightning, and caught the savage on the point of the jaw.

The Miami hit the earth with a thud, and lay there stunned. Paul turned and ran with all his might, and as he ran he heard the war cry behind him, and then the pattering of feet. But he heard no shots. He judged that the distance and the darkness kept the savages from firing, and he thanked God for the night.

He had sufficient presence of mind to remember the stream, and he kept closely to its course as he ran back swiftly toward the canoe.

"Up, Jim, up! The warriors have come!" he shouted, as he ran.

But Jim Hart, an awkward bean pole of a lion-hearted man, was already coming to meet him, and fired past him at a dusky, dancing figure that pursued. The death yell followed, the pursuit wavered for a moment, and then Jim Hart, turning, ran with Paul to the canoe, into which both leaped at the same time. But Hart promptly undoubled himself, seized the paddle, and with one mighty shove sent the boat out into the lake. Paul grasped the other paddle, and bent to the same task. Their rifles lay at their feet.

"Bend low, Paul," said Jim Hart. "We're still within range of the shore."

Paul almost lay down in the canoe, but he never ceased to make long, frantic sweeps with the paddle, and he was glad to see the water flashing behind him. Then he heard a great yell of rage and the crackle of rifles, and bullets spattered the surface of the lake about them. One chipped a splinter from the edge of the canoe and whistled by Paul's ear, singing, as it passed, "Look out! Look out!" But Paul's only reply was to use his paddle faster, and yet faster.

The boy did not notice that Jim Hart had turned the course of the canoe, and that they were running northward, about midway between the island and the mainland; but the rifle fire ceased presently, and Jim Hart said to him:

"You can take it easier now, Paul. We're out uv range, though not uv sight."

Paul straightened up, laid his paddle in the boat, and gasped for breath.

"Look over thar, Paul, ef you want to see a pleasant scene," said Jim Hart calmly.

Paul's gaze followed the long man's pointing finger, and he saw at least twenty warriors gathered on the bank, and regarding them now in dead silence.

"Mad!" said Jim Hart. "Mad clean through!"

"They've chased us on land, and now they are chasing us on water. I wonder where they will chase us next," said Paul.

"Not through the air, 'cause they can't fly, nor kin we," said Jim Hart sagely.

Paul looked back again at the ferocious band gathered on the shore, and, while he could not see their faces at the distance, he could imagine the evil passions pictured there. As he gazed the band broke up, and many of them came running along the shore. Then Paul noticed that the prow of their canoe was not turned toward the island, but was bearing steadily toward the north end of the lake, leaving the island well to the left. He glanced at Jim Hart, and the long man laughed low, but with deep satisfaction.

"Don't you see, Paul," he said, "that we kain't go to the islan' an' show to them that we've been livin' thar? That might wipe out all the spell uv the place. We got to let 'em think we're 'fraid uv it, too, an' that we dassent land thar. We'll paddle up to the head uv the lake, come down on the other side, an' then, when it's atween us an' them, we'll come across to our islan'.'"

They were still abreast of the island, and yet midway between it and the mainland. Paul saw the Indians running along the shore, and now and then taking a shot at the canoe. But the bullets always fell short.

"Foolish! Plumb foolish," said Jim Hart, "a-wastin' good powder an' good lead in sech a fashion!"

"That one struck nearer," said Paul, as a little jet of water spurted up in the lake. "Keep her off, Jim. A bullet that is not wasted might come along directly."

Hart sheered the boat off a little toward the island, and then took a long look at a warrior who had reached a projecting point of land.

"That thar feller looks like a chief," he said, "an' I kain't say that his looks please me a-tall, a-tall. I don't like the set uv his figger one little bit."

"What difference does it make?" said Paul. "You can't change it."

"Wa'al, now, I was a-thinkin' that maybe I could," drawled Jim Hart. "Hold the boat steady, Paul."

He laid down his paddle and took up his rifle, which he had reloaded.

"Them Injuns have guns, but they are not generally ez good ez ours," he said. "They don't carry ez fur. Now jest watch me change the set uv that savage's figger. I wouldn't do it, but he's just a-pinin' fur our blood an' the hair on top uv our heads."

Up went the long Kentucky rifle, and the moonlight fell clearly along its polished barrel. Then came the flash, the spurt of smoke, the report echoing among the hills about the lake, and the chief fell forward with his face in the water. A yell of rage arose from the others, and again bullets pattered on the surface of the lake, but all fell short. Jim Hart calmly reloaded his rifle.

"That'll teach 'em to be a little more keerful who they're a-follerin'," he said. "Now, Paul, let's paddle."

They sent the boat swiftly toward the north end of the lake, and Paul now and then caught glimpses of the Miamis trying to keep parallel with it, although out of range; but presently, as they passed the island, and could swing out into the middle of the lake, the last of them sank permanently from sight. But the two kept on in the canoe. The moonlight faded a little, and soon the hills on the shore could be seen only as a black blur.

"This is jest too easy, Paul," said Jim Hart, "With them runnin' aroun' that big outer circle, they couldn't keep up with us even ef they could see us. Let's rest a while."

Both put their paddles inside the canoe and drew long breaths. Each had a feeling of perfect safety, for the time at least, and they let the boat drift northward under the gentle wind from the south that rippled the surface of the lake.

"Water and darkness," said Paul. "They are our friends."

"The best we could have," said Jim Hart. "Are you rested now, Paul?"

"I'm fresh again."

They resumed the paddles, and, curving about, came down on the western side of the lake until they were opposite the island. Then they paddled straight for their home, and the word "home," in this case, had its full meaning for Paul. It gave him a thrill of delight when the prow of the canoe struck upon the margin of the little island, and the gloom of the great trees was friendly and protecting.

"We must hide the canoe good," said Jim Hart.

They concealed it in a thick clump of bushes, and then Hart carefully readjusted the bushes so that no one would notice that they had ever been disturbed, and they took their way to the hut in the glen. They did not light a fire, but they sat for a little while on the stones, talking.

"You're sure they won't come over to the Island?" said Paul.

"They'll never do it," replied Jim Hart confidently. "Besides, they ain't got the least suspicion that we've come here. Likely, they think we've landed at the north end uv the lake, an' they'll be prowlin' aroun' thar three or four days lookin' fur us. Jest think, Paul, uv all the work they'll hev fur nothin'. I feel like laughin'. I think I will laugh."

He kept his word and laughed low; but he laughed long, and with the most intense pleasure.

"Jest to think, Paul," he continued, "how we're guarded by dead Injuns theirselves!"

Presently the two went into the hut, and slept soundly until the next morning. They did not light a fire then, but ate cold food, and went down among the trees to watch the lake. They saw nothing. The water rippled and glowed in alternate gold and silver under the brilliant sunshine, and the hills about it showed distinctly; but there was no sign of a human being except themselves.

"Lookin' fur us among the hills," said Jim Hart. "You an' me will jest keep close, Paul, an' we won't light no fire."

The whole day passed without incident, and the following night also, but about noon the next day, as they watched from the shelter of the trees, they saw a black dot on the lake, far to the south.

"A canoe!" said Jim Hart.

"A canoe? How did they get it?" said Paul—he took it for granted that its occupants were Miamis.

"Guess they brought it across country from some river, and thar they are," replied Jim Hart. "They've shore put a boat on our lake."

His tone showed traces of anxiety, and Paul, too, felt alarm. The Miamis, after all, might defy their own superstition and land on the island. Presently another canoe appeared behind the first, and then a third and a fourth, until there was a little fleet, which the two watched with silent apprehension. Had Henry Ware been mistaken? Did the Miamis really believe it was a haunted island?

On came the canoes in a straight black file, enough to contain more than a score of warriors, and the man and the boy nervously fingered their rifles. If the Indians landed on the island, the result was sure. The two might make a good fight and slay some of their foes, but in any event they would certainly be taken or killed. Their lives depended upon the effect of a superstition.

The line of canoes lay like a great black arrow across the water. They were so close together that to the watchers they seemed to blend and become continuous, and this arrow was headed straight toward the island. Paul's heart went down with a thump, but a moment later a light leaped into his eyes.

"The line is turning!" he exclaimed. "Look, Jim, look! They are afraid of the island!"

"Yes," said Jim Hart, "I see! The ghosts are real, an' it's pow'ful lucky fur us that they are. The Miamis dassent land!"

It was true. The black arrow suddenly shifted to the right, and the line of canoes drew into the open water, midway between the island and the eastern mainland.

"Lay close, Paul, lay close!" said Jim Hart. "We mustn't let 'em catch a glimpse uv us, an' they're always pow'ful keen-eyed."

Both the man and the boy lay flat on their stomachs on the ground, and peered from the shelter of the bushes. No human eye out on the lake could have seen them there. The canoes were now abreast of the island, but were going more slowly, and both could see that the occupants were looking curiously at their little wooded domain. But they kept at a healthy distance.

"I think they're lookin' here because the place is haunted, and not because we are on it," said Jim Hart.

It seemed that he spoke the truth, as the Miamis presently swung nearer to the mainland and began to examine the shores long and critically.

"I guess they've been huntin' us all through the woods, an' think now we may be hid somewhar at the edge uv the lake," said Jim Hart.

It seemed so. The two lay there for hours, watching the little fleet of canoes as it circled the lake, keeping near the outer rim, and searching among all the hills and hollows that bordered the shores. Once, when it was on the western side, the fleet turned its head again toward the island, and again apprehension arose in the hearts of the boy and the man, but it was only for a fleeting moment. The line of canoes was quickly turned away, and bore on down the open water. Paul and Jim Hart were protected by Manitou.

The circumnavigation of the lake by the Miamis lasted throughout the remainder of the day, and when the twilight came, the canoes were lost in its shade toward the southern end of the sheet of water.

"We're safe," said Jim Hart, "but we've still got to keep close. They may hang about here fur days."

"What about Henry and Ross and Sol?" asked Paul anxiously. "On their way back they may run right into that wasp's nest."

"'Tain't likely," replied Jim Hart. "Our boys know what they're a-doin'. But I wish them Miamis would go away so's I could light a fire an' cook some fresh meat."

CHAPTER XII
THE BELT BEARERS

Paul and Jim Hart waited several days, never once venturing from the protecting shadows of the woods, and they found the burden very great. The little island was like a cage, and Jim Hart groaned, moreover, because he could not exercise his skill in the art of cooking.

"These cold victuals," he said, "besides bein' unpleasant to the inside, are a disgrace to me. I jest got to cook somethin'."

Finally, he built up a bed of coals on a very dark night, when it was impossible for anyone to see either their sheltered glow or the smoke they sent out, and he broiled juicy steaks from the body of a deer that they had hung up in a tree.

"Isn't it fine, Paul?" he said, as they ate hungrily.

"Fine's no name for it," replied Paul. "It's great, splendid, grand, magnificent, surpassing, unapproachable! Are those the terms, Jim?"

"I don't know jest what all uv 'em mean," replied Jim Hart, "but they shorely sound right to me."

They saw the Indian canoes on the lake once more, but the Miamis seemed to be fishing, and did not come anywhere near the island. Paul appreciated then how great had been their continual need of caution.

A day or two later there was a magnificent thunder storm, despite the lateness of the season. The heavenly artillery roared grandly, and lakes, hills, and forest swam at times in a glare that dazzled Jim Hart. After that it rained hard, and they clung to the shelter of their hut, which was fortunately water-tight now. The rain ceased by and by, but the clouds remained in the sky, and night came very thick and dark. Jim Hart suggested that it would be a good time to do a little fishing, and Paul was ready and willing.

They paddled out silently a short distance from the island, where the water was not too shallow, and let down the lines.

They waited some time and received no bites; but as this was nothing unusual, owing to the crudity of their fishing tackle, they persisted patiently. The night deepened and darkened, and they could not see the surface of the lake fifty yards away. The water, moved by a light wind, bubbled faintly against the sides of the canoe. Neither spoke, but sat in silence, waiting hopefully for a pull on the lines.

Presently Paul heard a faint, wailing sound, coming from the mainland, but at first he paid little attention to it. Then he noticed that Jim Hart had raised his head and was listening intently. Naturally Paul then listened, too, with the same eager attention, and the faint wailing sound, singularly weird and strange in the night, came a second, and presently a third time. But after that it was not repeated. Long Jim Hart looked at the boy.

"You know what that is?" he said.

"The cry of the whip-poor-will."

"The cry of the whip-poor-will, given three times! The signal! The boys are thar, an' we must go fur 'em."

"Of course," said Paul. "Do we need to return to the island for anything?"

"No; we have our rifles an' ammunition with us. We got to start right now, an' Paul, don't you splash any water with your paddle."

Paul understood as well as Jim Hart the need of extreme caution, as the Miamis might be abroad, and he made every stroke steady and sure. Jim Hart emitted the lonesome cry of the whip-poor-will once in return—signal for signal—and then they cut their way in silence through the dark.

They laid their course, according to agreement, for the drinking place at the mouth of the brook, and Paul's heart beat with relief and gladness. His comrades had come back, safe and sound. It did not occur to him that any one of them might have fallen in the venture. Half way to the mainland Jim Hart stopped the canoe, and listened a moment.

"I thought I heard somethin' down the lake that sounded like a splash," he said.

But he did not hear it again, and they resumed their progress. Paul now saw the loom of the land, a darker outline in the darkness, and his heart, already beating fast, began to beat faster. Suppose there should be some trick in the signal! Suppose they should find the Miamis, and not their comrades, waiting for them! He sought hard to pierce the darkness and see what might be there on the land before him.

The outline of the shore rose more distinctly out of the darkness, and the prow of the boat struck softly on the margin. Then Paul saw a figure rise from the bushes, and after it another, and then a third, and then no more. He could not see their faces, but it was the right number, and a vast relief surged up. The three figures came down confidently to the canoe, and then the welcome voice of Henry Ware said in a low tone:

"You are here, Paul! You and Jim are on time to the minute!"

"An' mighty glad I am, too," said Shif'less Sol, in the same tone. "I wuz never so tired before in all my life. I think I must have trotted a thousan' miles, an' now I'm willin' to let Jim Hart paddle me the rest o' the way in a canoe."

Tom Ross said nothing, merely showing his white teeth in a smile.

"The Miamis are about," said Paul. "They have been around the lake, and on it, for days, looking for something."

"We know it," said Henry. "In fact, we've seen some of them not so long since, though none of them saw us. There are big doings afoot, Paul, and we must have our part in them."

"Should we go back to the island, then?"

"For the present, yes. We need a base, and the island is safest and best."

The five got cautiously into the canoe, disposing their weight carefully, and Shif'less Sol, who had taken the paddle from Paul, raised it for the first sweep. But it did not come down into the water. Instead, he stopped it in its fall, and he and all the others listened. The same splash that Jim Hart thought he had heard came now to their ears, and it was repeated. Paul knew that it was made by paddles sweeping through water, and it was coming nearer.

"Push back into the bushes," whispered Henry.

They gently shoved the canoe far among the bushes in the shallow water, and waited. They were completely hidden, but even if seen they could spring instantly to the land. They waited, and the splashing steadily grew louder. Paul felt the pressure of Henry's hand on his arm, and he looked with all his eyes. The Miami navy was abroad that night! A canoe, a long one with seven or eight warriors in it, was abreast of them, and behind it came five others. They were not twenty yards away, and Paul, in fancy at least, saw the savage eyes and the painted faces. What had brought them out on the lake, what suspicion or precaution, Paul never knew, but there they were. All were brave hearts in the hidden canoe, but they held their breath while that silent file passed by. Then, when the last had gone and was lost in the darkness, they pushed out a little and listened, with all the keenness of forest-bred ears. Hearing no splash, they paddled in a straight course for the haunted island.

"I think they've gone toward the north end of the lake, and as they are likely to keep on their way, now is our time," said Henry.

They pushed farther into the lake, Ross and Shif'less Sol now handling the paddles with wonderful dexterity. They went very slowly, not wishing to make the faintest splash, and meanwhile the darkness thickened and deepened again. It felt very damp to the face, and Paul saw now that fog from the rain of the day was mingled with it. They could not see the faintest outline of the island, but held their course from memory.

They had been out about ten minutes when Ross and Sol, as if by simultaneous impulse, ceased paddling, and Henry whispered: "Don't anybody make any noise; it's for our lives!"

They heard that faint splash, which Paul had learned to hate, coming back. The Miami navy, from some unknown cause, had turned in its course. How Paul blessed the thick, fog-charged darkness!

"It's all chance now," whispered Henry, ever so low, and Paul understood.

Then they held their breath, and the Miami canoes steadily drew nearer. Would they come directly upon the white canoe or would they pass? They passed, but they passed so near that Paul could hear the Indians in the boats talking to each other. He also heard his heart beating in his body as the invisible file went by, and the loud beat did not cease until no more splashing of the paddles was heard.

"Is all my hair gray?" whispered Shif'less Sol.

Paul wanted to laugh in a kind of nervous relief, but he did not dare. Instead he whispered back:

"I can't see, Sol, but I'm sure mine is."

Ross and Shif'less Sol took up the paddles again, and now they reached the island without interruption. The boat was hidden again, and soon all were in the hut in the sheltered cove. Henry spoke with approval of the industry and forethought of Paul and Jim in their absence.

"This hut is a mighty good place on a raw night like this," he said. "Now, I'm going to sleep, and I'd advise you to do the same, Paul. I'll tell you to-morrow all that we've done and have seen and know."

While the others slept, Jim Hart, long-legged and captious, but brave, faithful, and enduring, watched. He saw the fog and the darkness clear away, and the moonlight came out, crisp and cold. A light wind blew and dead leaves fell from the trees, rustling dryly as they fell. Autumn was waning and cold weather would soon be at hand. When pale dawn showed, Jim roused his comrades, and they ate breakfast, though no fire was lighted. Then Henry talked.

"It's true," he said, "about a great league of all the tribes being formed to destroy forever the white settlements in Kentucky. They are alarmed about their hunting grounds, and they think they must all strike together now, and strike hard. We've spied upon several of their villages, and we know. Some renegades are with them, pointing the way, and among them is Braxton Wyatt, the most venomous of them all. I don't see how one who is born white can do such a thing."

But Paul had read books, and his mind was always leaping forward to new knowledge.

"It is the bad blood of some far-off ancestor showing," he said. "It is what they call a reversion. You know, Henry, that Braxton was always mean and sulky. I never saw anybody else so spiteful and jealous as he is, and maybe he thinks he will be a big man among the Indians."

"That's so," said Henry. "I can understand why anybody should love a life in the forest. Ah, it's such a glorious thing!"

He expanded his chest, and the light leaping into his eyes told that Henry Ware was living the life he loved.

"But," he added, "I can't see how anybody could ever turn against his own people."

"It's moral perversity," said Paul.

"Moral perversity," said Jim Hart, stumbling over the syllables. "Them words sound mighty big, Paul. Would you mind tellin' us what they mean?"

"They mean, Jim," put in Shif'less Sol, "that you won't be what you ought to be, an' that you won't, all the time."

"That's a good enough explanation," laughed Paul.

"Whatever is the reason," said Tom Ross, who used words as rarely as if they were precious jewels, "the tribes are comin' together to destroy the white settlements. Braxton is givin' them all kinds uv useful information, an' we've got to hinder these doin's, ef we kin."

The others agreed once more, and talked further of the new league. They did not go into much detail about their adventures while spying on the villages, rather looking now to the future.

"I told you, Paul, we ought to a-put a knife in that Braxton Wyatt when we had the chance," growled Shif'less Sol.

"I couldn't do it, Sol," replied Paul.

Later they held a conference beside a bed of coals that threw out no smoke, and Paul listened with absorbed attention while Henry stated the case fully.

"The Shawnees were somewhat daunted by their repulse at Wareville last year," he said, "but they hope yet to crush the white settlement before we grow too strong. They are seeking to draw the Miamis, Wyandottes, and all the other tribes up here into a league for that purpose, and they want to have it formed and strike while our people are not expecting it. Wareville, owing to her victory of last year, thinks she's safe, and it is not the custom of Indians to raid much in winter. See, cold weather is not far away."

Henry looked up, and the eyes of the others followed. The trees were still clothed in leaves, but the blazing reds and yellows and the dim mist on the horizon showed that Indian summer was at hand.

"Any day," continued Henry, "a cold wind may strip off all these leaves, and winter, which can be very cold up here, will come roaring down. Now, the Shawnees are more than willing to cross the Ohio again to attack us, but the Miamis, while ready enough to take white scalps up here, have not yet made up their minds to go south on the war trail. The Shawnees are sending war belts to them, because the Miamis are a powerful tribe and have many warriors. The first thing for us to do is to take the messengers with the war belts."

"An' to do that," said Shif'less Sol, "we've got to git off this islan' ez soon ez we kin, an' shake off the band o' Miamis. Thar is always work fur a tired man to do."

Paul laughed at his tone of disgust. The boy's spirits were high now; in fact, he was exuberant over the safe return of his comrades, and the entire enterprise appealed with steadily increasing force to him. To hinder and prevent the Indian alliance until the white settlements were strong enough to defy all the tribes! This was in truth a deed worth while! It was foresight, statesmanship, a long step in the founding of a great state, and he should have a part in it! Already his vivid mind painted the picture of his comrades and himself triumphant.

"We must go to-night, if it is dark," said Henry.

"That's so," said Tom Ross emphatically.

The three had captured fresh supplies of ammunition while they were gone, and they replenished the powder-horns and bullet pouches of Paul and Jim Hart. Moreover, they had taken blankets, of a fine, soft, light but warm make, probably bought by the Indians from European traders, and they gave one each to Paul and Jim Hart.

"It's getting too cold now," said Henry, "to sleep in our clothes only on the ground in the forest."

They made up the blankets in tight little rolls, which they fastened on their backs, and Paul and Jim Hart put in a tanned deerskin with each of theirs.

"They're pow'ful light, an' they may come in mighty handy," said Long Jim.

The night fortunately was dark, as they had hoped, and about eleven o'clock they embarked in the canoe, paddling straight for the

103

western shore. Paul looked back with some regret at the island, which at times had been a snug little home. The ancient, mummified bodies in the trees had protected them, as if with a circle of steel, and he was grateful to those dead of long ago.

They saw no sign of the Indian canoes, and both Henry and Ross were certain that they were in camp somewhere on the eastern shore. The little party reached the dense woods on the west without incident whatever, and there they partly sank the canoe in shallow water among dense bushes. Then they plunged into the forest, and traveled fast. Shif'less Sol spoke after a while, and apparently his groaning voice was drawn up from the very bottom of his chest.

"Oh, that blessed canoe!" he said. "I wuz so happy when I wuz a-ridin' in it, an' somebody else wuz a-paddlin'. Now I hev to do all my own work."

"You wouldn't be truly happy, Sol Hyde," said Jim Hart, "'less you wuz ridin' in a gilt coach drawed by four white horses, right smack through the woods here."

"That's heaven," said the shiftless one, with a deep sigh. "I don't ever dream o' sech a thing ez that, and please don't call it up to my mind, Jim Hart; the contras' between that an' footin' it ez I am now is too cruel an' too great."

Paul smiled. The little by-play between those two good friends amused and brightened him, but nothing else was said for a long time. Then it was Henry who spoke, and he called a halt.

"The big Miami village is not more than a dozen miles away," he said, "and the warriors there are expecting messengers from the Shawnees, with war belts. The messengers will pass near here, and we'll wait for them. The rest of you will go to sleep, and Tom and I will watch."

Paul, Jim Hart, and Shif'less Sol rolled themselves in their blankets and lay down under a tree, the shiftless one murmuring, "Now, this is what I like," and the others saying nothing. Paul was devoutly grateful for the blanket, because the air was now quite cold, but in five minutes all emotions were lost in deep and dreamless sleep.

When Paul awoke from his slumber he started up in horror. Three powerful, painted Shawnees stood over him. He was so much overwhelmed by the catastrophe that he could only utter a kind of gasp. But the blood flowed back from his heart into his veins when he heard the dry laugh of Long Jim Hart.

"Paul," said Jim, "I'd like to introduce you to the three new Shawnee warriors that you used to know, when they were white, an' that you called then Henry Ware, Tom Ross, and Sol Hyde."

104

"Why, what has happened?" asked Paul, still in the depths of astonishment.

Then Henry spoke, and he spoke gravely.

"Sol did not sleep long, Paul," he said, "and when he awoke he joined us. Then we went to meet the three Shawnee messengers, carrying war belts and peace belts, for the Miamis to choose. It was not a business for you, Paul. We met them, there was a fight—well, they will never appear in the Miami village, and we are here in their place."

Paul understood, and he shuddered a little at the deadly conflict that must have raged out there in the forest while he slept. Then he looked curiously at the three. He never would have known any one of them anywhere. They were savages in every aspect—painted and garbed like them, and with their hair drawn up in the defiant scalp lock.

"What are you going to do?" he asked.

"Deliver the belts at the Miami village," replied Henry Ware, "but they will be peace belts, not war belts."

"It is death," said Paul in protest.

"It is not death," replied Henry. "We will come back safely, and it is for a great stake. You and Jim must remain here in the woods, waiting for us again, and we'll trust to your skill and caution not to be caught. If the warriors become too thick around here you might retreat to the island. Anyway, the signal will be as before—three wails of the whip-poor-will."

Paul was impressed by his words, which were spoken with gravity and emphasis.

"Yes, it's in a great cause, Henry," he said, "and we'll wait, expecting you to come back."

Five minutes later the three newly made warriors took their path through the forest, and they never looked back. Yet Henry Ware felt emotion. Although he regarded Paul Cotter almost as a younger brother, he respected him as a high type of one kind of being, and they were comrades true as steel. Moreover, he knew that he and Ross and Sol were engaged upon the most dangerous of tasks, and the chances were that they would not come back. Yet he faced them with a high heart and dauntless courage.

The three walked swiftly and silently in single file, and neither Shawnee nor Miami eye would have known that they were not Indian. They walked, toes in, as Indians do, and they had every trick of manner or gesture that the red men have. All trace of civilization was gone. Henry Ware, Thomas floss, and Solomon Hyde had disappeared. In their places were Big Fox, Brown Bear, and The Bat, Shawnee warriors who bore belts to the Miami village, and who would talk about the war to be made upon the white intruders far to the south of the Ohio.

Shortly before noon Big Fox, Brown Bear, and The Bat approached the Miami village, pitched in a pleasant valley, where wood and water were in plenty. Then they uttered the long whoop of the Shawnees, and it was answered from the Miami village; but Big Fox, Brown Bear, and The Bat, assured of a welcome, never stopped, keeping straight on for the village. Squaws and children clustered around them, and openly spoke their admiration of the three stalwart, splendidly proportioned warriors who had come from the friendly tribe; but Big Fox, Brown Bear, and The Bat, in accordance with the Indian nature, took no notice. It was only warriors and chiefs to whom they would condescend to speak, and they were silent and expressionless until the right moment should come. They passed straight through the swarm of old men, women, children, and dogs, toward the center of the village, where a long, low cabin of poles stood. An ancient and reverend figure stood in the doorway to meet them. It was that of Gray Beaver, head chief of the Miamis, an old, old man, gray with years and wise like the beaver, from which he took his name.

"My Shawnee brethren are welcome to the Council House," he said. "You have come far, and you shall rest, and the squaws shall bring you food before we talk."

"It is sufficient to us to see the great and wise chief, Gray Beaver," said Henry. "Though we come from a long journey, it makes us strong and brave again."

The old chief bowed, but his grave features did not relax. Nevertheless, he was pleased in his secret soul at the gallant bearing and polite words of the young warrior who addressed them. He led the way into the Council House, and a half dozen underchiefs followed them, hiding their interest beneath their painted masks of faces.

The Council House was large—fifty warriors could have sat in it—and robes of the buffalo, beaver, and other animals were spread about. Big Fox, Brown Bear, and The Bat sat down gravely, each upon a mat of skins, and were served by the warriors with food and drink, which the squaws had brought to the door, but beyond which they could not pass. The three Shawnee belt bearers ate and drank in silence and dignity, and they appreciated the rest and refreshment so needful to those who had traveled far. Neither did anyone else speak. The venerable Gray Beaver sat on a couch of skins a little higher than the others, and his eyes rested steadily on the belt bearers. The subchiefs, silent and motionless on their mats of skins, also watched the belt bearers. At one end of the great room, in a kind of rude chimney, smoldered the council fire, a bed of coals.

More than half an hour passed, and when the guests had eaten and drunk sufficiently, the venerable chief waved his hands, and the remains of the food and drink were taken away. Then Gray Beaver drew from beneath his robe a beautifully ornamented pipe, with a curved horn stem and a carven bowl. He pressed into the bowl a mixture of tobacco and aromatic herbs, which he also drew from beneath his robe, and lighted it with a coal which one of the chiefs brought from the fire. Then he took three whiffs and gravely and silently passed the pipe to the chief of the Shawnee belt bearers, Big Fox. It was a curious fact, but no one had said that Big Fox was the chief of the three. Something in his manner made all take it for granted, and Big Fox, too, unconsciously accepted it as a matter of course.

The magnificent young warrior took three whiffs at the pipe of peace, and passed it to Brown Bear, who, after doing the same, handed it in his turn to The Bat. Then it was passed on to all the subchiefs, and everyone smoked it in gravity and silence. The smoke circled up in rings against the low roof, and every man sat upon his mat of skins, painted, motionless, and wordless. The young chief, Big Fox, waited. Though his eyes never turned, he saw every detail of the scene, and he was conscious of the tense and breathless silence. He was conscious, too, of the immense dangers that surrounded his comrades and himself, but fear was not in his heart.

"My brethren have come to the Miami village with a message from their friends, the Shawnees," said the ancient chief at last.

"It is so," said Big Fox.

"The hearts of the Shawnees are filled with hatred of the white men, who have come into the hunting grounds beyond the Ohio, and who cut down trees and build houses there."

"It is so."

Big Fox's gaze never wavered. He continued to look straight at the council fire, and the tense silence came again. Big Fox was conscious that the air in the Council House was heavy, and that all were watching him with black, glittering eyes.

"The Shawnees would destroy the white villages, and would seek the help of all the tribes that know them," continued Gray Beaver.

Then Big Fox spoke.

"It is true," he said gravely and slowly, "that the Shawnees would wish the white settlements destroyed, every house burned, and every warrior, squaw, and child killed, that the forest might grow again where they live, and the deer roam again unafraid."

107

Big Fox paused, and for the first time looked away from the council fire. His piercing gaze swept the circle of the Miamis, and every man among them drew a deep breath. There was something extraordinary in this belt bearer, a majesty and magnetism that all of them felt, and they hung upon his words, listening intently.

"The Shawnees are warriors," resumed Big Fox, "and they do not fear battle. They went last year against the white settlements, and they went alone. The Miamis know that."

There was a deep murmur of assent.

"The Shawnees are wise as well as brave," resumed Big Fox. "Their old chiefs have talked over it long. It is a great war trail upon which we would go, and he who would travel far and long should prepare well. The white men are brave. From their wooden walls last year they beat us off, and many Shawnees fell afterwards in the battle with them in the forest."

Big Fox paused, and swept the circle again with his glittering eyes. As before, every man among them drew a deep breath when that hypnotic gaze fell upon him. But they were hearing words that they had not expected to hear, and after the tremendous gaze had passed there came a faint murmur of surprise. But Big Fox did not seem to notice it. Instead he continued:

"The winter is at hand. Already the dead leaves fall, and soon the bitter winds will sweep the forests and the prairies. The warrior would go forth to battle, chilled and stiff. The gun would fall from his frozen hands."

Again he paused and looked straight at Gray Beaver. The old chief stirred in his furred robe beneath that piercing gaze.

"We would not go forth to war until we are ready for war, until the season is ripe for war," resumed Big Fox. "When we would strike, we would strike with all the strength of all the allied tribes, that nothing of the white man might be left. We would send to Canada for more rifles, more powder, and more bullets, and to do all these things it must be long before we go on the great war trail. So I bring you, for the present, peace."

He took from beneath his robe the peace belts, message of the Shawnee nation, and handed them to the old, old chief, Gray Beaver. The murmur from the Miamis became deep and long, but Big Fox gazed once more at the fire, painted, silent, and immovable.

"It was war when I was in the Shawnee village, a moon ago," said a chief, Yellow Panther, "and it was war belts that we expected. Why have the Shawnees changed their minds?"

Murmurs of approval greeted his words, but Big Fox never stirred.

"The old men, the wise men of the Shawnees have so decided," he replied. "It is not for the bearer of the belts to question their wisdom."

"If the Shawnees wish to wait long to prepare, the Miamis must wait, too," said the chief, Gray Beaver, in whose veins flowed the cold and languid blood of old age.

The younger chiefs murmured again. Big Fox was conscious that a powerful faction of the Miamis wished to go on a winter war path, and strike the settlements at once. But Big Fox was still unafraid. He was a forest diplomatist as well as a forest warrior, and he played for the most precious of all stakes, the lives of his people.

"The great chiefs of the Shawnees have lived long," he said. "Their heads are heavy with age and with wisdom. It is not well to waste our strength with a blow which will not reach the mark, but it is good to wait until we can strike true."

The chief, Yellow Panther, arose. He was a tall and ferocious savage, with a cunning countenance.

"The Shawnees change their minds quickly," he said, in tones of subtle and insulting insinuation. "There is one here who came from their village but three days since, and then they looked not so kindly upon the peace belts. It is well to bring him to this council of the Miamis."

He glanced at Gray Beaver and the ancient chief nodded. Then Yellow Panther stepped from the Council House.

The heart of Big Fox stirred within him ever so slightly. What did Yellow Panther mean by "one who had come but three days since"? A new factor was entering the terrible game. But he showed no emotion, nor did his comrades, the other two belt bearers, Brown Bear and The Bat. Neither of the latter had spoken since he entered the Council House.

The murmurs ceased, and all sank back on their skin mats. Silence resumed absolute sway in the long room. The little eddies of smoke still curled against the roof, and the air was surcharged with suspense.

The buffalo robe over the entrance was lifted, and Yellow Panther returned. Behind him came a second figure.

The eyes of Big Fox turned slowly from the council fire, and looked straight into those of Braxton Wyatt.

CHAPTER XIII
BRAXTON WYATT'S ORDEAL

The blood of Big Fox leaped for a moment in his veins, but it did not show under the paint of his face. His figure never quivered. He still knew all the danger, and he knew, moreover, how it had increased since the entrance of Braxton Wyatt, but he said, in slow, cold tones, full of deadly meaning:

"It is the white youth who left his own people to come to our village and join our people. We have received him, but the eyes of the warriors are still upon him."

The insinuation was evident. The renegade could not be trusted. Already, with the first words spoken, Big Fox was impeaching his character.

Braxton Wyatt stood with his back to the buffalo robe, which had fallen again over the entrance, and looked around at the circle of chiefs who had resumed their seats on the skin mats. Then his eyes met the stern, accusing gaze of Big Fox, the Shawnee belt bearer, and were held there as if fascinated. But Braxton Wyatt was not without courage. He wrenched his eyes away, turned them upon the ancient chief, Gray Beaver, and said:

"I have been long in the Shawnee lodges, great chief of the Miamis, but I do not know these belt bearers."

There was a murmur, and a stir on the skin mats.

Big Fox scorned to look again at Braxton Wyatt. He gazed steadily at the council fire, and said in tones of indifference:

"The white youth who left his own people has been in the lodges, where the old men and women stay; we have been on the war trail with the warriors. The day we returned to the village we were chosen to bring the peace belts to our good friends, the Miamis."

"The belt bearers are Big Fox, Brown Bear, and The Bat," said Yellow Panther, looking at Braxton Wyatt. "You have heard of them? The Shawnee villages are full of their fame."

"I never saw them, and I never heard of them before," replied Braxton Wyatt, in a tone of mingled anger and bewilderment, "but I do know that all the Shawnees wish the Miamis to go south with them at once, on the great war trail against the white settlements."

The old chief, Gray Beaver, looked from the belt bearers to

Braxton Wyatt and from Braxton Wyatt to the belt bearers. His aged brain was bewildered by the conflicting tales, but he put little trust in the white youth. Already Big Fox had sowed in his mind the seeds of unbelief in the words of Braxton Wyatt.

"Scarcely a moon ago the Shawnees, as we all know, wished to go on the great war trail at once," said Yellow Panther, "but now three come, who say they are from them, bearing peace belts. Moreover, here is another who says that the Shawnees would send war belts. What shall the Miamis think?"

There was another murmur, and then silence. The surcharged air was heavy in the great lodge. But Big Fox merely shrugged his shoulders slightly, and answered in tones of lofty indifference:

"Big Fox, Brown Bear, and The Bat were sent by the old chiefs of the Shawnees to deliver peace belts to the chiefs of the Miamis, and they have delivered them."

Brown Bear and The Bat nodded, but said nothing. Yellow Panther looked at Braxton Wyatt, who was shaken by varying emotions. As he truly said, he had long been in the Shawnee villages, but he had never seen or heard of the three warriors who now sat calmly before him—Big Fox, Brown Bear, and The Bat. Yet he could not say that no such men existed, because small parties had roved far and long on the hunt or the war trail. He gazed at them before answering. He, too, was struck by the splendid figure and pose of Big Fox, and he was impressed, moreover, by a sense of something familiar, though he could not name it. It haunted him and troubled him, but remained a mystery. He collected his shrewd wits and said:

"As I told you, the warriors who bring the peace belts are strangers to me. Yet the Shawnees, when I left the head village, but a few days ago, wished war at once against the white settlements, and the Shawnees do not change their minds quickly."

"Is the word of a renegade, of one who would slay his own people, to be weighed against that of a warrior?"

Big Fox spoke with lofty contempt, not gazing at Braxton Wyatt, but straight into the eyes of Gray Beaver. The old chief felt the power of that look, and wavered under it.

"It is true," he said, "that the Shawnees, a moon ago, were for war; but Big Fox, Brown Bear, and The Bat have come, bearing peace belts from them, and what our eyes see must be true."

There was a murmur again, but it was very faint now. The authority of Gray Beaver, in his time a mighty warrior, and now wise with years and experience, was great, and the under chiefs

111

were impressed—all but Yellow Panther, whose eyes flashed vindictively at the belt bearers. Angry blood also flushed Braxton Wyatt's face, and he did not know at the moment what to say or do.

"It is true that I was born white," he said, "but I have become one of the Shawnees, and I shall be faithful to them. I have spoken no lies. The Shawnees were for war, and I believe they are so yet."

"The Shawnees from whom I have come," said Big Fox, in his grave tones, wholly ignoring Braxton Wyatt, "expect peace belts in return. Will the messengers depart with them to-morrow?"

He spoke directly to Gray Beaver, and his powerful gaze still rested upon him. The withered frame of the old chief trembled a little within his furred robe, and then he yielded to the spell.

"The Miami messengers will start to-morrow with peace belts for the Shawnees," he said.

A thrill of triumph ran through the frame of Big Fox, but he said nothing. The eyes of both Braxton Wyatt and Yellow Panther flashed vindictively, but they, too, said nothing. Big Fox judged that they were not yet wholly beaten, but he had accomplished much; if each tribe received peace belts from the others, it would take a long time to untangle the snarl, and unite them for war. Meanwhile, the white settlements were steadily growing stronger.

"Our Shawnee brethren, the belt bearers, will stay with us a while," said the crafty Yellow Panther. "They have traveled far, and they need rest."

Big Fox knew that it would not do to be too hasty; a desire to depart at once would only arouse suspicion, and he and his comrades, moreover, had further work to do in the Miami village. So he gravely accepted the offer of hospitality, and he and Brown Bear and The Bat were conducted to a lodge in the center of the village, where they ate again, and reclined luxuriously upon buffalo robes and deerskins. Yellow Panther followed them there, and was very solicitous for their comfort. All his attentions they received with grave courtesy, and when there was nothing more that he could do or say he withdrew, letting the covering of the lodge door fall behind him. Then the three belt bearers, putting their ears against the skin walls of the lodge, listened intently. Nothing was stirring without. If any person was at hand, or listened there, they would have known it; so they spoke to each other in low tones.

"Your plan seems to have worked so far, Henry," said Ross, "even if Braxton Wyatt did come."

"Yes—so far," replied Henry Ware; "but Braxton is sure that something is wrong, and so is that cunning wolf, Yellow Panther.

They want to hold us here in the village until they find out the truth; but we are willing to stay, that we may checkmate what they do. I can work on old Gray Beaver, whose age makes him favor caution and peace."

"An' while you are thinkin' it over," said Shif'less Sol, "jest remember that I'm a belt bearer who has traveled a long way, an' that I'm pow'ful tired; so I guess I'll take a nap."

He rolled over on the softest of the skins, and was as good as his word. In five minutes he was sound asleep. Tom Ross leaned back against the skin wall and meditated. Henry Ware arose and walked in the village; but the moment he stepped from the lodge, all trace of the white youth was gone, and he was again Big Fox, the chief of the belt bearers from the Shawnees.

The village was the scene of an active savage life. It had been a season of plenty. Game and fish abounded, and, according to the Indian nature, they ate and overate of that plenty, thinking little of the morrow. Hence this life, besides being active, was also happy in its wild way. Big Fox noticed the fact, with those keen eyes of his that nothing escaped.

And all in their turn noticed Big Fox here, as he had been noticed in the Council House. Old and young alike admired him. They thought that no such splendid warrior had ever before entered their village. Surely the Shawnees were a nation of men when they could produce such as he. His height, his straight, commanding glance, the wonderful, careless strength and majesty of his figure, all impressed them. He looked to them like one without fear, and moreover, with such strength and quickness as his, he seemed one who had little to fear. But as he walked there, Yellow Panther came again, and spoke to him with sly, insinuating manner:

"The belt bearer is not weary, though he has traveled far."

"No," replied Big Fox. "Manitou has been kind to me, and has given me strong limbs and muscles that do not tire."

"Did Big Fox, in his journey from the Shawnee village, hear of white men? It is said that a band of them have been in this region about the lake, there to the southward. One of our warriors was slain, but we could not find those whom we pursued."

Big Fox wondered if it was a chance shot, but he looked straight into the eyes of Yellow Panther, which fell before the gaze of his, and replied:

"I came bearing belts, and I thought only of them. If there are white men in the Miami woods, the Miamis are warriors enough to take them."

113

Yellow Panther turned aside, but he followed the tall figure with a look of the most vindictive hate. Like Braxton Wyatt, he felt that something was wrong, but what it was he did not yet know. Big Fox mingled freely in the village life throughout the day, and never once did he make a mistake. All the Indian ways were familiar to him, and when he talked with the warriors about the Northwestern tribes, he showed full knowledge. Old Gray Beaver was delighted with him. The deference of this splendid young warrior was grateful to his heart.

That night the three belt bearers, calm and unconcerned, lay down in the great lodge that had been assigned to them, and slept peacefully. Far in the darkness, Yellow Panther and Braxton Wyatt crept to the side of the lodge and listened. They heard nothing from within, and at last the Miami carefully lifted the buffalo hide over the entrance. His sharp eyes, peering into the shadows, saw the three belt bearers lying upon their backs and sleeping soundly. Apparently they were men without fear, men without the cause of fear, and Yellow Panther, letting the tent flap fall softly back, walked away with Braxton Wyatt, both deeply disappointed.

They did not know that a pair of hands had lifted the tent flap ever so little, and that a pair of keen eyes were following them. The wonderful instinct of Henry Ware had warned him, and he had awakened the moment they looked in. But his eyes had not opened. He had merely felt their presence with the swish of cold air on his face, and now, after they had disappeared among the lodges, he wished to deepen the impression the belt bearers had made. Then he and his comrades must go back to Paul and Jim Hart, who lay out there in the forest, patiently waiting.

The next morning Big Fox, Brown Bear, and The Bat saw three Miami belt bearers depart with peace belts for the Shawnee village, but as for themselves, they would remain a while longer, enjoying the Miami hospitality.

In an open space just north of the village, Miami boys were practicing with the bow and arrow, shooting at the bodies of some owls tied on the low boughs of trees. Warriors were looking on, and the belt bearers, Big Fox, Brown Bear, and The Bat, joined them. By and by some of the warriors began to take a share in the sport and practice, using great war bows and sending the arrows whistling to the mark. At last the chief, Yellow Panther, himself handled a bow and surpassed all who had preceded him in skill. Then, turning with a malicious eye to Big Fox, he said:

"Perhaps the Shawnee belt bearers would like to show how

well they can use the bow. Surely they are not less in skill than the Miamis?"

His look was full of venom. Shawnees, though armed now with rifles, were good bowmen, and whatever he suspected might be confirmed by the failure of the belt bearers to show skill, or not to shoot at all. He held in his hand the great bow that he had used, and, barring the malice of his eyes, his gesture was full of politeness.

Big Fox did not hesitate a moment. He stepped forward, took the bow and arrow from the hand of Yellow Panther, glanced at the great owl at which the chief had shot, and then walked back fifteen yards farther from it. A murmur of applause came from the crowd. He would shoot at a much greater distance than Yellow Panther had shot, and the chief and Braxton Wyatt, too, who had drawn near, frowned.

Big Fox glanced once more at the body of the great owl, and then, fitting the arrow to the string, he bent the bow. An involuntary cry of admiration came from a people who valued physical strength and skill when they saw the ease and grace with which he bent the tough wood. Not in vain had nature given Big Fox a figure of power and muscles of steel! Not in vain had nature given him an eye the like of which was not to be found on all the border! Not in vain had he achieved surpassing skill with the bow in his life among the Northwestern Indians!

There was silence as the bow bent and the arrow was drawn back to the head. Then that silence was broken only by the whizz of the feathered shaft as it shot through the air. But a universal shout arose as the arrow struck fairly in the center of the owl, pierced it like a bullet, and flew far beyond.

Big Fox turned and handed back the bow to Yellow Panther.

"Is it enough?" he asked gravely. "Can the Shawnee belt bearers use the bow and arrow?"

"It is enough," replied the chief, seeking in vain to hide his chagrin.

"It wuz great luck," whispered The Bat to Brown Bear, a little later, "that the challenge to the bow an' arrow should a-been made to perhaps the only white in all the West who could a-done sech a thing."

The belt bearers spent a second night in the same lodge, and on the morning of the third day they announced that they must depart for their own village. Gray Beaver hospitably, and Yellow Panther craftily, urged them to stay longer, but Big Fox replied that the Shawnees were going on a great hunt into the Northwest before the winter came, and the belt bearers would be needed. Braxton Wyatt knew nothing of the projected hunt, but for the present he was silent. Throughout the contest he had shown at a disadvantage against the diplomacy of Big Fox. Now the belt bearers courteously invited him to return home with them, but he declined, replying that he would not depart for some days. He did not say it aloud, but nothing could have induced him to go with the belt bearers.

Big Fox noticed that neither Yellow Panther nor Braxton Wyatt made any opposition to their going, and it was a fact that he did not forget, drawing from it his own inference. His power to read the faces of men was scarcely inferior to his wonderful skill in reading every sign of the forest.

Gray Beaver, and behind him a rabble, accompanied the Shawnee belt bearers to the edge of the woods, and there the aged chief said graciously to Big Fox:

"My son, my heart is warm toward you, and I am glad to have seen you in the lodges of the Miamis."

"Farewell, Gray Beaver," said Big Fox.

Then he and his two comrades turned, and disappeared like phantoms in the forest, so swiftly they went.

Autumn had made further advance. The dying leaves were falling fast, and the wilderness was more open. A crisp wind blew in the faces of the three belt bearers—now belt bearers no longer, but Henry Ware, Tom Ross, and Solomon Hyde, white of skin and white of heart. They sped forward on fleet foot many miles, and it was Shif'less Sol who spoke first.

"Shall we stop at this spring," he said, "an' wash the paint off our faces? I want to look like a white man agin, jest ez I am. I don't feel nat'ral at all ez an Injun."

"Neither do I," said Tom Ross, "I don't like to change faces, an' right here I wash mine."

The three stooped down to the spring, and as they rubbed off the paint they felt their right natures returning.

"I'm thankful I wuz born white," said Shif'less Sol. "Why, what is it, Henry?"

Henry Ware had raised his head in the attitude of one who listens. His eyes were intent and nostrils distended like those of a deer that suspects an enemy.

"We're followed," he said. "I thought we would be."

"Yellow Panther, uv course!" said Tom Ross, with emphasis.

"Of course! And like as not Braxton Wyatt is among those who are with him."

Sol Hyde looked at Henry. There was a queer light in the eyes of the shiftless one.

"Do we want 'em to ketch us?" he asked.

"I think we'd better wait and see."

It was in no tone of boasting that either spoke. Three borderers such as they could shake off the pursuit of any men who lived.

"S'pose we lead 'em on a while," said Tom Ross.

Henry nodded, and the three ran in a sort of easy trot toward the southeast. They took no trouble to hide their trail, and as the forest at this point was free from undergrowth, they were visible at a considerable distance. This easy trot they kept up for hours, and the extraordinary powers, or intuition, of Henry Ware told him that the Miamis were always there, a quarter of a mile, perhaps, behind. But the three men were never troubled. There was no fear in their minds. This was only sport to them.

They crossed brooks and little creeks, and at last, when they came to one of the latter a little larger than the others, Henry Ware said:

"I think it's time to bother 'em now. We'll wade here."

They entered the creek, which had a hard, pebbly bed, and walked rapidly against the stream for at least a quarter of a mile. Then they emerged in dense undergrowth, and turned backward in a course parallel to that by which they had come. But before going far they sank down in a dense thicket, and lay quite still. Then they saw the Miami band pass—fifteen or sixteen warriors, led by Yellow Panther, with Braxton Wyatt trailing at the rear. "The renegade!" said Shif'less Sol savagely, under his breath.

The band passed on, but the three borderers did not stir. They knew that the trail would be lost presently, and some, at least, of the warriors would come back seeking it.

Fifteen minutes, a half hour, passed, and then they heard distant footsteps. Henry Ware, peering above the bushes, saw a face that belonged to a white youth, and suddenly a daring project formed itself in his mind. Braxton Wyatt was alone! Other members of the Miami band must be near, but they were not in sight, and, above all, Braxton Wyatt was for the present alone! Only a few minutes were needed!

"Watch what I do!" whispered Henry Ware to his comrades—he knew that their keen minds would need no other hint.

Braxton Wyatt came back, looking on the ground, his rifle lying loosely across his shoulder. He dreamed of no danger. The three suspected belt bearers must be fleeing fast. Moreover, Yellow Panther and his Miami friends were near. He walked on, and the fiend he served gave him no warning.

He came to a dense clump of bushes, and turned to go around it. There was a sudden rustling in those bushes, and he looked up. A terrifying form threw itself upon him and bore him to the ground. A heavy hand was clapped upon his mouth, and the cry that had risen to his lips died in his throat. He looked up and saw the face of Henry Ware. Beside him stood two others whom he knew—Tom Ross and Shif'less Sol. He became blue about the lips, and expected a quick death.

"Listen!" said Henry Ware, and every word that he said was burned into Braxton Wyatt's wretched soul. "You are not to die, not at this time. But you are to do what we say. Go back there, under those trees by the big rock, and when Yellow Panther and the other Miamis come up, tell them that you have lied! We were the belt bearers, and you are to say to Yellow Panther that you knew us as real Shawnees, but you were so anxious for the war that you denied us. Tell it as if it were true. Don't tremble! Don't look once at these bushes! Our three rifles will be aimed at you all the time, and if you say a single word that will make them suspect, we fire, and you know that no one of us ever misses. Do as we say!"

He was released, the heavy hand was taken away from his mouth, and his captors disappeared so suddenly and silently in the bushes that it was almost unbelievable. Then Braxton Wyatt rose to his feet and trembled violently. Though he could not see them now, he must believe. He could feel that powerful grasp yet upon his arms, and that heavy hand yet upon his mouth. He knew, too, as well as he knew that he was living, that the unseen muzzles were there, trained upon him. As Henry Ware truly said, no one of the three ever missed, and he had no chance.

He stopped his trembling with an effort of the will and walked to the rock under the trees, thirty or forty yards away. Already he saw Yellow Panther and the other Miamis coming, and he rebelled at the deadly menace from the bushes. But the love of life was strong within him. He looked at Yellow Panther, who was approaching with five or six warriors, and then he tried to form a rapid plan. He would talk with the chief, saying at first what his terrible enemies wished, and then, gradually drawing him away, he would tell the truth, and thus achieve the destruction of the three whom he hated and feared so horribly.

Braxton Wyatt raised one hand and wiped the perspiration

118

from his face. Then, when a deadly fear struck him, he composed his features. Henry Ware had said he must tell a tale that seemed true. There must be no suspicion. The fatal muzzles were trained on him, he well knew, and the sharpest of eyes and ears were watching. He longed to cast one look at the bushes, only one, but he dared not for his life. It was forbidden!

Yellow Panther was at hand now, plainly showing annoyance. The lost trail could not be found, and wrath possessed him. He looked at the renegade, and uttered his discontent.

Braxton Wyatt longed more than ever to tell; they were there so near, it seemed he must tell; but the deadly rifles held him back. No one of their bullets would miss!

"Yellow Panther," he said, and his voice faltered, "let us abandon the trail and go back."

Yellow Panther looked at him, astonished by words and manner alike.

"Go back!" he said. "Did you not tell me that they were false, that there were no such warriors in the Shawnee village?"

Braxton Wyatt trembled, and the cold sweat came again on his forehead. If only those rifles were not there in the thicket! A mighty power seemed to draw him about for one look, only one! But he did not dare—it was death!—and with a supreme effort he wrenched himself away.

"I was wrong," he said. "I was eager for war, eager to see the Shawnees and Miamis go together against the white settlements in the south—so eager that I forgot the men. But I remember them now."

"Have you a crooked tongue?" asked Yellow Panther.

"No, no!" cried Braxton Wyatt, in mortal terror of the three rifles. "I had, but I have not now! I am telling you the truth! As I live I am, Yellow Panther! I was anxious for the war, anxious as you are, and it brought a cloud before my eyes. I could not remember then, but I remember now! The men were true Shawnees, and the Shawnee nation does not wish to go on the great war trail this year."

Yellow Panther looked at him with indignation and contempt, and hesitated. Braxton Wyatt trembled once more. Would the chief believe? He must believe! He must make him believe, or he would die!

"I wished to tell you before we started, Yellow Panther," he said, "but I feared then your just anger. Now we have lost the trail, and I must save you from further trouble. Why should I tell you this now if it is not true? Why else should I avow that I have spoken false words?"

Yellow Panther looked at the unhappy figure and face, and believed.

"It is enough," he said. "We will go back to our own village. Come!"

He spoke to his warriors, and they returned swiftly on their own tracks to the Miami village. Braxton Wyatt went with them, and he dared not look back once at that fateful clump of bushes.

When they were gone far beyond sight, Henry Ware, Tom Ross, and Shif'less Sol rose up, looked at each other, and laughed.

"That wuz well done, Henry," said Shif'less Sol lazily. "I never knowed a purtier trick to be told. He's clean caught in his own net. If he wuz to tell the truth now to the chief, Yellow Panther wouldn't believe him."

"And if he were to believe him, Yellow Panther, in his anger, would tomahawk him," said Henry Ware, "No, Braxton Wyatt will not dare to tell."

"And now we may take it easy," said Tom Ross. "But I wouldn't like to be in your place, Henry, ef ever you wuz to fall into the hands uv Yellow Panther an' that renegade."

"I'll take care that I don't have any such bad luck," said Henry. "And now we must find Paul and Jim."

Serenely satisfied, they resumed their journey, but now they went at a slower gait.

CHAPTER XIV
IN WINTER QUARTERS

The three walked slowly on for a long time, curving about gradually to the region in which Paul and Jim Hart remained hidden. They did not say much, but Shif'less Sol was slowly swelling with an admiration which was bound to find a vent some time or other.

"Henry," he burst out at last, "this whole scheme o' yours has been worked in the most beautiful way, an' that last trick with Braxton Wyatt wuz the finest I ever saw."

"There were three of us," said Henry briefly and modestly.

"It's a great thing to use your brain," said the shiftless one sagely. "I'm thinkin' o' doin' it hereafter myself."

Tom Ross laughed deeply and said:

"I'd make a beginning before it wuz too late, ef I wuz you, Sol."

"How long do you think it will take the Shawnees an' the Miamis to straighten out that tangle about the great war trail?" asked the shiftless one of Henry.

"Not before snow flies," replied the youth; "and then there will be so much mutual anger and disgust that they will not be able to get together for months. But we must stop up here, Sol, and watch, and egg on the misunderstanding. Don't you think so, Tom?"

"Of course!" replied Ross briefly, but with emphasis. "We've got to hang on the Injun flanks."

Late in the afternoon they reached familiar ground, or at least it was so to the sharp eyes of these three, although they had seen it but once. Here they had left Paul and Jim Hart, and they knew that they must be somewhere near. Henry gave forth the whip-poor-will cry—the long, wailing note, inexpressibly plaintive and echoing far through the autumn woods. It was repeated once and twice, and presently came the answering note.

The three walked with confidence toward the point from which the answer had come, and soon they saw Paul and Jim Hart advancing joyously to meet them.

Paul listened with amazement to the story of their wonderful adventure, told in a few brief phrases. Not many words were needed for him. His vivid imagination at once pictured it all—the deadly play of words in the Council House, the ambushing of Braxton Wyatt, and the triumphant result.

121

"That was diplomacy, statesmanship, Henry," he said.

"We're going to stay up here a while longer, Paul," said Henry. "We think our presence is needed in these parts."

"I'm willing," said Paul, wishing to have assurances, "but what about the powder for Marlowe, and what will our people at Wareville think has become of us?"

"As long as we can keep back these tribes, Marlowe will not need the powder, and some of the buffalo hunters have taken word to Wareville that we have come into the North."

"I purpose," said Shif'less Sol, "that so long ez we're goin' to stay in these parts that we go back to the haunted islan' in the lake. It's in the heart o' the Injun country, but it's the safest spot within five hundred miles o' us."

"I think with Sol," said Henry. "We can prepare there for winter quarters. In fact, we've got a hut already."

"An' I won't have nothin' to do," said the shiftless one, "but lay aroun' an' hev Jim Hart cook fur me."

"You'll hev to be runnin' through the frozen woods all the time fur game fur me to cook, that's what you'll hev to do, Sol Hyde," retorted Jim Hart.

The idea of going into winter quarters on the island appealed to Paul. He had grown attached to the little hollow in which he and Jim Hart had built the hut, and he thought they could be very snug and warm. So he favored Sol's proposition with ardor, and about twilight they brought the hidden canoe again from the bushes, paddling boldly across the lake for the island. The place did not now have an uncanny look to Paul. Instead, it bore certain aspects of home, and he forgot all about the mummies in the trees, which were their protection from invasion.

"It's good to get back again," he said.

They landed on the island, hid the canoe, and went straight to the hollow, finding everything there absolutely undisturbed.

"We'll sleep to-night," said Henry, "and in the morning we'll plan."

Paul noticed, when he rose early the next day, that the whole earth was silver with frost, and he felt they were particularly fortunate in having found some sort of shelter. The others shared his satisfaction, and they worked all day, enlarging the hut, and strengthening it against the wind and cold with more bark and brush. At night Henry and Ross took the canoe, went to the mainland, and came back with a deer. The next day Jim Hart and Shif'less Sol were busy drying the venison, and Paul spent his time fishing with considerable success.

122

Several days passed thus, and they accumulated more meat and more skins. The latter were particularly valuable for warmth. Paul draped them about their hut, arranging them with an artistic eye, while Jim Hart and Shif'less Sol, with a similar satisfaction, watched their larder grow.

"This is the finest winter camp in all the wilderness," said Shif'less Sol.

"You couldn't beat it," said Jim Hart.

These were happy days to Paul. Knowing now that a message had been sent hack to Wareville, he was released from worry over the possible anxiety of his people on his account, and he was living a life brimful of interest. Everyone fell almost unconsciously into his place. Henry Ware, Ross, and Shif'less Sol scouted and hunted far and wide, and Paul and Jim Hart were fishermen, house builders, and, as Paul called it, "decorators."

The hut in the hollow began to have a cozy look. Henry and Ross brought in three buffalo skins, which Jim promptly tanned, and which Paul then used as wall coverings. Wolfskins, deerskins, and one beautiful panther hide were spread upon the floor. This floor was made mainly of boughs, broken up fine, and dead leaves, but it did not admit water, and the furs and skins were warm. In one corner of the place grew up a store of dried venison and buffalo meat, over which Jim Hart watched jealously.

All of the cooking was done at night, but in the open, in a kind of rude oven that Jim Hart built of loose stones, and never did food taste better in the mouth of a hungry youth than it did in that of Paul. The air was growing much colder. Paul, who was in the habit of taking a dip in the lake every night, found the waters so chill now that he could not stay in long, although the bath was wonderfully invigorating. Whenever the wind blew the dead leaves fell in showers, and Paul knew he would soon be deeply thankful they had the hut as a retreat.

About ten days after their return Henry came back from a scout around the Miami village, and he brought news of interest.

"Braxton Wyatt is still there," he said, "and he is so mixed up that he does not know just what to do for the present. After saying one thing and then denying himself, he is in the bad graces of both parties of the Miamis. For the same reason he doesn't dare to go back for a while to the Shawnees, so he is waiting for things to straighten themselves out, which they won't do for a long time. The Miami belt bearers have not yet returned from the Shawnee village, and then belts will have to go back and forth a dozen times each before either tribe can find out what the other means."

"An' if we kin keep 'em misunderstandin' each other," said Shif'less Sol, "they can't make any attack on the white settlements until away next spring, an' by that time a lot more white people will arrive from over the mountains. We'll be at least twice ez strong then."

"That's so," said Henry; "and the greatest work we five can do is to stay here and put as many spokes as we can in the Indian alliance."

"And I am glad to be here with all of you," said Paul earnestly. It seemed to him the greatest work in the world, this holding back of the tribes until their intended victim should acquire strength to beat them off, and his eyes shone. Besides the mere physical happiness that he felt, there was a great mental exhilaration, an exaltation, even, and he looked forward to the winter of a warrior and a statesman.

Paul's body flourished apace in the cold, nipping air and the wild life. There were discomforts, it is true, but he did not think of them. He looked only at the comforts and the joys. He knew that his muscles were growing and hardening, that eye, ear, all the five senses, in truth, were growing keener, and he felt within him a courage that could dare anything.

Henry made another expedition, to discover, if he could, whether the Miamis suspected that the haunted island harbored their foes. They did not ask him what means he used, how he disguised himself anew, or whether he disguised himself at all, but he returned with the news that they had no suspicion. The island was still sacred to the spirits—a place where they dare not land. This was satisfying news to all, and they rested for a while.

Three or four days after Henry's return a strong wind stripped the last leaves from the trees. All the reds and yellows and browns were gone, and the gusts whistled fiercely among the gray branches. The surface of the lake was broken into cold waves, that chased each other until they died away at the shore.

The next day heavy rolling clouds were drawn across the sky, and all the world was somber and dark. Paul stood at the entrance to the hut, and now, indeed, he was thankful that they had that shelter, and that they had furs and skins to reinforce their clothing. As he looked, something cold and wet came out of the sky and struck him upon the face. Another came, and then another, and in a few moments the air was full of flakes whirled by the wind.

"The first snow," said Paul.

"Yes," said Henry, "and let us pray for snows—many, hard,

and deep. The fiercer the winter the easier it will be to hold back the allied tribes."

It was not a heavy snow, but it gave an earnest of what might come. The bare boughs were whipped about in the gale, and creaked dismally. The ground was covered with white to the depth of about two inches, and dark, rolling waves, looking very chill, chased one another across the lake. Jim Hart and Paul had managed to build of stones, in one corner of their hut, a rude oven or furnace, with an exterior vent. They had plastered the stones together with mud, which hardened into a sort of cement, and in this furnace they kindled a little fire. They did not dare to make it large, because of the smoke, but they had enough coals to give out a warm and pleasant glow.

All of them retreated for a while to the "mansion," as Paul rather proudly called it, and Henry. Ross, and Shif'less Sol busied themselves with making new and stout moccasins of deerskin, fastened with sinews and lined with fur. Shif'less Sol was especially skillful at this work; in fact, the shiftless one was a wonderfully handy man at any sort of task, and with only his hunting knife, a wooden needle of his own manufacture, and deer sinews, he actually made Paul a fur-lined hunting shirt, which seemed to the boy's imaginative fancy about the finest garment ever worn in the wilderness. All of them also put fur flaps on their raccoon-skin caps, and Shif'less Sol even managed to fashion an imitation of gloves out of deerskin.

"I wouldn't advise you to try to use your hands much with these gloves on," he said; "leastways, not to shoot at anything till you took 'em off; but I do say that so long ez your hands are idle, they'll be pow'ful warmin' to the fingers."

"We don't have to go out very much just now," said Paul, "and if we only had two or three books here, we could pass the time very pleasantly."

"That's so," said Shif'less Sol musingly. "You an' me, Paul, wuz intended to be eddicated men. Ez fur Jim Hart here, he's that dull he'd take more pride in cookin' in a stone furnace than in writin' the finest book in the world."

"When I cook I git's somethin' that I kin see," said Jim Hart. "I never read but one book in my life, an' I didn't find it very sustainin'. I guess if you wuz starvin' to death here in the wilderness, you'd ruther hev a hot hoe cake than all the books in the world."

"'Tain't worth while, Paul, to talk to Jim Hart," said Shif'less

Sol sadly. "He ain't got no soul above a hoe cake. I've allus told you, Paul, that you an' me wuz superior to our surroundings. Ef Jim Hart wuz locked up in a schoolhouse all his life he'd never be an eddicated man, while ez fur me, I'm one without ever gittin' a chance, jest because it's in my natur'."

Paul laughed at them both, and drew a little closer to the bed of red coals. The warmth within and the cold without appealed to all the elements of his vivid and imaginative nature. Not for worlds would he have missed being on this great adventure with these daring men.

"I'm a-thinkin'," said Ross, as he lifted the buffalo robe over their door and looked out, "that ez soon ez the wind dies the lake will freeze over."

"An' it will be harder than ever then," said Paul, "to catch fish."

"I guess we kin do about ez well through holes in the ice," said Ross.

Ross's prediction soon came true. When they awoke on the morning two days afterwards the lake curved about them in a white and glittering sheet, reflecting back a brilliant sun in a million dazzling rays.

"I'm glad all of our party are here on the island together," said Henry, "because the ice isn't thick enough to support a man's weight, and it isn't thin enough to let a canoe be pushed through it. We're clean cut off from the world for a little while."

"An' this is whar poor old Long Jim becomes the most vallyble uv us all," said Jim Hart. "It's a lucky thing that I've got a kind uv stove an' buffalo meat an' venison an' other kinds uv game. I'm jest willin' to bet that you four hulkin' fellers will want to lay aroun' an' eat all the time."

"I wouldn't be surprised, Jim, if we didn't get hungry once in a while," said Henry, with a smile.

Two more days passed, and the ice on the lake neither melted nor grew thicker, and they were as well shut in and others were as well shut out as if they had been on a lone island in the Pacific Ocean. Once they saw a thin column of smoke, only a faint blue spire very far away, which Henry said rose from an Indian camp fire.

"It's several miles from here," he said, "and it's just chance that they are there. They don't dream that we are here."

Nevertheless, they did not light the fire in their furnace again for two days. Then, when the skies grew too dark and somber for a

126

faint smoke to show against its background, they kindled it up again, and once more enjoyed warm food.

"Ef I jest had a little coffee, an' somethin' to b'il it in, I'd be pow'ful happy," said Jim Hart. "I'd jest enjoy b'ilin' a gallon or two apiece fur you fellers an' me."

"Wa'al, ez you ain't got any coffee an' you ain't got anythin' to b'il it in, I reckon we'll hev to be jest ez happy without it," said Shif'less Sol.

The night after this conversation Paul was awakened by a patter upon their skin and thatch roof. It must have been two or three o'clock in the morning, and he had been sleeping very comfortably. He lay on furs, and the soft side of a buffalo robe was wrapped close about him. He could not remember any time in his life when he felt snugger, and he wanted to go back to sleep, but that patter upon the roof was insistent. He raised himself up a little, and he heard along with the patter the breathing of his four comrades. But it was pitch dark in the hut, and, rolling over to the doorway, he pulled aside a few inches the stout buffalo hide that covered it. Something hard and white struck him in the face and stung like shot.

It was hailing, pouring hard and driven fiercely by the wind. Moreover, it was bitterly cold, and Paul quickly shut down the buffalo flap, fastening it tightly. "We're snowed in and hailed in, too," he murmured to himself. Then he drew his buffalo robe around his body more closely than ever, and went back to sleep. The next morning it rained on top of the hail for about an hour, but after that it quickly froze again, the air turning intensely cold. Then Paul beheld the whole world sheathed in glittering ice. The sight was so dazzling that his eyes were almost blinded, but it was wonderfully beautiful, too. The frozen surface of the lake threw back the light in myriads of golden sheaves, and every tree, down to the last twig, gleamed in a silvery polished sheath.

"It 'pears to me," said Shif'less Sol lazily, "that we ain't on an islan' no longer. The Superior Powers hev built a drawbridge, on which anything can pass."

"That's so," said Paul. "The ice must be thick enough now to bear a war party."

"Ef that war party didn't slip up an' break its neck," said Shif less Sol. "All that meltin' stuff froze hard, an' it's like glass now. Jest you try it, Paul."

Paul went out in the hollow, and at his very first step his feet flew from under him and he landed on his back. Everywhere it was the same way—ice like glass, that no one could tread on and yet feel secure.

"We have our drawbridge," said Paul, "but it doesn't seem to me to be very safe walking on it."

Nevertheless, Henry and Ross slipped away two nights later, and were gone all the next day and another night. When they returned they reported that the Miami village was pretty well snowed up, and that the hunters even were not out. Braxton Wyatt was still there, and they believed he would soon be up to some sort of mischief—it was impossible for him to remain quiet and behave himself very long.

"Meanwhile what are we to do?" asked Paul.

"Just stay quiet," said Henry. "We'll wait for Braxton and his savages to act first."

But the ice did not remain long, all melting away as the fickle northwestern weather turned comparatively warm again, and the five once more began to move about freely.

CHAPTER XV
WORK AND PLAY

Henry and Ross were gone to the mainland, and Paul, Shif'less Sol, and Jim Hart were left on the island. Shif'less Sol stood at the edge of the hollow, hands on hips, admiring the hut.

"Paul," he said, "I think that thar house is jest about the finest I ever built."

"You built!" exclaimed Jim Hart indignantly. "Mighty little you had to do with it, Sol Hyde, but eat in it an' sleep in it, which two things you are willin' enough to do any time! It's me an' Paul who have reared that gran' structure."

"It appeals to my instincts as an eddicated man," went on Sol, calmly disregarding Jim. "We've got up the house without sp'ilin' the surroundin's. It jest blends with rock an' bush, an' we've helped natur' without tryin' to improve it."

"I believe you've got the truth of it, Sol," said Paul. "I'm getting fond of this place. How long do you think we'll stay here, Sol?"

Shif'less Sol cocked up his weather eye, and a look of surpassing wisdom came over his face.

"When the ground hog come out o' his hole in the fall an' saw his shadder, he went right back ag'in," he replied, "an' that means a hard winter. Besides, we're pretty far north, an' all the hunters say they have lot o' snow hereabouts. We're goin' to have cold an' snow right along. That's the opinion o' me, Solomon Hyde. Jim Hart may say somethin' else, but he ain't worth listenin' to."

"I said this mornin' that it wuz goin' to be a hard winter," growled Jim Hart. "You heard me sayin' so, an' that's the reason you're sayin' so now."

"Oh, Jim, Jim! Whatever will become o' you?" exclaimed Shif'less Sol sadly. "An' I've always tried to teach you that the truth wuz the right thing."

Paul laughed.

"Sol," he asked, "did you ever see a game of chess?"

"Chess? What's that? Is it a mark you shoot at?"

"No; you play it on a board with little figures made of wood, if you haven't got anything else. My father has a set of chessmen, and he plays often with Mr. Pennypacker, our school teacher. He's

129

played with me, too, and I can show you how to make the things and to play."

A look of interest came into Sol's eyes.

"We've got lots o' time," he said. "S'pose you do it, Paul. I know I kin learn. I ain't so sure o' Jim Hart thar."

Jim was also interested, so much so that he forgot to reply to Shif'less Sol.

"How'll you do it?" he asked.

Paul's reply was to begin at once. He cut a big square piece of white fanned deerskin, and upon this he marked the little squares with coal-black. Then the three of them went to work with their sharp hunting knives, carving out the wooden figures. The results were crude, but they had enough shape for identification, and then Paul began to teach the game itself.

Sol and Jim were really men of strong intellect, and they had plenty of patience. Paul was surprised at their progress. They were soon thinking for themselves, and when Paul himself did not want to play, the two would fight it out over the deerskin.

"It's a slow game, but good," said Shif'less Sol. "It 'pears to me that a man to be at the head o' 'em all in this would hev to do nothin' else all his life."

"That is so," said Paul.

"Jim, thar ain't no earthly chance for you," said Shif'less Sol.

"I guess I've got you this time, anyhow," said Jim, with a deep chuckle of satisfaction. "Jest look at that thar board, Sol Hyde. Ef you ain't druv into a corner so you can't move this way nor that, then you can hev the huntin' shirt right off my back."

Shif'less Sol examined the deerskin square attentively.

"Blamed ef it ain't so," he said in a tone of deep disgust. "It wuz an accident, nuthin' but an accident, or else I've been talkin' too much."

"That's what you're always doin', Sol Hyde—talkin' too much."

"Then we'll jest try it over ag'in, an' I'll show you what it is to play ag'inst a real smart man."

They were deep in a fresh game a few moments later, and Paul went outside. He was glad to see them so interested, because he knew that otherwise the curse of dullness might fall upon them.

The air was raw and chill, and, although the snow and ice were gone, the lake and the hills beyond looked singularly cold. But Paul was neither uncomfortable nor unhappy. He was clothed warmly, and he had food in abundance and variety. Trusty comrades, too, surrounded him. Life at present seemed very pleasant.

He strolled up the island toward the trees that contained the

Indian bodies, and after a while returned toward the home in the hollow. A warm, mellow light gleamed from its rude window, and Paul's heart throbbed with something of the feeling that one has only toward "home."

He opened the door and entered, just in time to hear Shif'less Sol's cry of triumph:

"Thar, Jim Hart, ef that don't settle you, I'd like to know what will! Now, who's doin' too much talkin'?"

"I can't see jest how it happened," said Jim Hart ruefully.

"No, an' you never will. Them things are too deep fur you. It's only eddicated men, like me an' Paul, that kin see to the bottom o' 'em."

"You're even, as it's game and game," said Paul, "so let's rest now. Henry and Tom ought to be coming pretty soon."

"An' they'll be ez hungry ez a hull pack uv wolves," said Jim Hart, "so I guess I'd better be cookin'. Here, Sol, give me them strips uv deer meat an' buffalo."

"I shorely will," said Shif'less Sol. "Thar is one thing, ef it is only one, that you kin do well, Jim Hart, an' it's cook."

The two, in the most friendly fashion, went about preparing the supper. They had many kinds of game to choose from, and once Ross had brought a bag of ground corn, perhaps taken by stealth from an Indian village, and now and then Jim made from it a kind of bread. He was to bake some to-night, in honor of the returning two, and soon the place was filled with pleasant odors.

Twilight was deepening, the supper was almost ready, and Paul went forth to see if Henry and Tom were yet in sight. Presently he saw them coming—two black figures against the setting sun, with the body of a deer that they had killed and dressed. He hastened to meet them and give them a helping hand, and together they approached the house.

First they swung the body of the deer from a bough, and then they opened the door. Deep silence reigned within. No friendly voice greeted them. The heads of Jim Hart and Shif'less Sol almost touched over a square of deerskin, at which both were looking intently. With the supper ready, and nothing else to do, they had got out the chessmen, and were playing the rubber. So absorbed were they that they neither heard nor saw.

"Now what under the sun is this?" exclaimed Tom Ross.

"It's a game I taught 'em while you and Henry were gone," explained Paul. "It's called chess."

Shif'less Sol and Jim sprang up, but Sol quickly recovered his presence of mind.

131

"I jest about had him cornered, an' your comin' saved him," he said.

"Cornered!" said Jim Hart. "He ain't even seed the day when he kin beat me!"

The chessmen were put aside for the time, and five hungry beings ate as only borderers could eat. Then Tom Ross demanded a look at the game. After the look he asked for instruction.

"I saw a set uv them fellers once when I wuz at Fort Pitt," he said, "but I never thought the time would come when I'd play with 'em. Push up the fire thar a little, will you, Jim, so I kin see better."

Paul and Henry looked at each other and smiled. Soon Tom himself, the senior of the party, was absorbed in the new game, and it was a happy thought of Paul's to introduce it, even with the rude figures which were the best that they could make.

Paul brought up again the next morning the subject of their weather prospects, and Tom and Henry agreed with the others in predicting a great deal of snow and cold.

"All signs show it," said Henry. "The rabbits are burrowing deeper than usual under the bushes, and I notice that the birds have built their nests uncommonly thick. I don't understand how they know what's coming, but they do."

"Instinct," said Paul.

"We know that a hound kin follow by smell the track of a man who has passed hours before," said Shif'less Sol, "when no man in the world kin smell anything at all o' that track. So it ain't any more strange that birds an' beasts kin feel in their bones what's comin' when we can't."

"Ef you'll imitate them squirrels an' rabbits an' birds an' things," said Jim Hart, "an' lay up lots uv things good to eat fur the winter, it'll give me pleasure to cook it ez it's needed."

"I've noticed something besides the forethought of the animals," added Henry. "The moss on the north side of the trees seems to me to be thicker than usual. I suppose that nature, too, is getting ready for a long, hard winter."

"When nature and the animals concur," said Paul, "it is not left to man to doubt; so we'd better be providing the things Jim promises to cook so well."

They had learned the border habit of acting promptly, and Henry Ross and Sol were to depart the very next morning for the mainland on a hunt for deer, while Long Jim was to keep house. Paul otherwise would have been anxious to go with the hunters, but he had an idea of his own, and when Henry suggested that he accompany them, he replied that he expected to make a contribution of a different kind.

All these plans were made in the evening, and then every member of the five, wrapping himself in his buffalo robe, fell asleep. The fire in Jim Hart's furnace had been permitted to die down to a bed of coals, and the glow from them barely disclosed the five figures lying, dark and silent, on the floor. They slept, clean in conscience and without fear.

Henry, Shif'less Sol, and Ross were off at dawn, and Paul, using a rude wooden needle that he had shaped with his own pocketknife, and the tendon of a deer as thread, made a large bag of buckskin. Then he threw it triumphantly over his shoulder.

"Now what under the sun, Paul, are you goin' to do with that?" asked Jim Hart.

"I'm going to add variety to our winter store. Just you wait, Jim Hart, and see."

Bearing the bag, he left the house and took his way to the north end of the island. He had not been above learning more than one thing from the squirrels, and he had recalled a grove of great hickory trees growing almost to the water's edge. Now the ground was thickly covered with the nuts which had fallen when the severe frosts and the snow and ice came. There were several varieties, including large ones two inches long, and the fine little ones known to boys throughout the Mississippi Valley as the scaly bark. Paul procured two stones, and, cracking several of them, found them delicious to the taste. Already in his Kentucky home he had become familiar with them all. The hogs of the settlers, running through the forest and fattening upon these nuts and acorns, known collectively as "mast," acquired a delicious flavor. Boys and grown people loved the nuts, too.

The nuts lay about in great quantities, and the thick, barky coverings, known to the boys as "hulls," almost fell off at a touch. Soon the ground was littered with these hulls, while the big buckskin bag was filled with the clean nuts. Then, lifting it to his shoulder, Paul marched off proudly to the house.

"Now, why didn't I think uv that?" said Jim Hart, as Paul threw down the bag before him and disclosed its contents. "An' all them hick'ry nuts jest layin' thar on the ground an' waitin' fur me."

"It's because you had so much else to do, Jim," said Paul; "and as I'm idle a good deal of the time, the thought occurred to me."

"You shorely do have the gift uv sayin' nice things, an' makin' a feller feel good, Paul," said Jim admiringly.

Paul laughed. Jim's words pleased him.

"I told nothing but the truth," he said. "Now, Jim, I'm going back for more, and I'd like to do this job all by myself. I think I can gather at least six bagfuls, and we'll heap them here by the wall."

"An' mighty good seas'nin' they'll be to deer an' buffalo an' b'ar meat," said Jim Hart. "It wuz a good thought uv yours, Paul."

Paul worked the whole morning, and when he had gathered all the nuts in the house he estimated the quantity at several bushels. Although he sought to conceal his pride, he cast more than one triumphant look at the great heap by the wall.

He and Jim went forth together in the afternoon with rude spades, made of wood and hardened at the edges in the fire, to dig for Indian turnip.

"It ain't much of a veg'table," said Jim, "but we might find it useful to give a new taste to our meat, or it might be uv some help doctorin', in case any uv us fell sick."

They found two or three of the roots, and the remainder of the afternoon they devoted to strengthening their house. They did this with huge slabs of bark lying everywhere on the ground, fallen in former seasons. Some they put on the roof, thatching in between with dry grass and leaves, and others they fastened on the sides.

"It ain't purty," said Jim, "but it turns rain an' snow, an' that's what we're after."

"I take another view," said Paul. "It does look well. It blends with the wilderness, and so it has a beauty of its own."

The three hunters were not to return that night, and Paul and Jim kept house. Jim slept lightly, and just before the dawn he rolled over in his buffalo robe and pushed Paul's shoulder.

Paul awoke instantly, and sat up.

"What is it, Jim?" he asked anxiously. It was his natural thought that some danger threatened, and it was so dark in the cabin that he could not see Jim's face.

"Do you hear that hoo-hooing sound?" asked Jim Hart.

Paul listened and heard faintly a low, mellow note.

"What is it, Jim?" he asked.

"The call of the wild turkey."

"What, Indians again?"

"No, it's the real bird, talkin'. An old gobbler is tellin' his hens that day is comin'. It's a plumb waste on his part, because they know it theirselves, but he must jest let 'em know what a smart bird he is. An' it's that pride uv his that will be his ruin. Git up, Paul; we must have him an' one uv his hens to eat."

"Where do you think they are?" asked Paul.

"In the hick'ry grove. I guess they lighted thar fur the night, when flyin' 'cross the lake."

The two hurried on their clothes, took their rifles, and stole out. A faint tinge of light was just showing under the horizon in the

134

east, but the air was not yet gray. It was very cold at that early hour, and Paul shivered, but he soon forgot it in the ardor of the chase.

"Slip along softer nor a cat, Paul," said Jim. "We don't want to give old Mr. Gobbler any warnin' that his time hez come. Thar, hear him? The tarnal fool! He's jest bound to show us where he is."

The mellow call arose again, very clear and distinct in the silent air, and as they approached the edge of the hickory grove, Jim pointed upward.

"See him thar on the limb," he said, "the big feller with the feathers all shinin' an' glistenin'? That's the gobbler, an' the littler ones with the gray feathers are the hens. I'm goin' to take the gobbler. He may be old, but he's so fat he's bound to be tender; an' s'pose, Paul, you take that hen next to him. When I say 'Now,' fire."

The two raised their guns, took careful aim, and Jim said "Now." They fired together, aiming at the necks or heads. The big gobbler fell like a stone from the bough and lay still. The hen fell, too, but she fluttered about on the ground. The rest flew away on whirring wings. Paul ran forward and finished his bird with a stick, but Jim lifted the great gobbler and looked at him with admiring eyes.

"Did you ever see a finer turkey?" he said. "He must weigh all uv forty pounds, an' he's as fat as he can be with the good food uv the wilderness. An' he's a beauty, too! Jest look at them glossy blue-black feathers. No wonder so many hens wuz in love with him. I could be pop'lar with the women folks, too, ef I wuz ez handsome ez Mr. Gobbler here."

They picked and cleaned the turkeys, and then hung the dressed bodies from the boughs of a tree near the hut, where they would be frozen, and thus keep.

The hunters returned that afternoon with two deer, and were delighted with Jim and Paul's zeal and success.

"Ef things go on this swimmin' way," said Shif'less Sol, "we'd be able to feed an army this winter, ef it wuz needed."

It was very cold that evening, and they built the fire higher than usual. Great mellow rays of heat fell over all the five, and lighted up the whole interior of the cabin with its rich store of skins and nuts and dressed meats, and other spoil of the wilderness. The five, though no one of them ever for a moment forgot their great mission of saving Kentucky, had a feeling of content. Affairs were going well.

"Paul," said Shif'less Sol, "you've read books. Tell us about some o' them old fellers that lived a long time ago. I like to hear about the big ones."

"Well," said Paul, "there was Alexander. Did you ever hear of him, Sol?"

Shif'less Sol shook his head and sighed.

"I can't truly call myself an eddicated man," he replied, "though I have the instincts o' one. But I ain't had the proper chance. No, Paul, me an' Alexander is strangers."

"Then I'll make you acquainted," said Paul. He settled himself more comfortably before the fire, and the others did likewise.

"Alexander lived a long, long time ago," said Paul. "He was a Greek—that is, he was a Macedonian with Greek blood in him—I suppose it comes to the same thing—and he led the Greeks and Macedonians over into Asia, and whipped the Persians every time, though the Persians were always twenty to one."

"Who writ the accounts o' them thar battles?" asked Shif'less Sol.

"Why, the Greeks, of course."

"I thought so. Why, Jim Hart here must be a Greek, then. To hear him tell it, he's always whippin' twenty men at a time. But it ain't in natur' for one man to whip twenty."

"I never said once in my life that I whipped twenty men at a time," protested Jim Hart.

"We'll let it pass," said Paul, "and Sol may be right about the Greeks piling it up for themselves; but so they wrote it, and so we have to take it. Well, Alexander, although he wasn't much more than a boy, kept on whipping the Persians until at last their king, Darius, ran away with his wives."

Shif'less Sol whistled.

"Do you mean to tell me, Paul," he said, "that any white man ever had more than one wife! I thought only Injun chiefs had 'em?"

"Why, it was common a long time ago," replied Paul.

"What a waste!" said Shif'less Sol. "One man havin' a lot uv wives, an' Jim Hart here ain't ever been able to get a single one."

"An' you ain't, either, Sol Hyde," said Jim Hart.

"Oh, me!" replied Shif'less Sol carelessly. "I'm too young to marry."

"Let him go on about Alexander, the fightin' feller," interrupted Tom Ross.

"Alexander conquered all Asia," resumed Paul, "but it didn't agree with him. The more he conquered the more he wanted to conquer."

"Jest like a little boy eatin' turkey," said Shif'less Sol. "Can't hold enough to suit him. Stummick ain't ez big ez his appetite, an' he hez to cry about it. I don't think your Alexander wuz such a big man, after all."

136

"He was not, from one point of view, Sol, but he was certainly a general. After conquering all the world, he fell to drinking too much, and quarreling with his best friends. One day he got raging drunk, which made him hot all over, and he jumped into an icy river to cool off. That gave him a fever, and he died right away. He was only thirty-two."

Shif'less Sol sniffed in disgust.

"Dead at thirty-two!" he said. "Now, I call him a plumb failure. With fightin' goin' on all the time, an' fevers layin' aroun' fur you, I call it somethin' jest to live, an' I mean to stay in these parts till I'm a hundred. Why, that Alexander never had time, Paul, to think over what he'd done. I wouldn't change places with him, I think I'm a heap sight better off."

"I agrees with Sol ag'in," said Tom Ross, who had been in deep thought. "In dang'rous times it's doin' a heap jest to live, an' a man who dies off at thirty-two, all through his own foolishness, ain't much to brag about."

Henry laughed.

"Paul," he said, "you'll have to bring out better examples of greatness to satisfy Sol and Tom."

Paul laughed, too.

"I just tell things as they are," he said. "Maybe they are right."

Henry went to the door and looked out. The air was full of raw chill, and he heard the leafless boughs rustling in the winter wind. All around him was the dark wilderness, and, natural hunter and warrior though he was, he was glad to have the shelter, the fire, and his comrades. He turned back and closed the door tightly, in order to shut out any stray gust that might be of an unusually penetrating quality.

"I'm thinking that we'd better start away hunting again very early in the morning," he said. "The big snows are bound to come soon. That first little one was only a taste of what we're going to get."

They were off again at daybreak, and this time Paul went with them. The party turned to the southward, in order to avoid the chance of meeting Shawnees or Miamis, and soon had the luck to run into a small buffalo herd. They killed only what they could carry, and then returned with it toward the island. Henry continually watched the skies as they traveled, and he uttered an exclamation of relief when they landed. The heavens all the while had been leaden and somber, and there was no wind stirring.

"See," he said, "the great snow comes!"

The sullen skies opened, and big white flakes dropped down as they hurried with their fresh supplies to the cabin.

137

CHAPTER XVI
NOEL

The snow fell three days and nights without ceasing, and they rejoiced greatly over their foresight in preparing so well for it, because it was a big snow, a very big snow. "It ain't jest snowin'," said Shif'less Sol; "the bottom o' the sky hez dropped out, an' all the snow's tumblin' down."

The great flakes never ceased for a moment to fall. The sun did not get a single chance to shine, and as fast as one cloud was emptied, another, huge and black, was drawn in its place across the sky. The island ceased to be an island, because the snow heaped up on the frozen surface of the lake, and it was impossible to tell where land ended and water began. The boughs of the trees bent and cracked beneath their load, and some fell to the ground. At times the sound of snapping boughs was like stray rifle shots.

Paul watched the snow deepen before their door. First an inch, then two, then four, then six, and on and on. The roof began to strain and creak ominously beneath the great weight. All rushed forth at once into the storm, and with poles and their rude shovels they thrust the great mass of accumulated snow from the roof. This task they repeated at intervals throughout the three days, but they had little else to do, except cook, eat, and sleep. They had recourse again to the chessmen and Paul's stories, and they reverted often to their friends and relatives at Wareville.

"At any rate," said Henry, "Kentucky is safe so long as this great snow lasts. What holds us holds the Shawnees and the Miamis, too; they can't go south through it."

"That's so," said Paul, with intense satisfaction, as he ran over all the chances of success or failure in their great task.

At the end of the third day the snow ceased. It lay three feet deep on the level, and deeper in the hollows and gullies. Then all the clouds floated away, the sun came out, and the whole world was a dazzling globe of white, so intense that it hurt Paul's eyes.

"We've got to guard against snow-blindness," said Shif'less Sol, "an' I'm thinkin' o' a plan that'll keep us from sufferin'."

He procured small pieces of wood, and fitted them together so there would be only a narrow slit between. These were placed over the eyes like spectacles, and fastened with deerskin string, tied behind the head. The range of vision was then very narrow, but all the glare from the snow was shut out. Shif'less Sol unconsciously had imitated a device employed by the Esquimaux of the far north to protect their eyesight. Sets were made for all, and they used them a few days until their eyes grew accustomed to the glare.

All had a great sense of coziness and warmth. The snow pushed from the roof had gone to reinforce that on the ground, and it now lay heaped up beside the house to a depth of five or six feet, adding to the snugness and security of their walls. They had gathered an ample supply of firewood, and a deep bed of coals always threw out a mellow and satisfying glow.

They did not spend their time in idleness. The narrow confines of their house would soon grow irksome to five able-bodied boys and men, and every one of them knew it. They went forth with rude wooden shovels, and began to clear paths in the snow—one to a point among the trees where the fallen brushwood lay thickest, another to the edge of the lake, where they broke holes in the ice and caught pickerel, and two or three more to various points around their little domain. This task gave them healthy occupation for two or three days, and on the fourth day, while Henry, Ross, and Jim Hart were fishing, Paul and Shif'less Sol sat together in the house.

"This snow is goin' to last a long time, Paul," said Sol, "an' we've got to stay here till at least most o' it's gone. The warriors won't be movin', nor will we. While we're idlin', I wish we had three or four o' them books that your father an' Mr. Pennypacker brought over the mountains with 'em."

"So do I," said Paul, with a sigh. He was thinking of an interminable romance, translated from the French of a certain Mademoiselle de Scudéry, which his teacher, Mr. Pennypacker, had among his possessions, and which he had once secretly shown to Paul, who was his favorite pupil. But he added, resignedly: "You'd never find a book in all this region up here, Sol. We'd better make up our minds to some monotonous days."

Shif'less Sol had been leaning lazily against a heap of firewood, and suddenly he sat up with a look of interest in his eyes. His acute ear had detected a sound on the hill above them—a faint crunching in the snow.

"It's one o' the boys, I s'pose," he said. "Now, I wonder what he wants to be tramping around in the deep snow up thar fur."

"Yes, I hear him," said Paul, "and he's lumbering about queerly."

"He's comin' down toward the house," said Shif'less Sol. "Now, what in thunder is that?"

There was the sound of an angry "snuff!" a sudden, wild

threshing in the snow, and the next instant a tremendous weight struck the roof of their house. A rending of bark and thatch followed, and a massive black form shot down into the center of the room and lay there a moment, stunned. Paul, too, was dizzy. He had been struck a glancing blow on the shoulder by the big black body in its fall, and hurled into a heap of furs. Shif'less Sol had been sent spinning in another direction.

When both rose to their feet the big black body also rose, growling savagely and extending long, powerful paws, armed with cruel claws. A bear, prowling in the snow, had fallen through the roof of their house, and it was furiously angry.

"Jump back, Paul, jump back!" shouted Shif'less Sol, "an' get to the door, ef you kin!"

Paul obeyed a part of his command instinctively and sprang away, just in time to escape the cruel claws. But he was compelled to press against the wall. The enraged animal was between him and the door. Shif'less Sol himself was darting here and there in an effort to keep out of the way. Both Paul's rifle and Shif'less Sol's stood in a corner far from reach.

The bear, blind with rage, fright, and astonishment, whirled around ripping into the air with his long claws. The man and the boy not able to reach the door, hopped about like jumping jacks, and the cold air poured down upon them from the huge hole in their damaged roof. The bear suddenly ran into Jim Hart's furnace and uttered a roar of pain. He stopped for a moment to lick his singed flank, and Shif'less Sol, seizing the opportunity, leaped for his rifle. He grasped it, and the next instant the cabin roared with the rifle shot. The great bear uttered a whining cry, plucked once or twice at his breast, and then stretched himself out in front of Jim Hart's furnace, quite dead. Paul stopped dancing to and fro, and uttered a gasp of relief.

"You got that rifle just in time, Sol," he said.

"We shorely did need a gun," Shif'less Sol said. "I guess nobody ever had a more sudden or unwelcome visitor than you an' me did, Paul. But I believe that thar b'ar wuz ez bad skeered ez we wuz."

"And just look at our house," said Paul ruefully. "Half the roof smashed in, our furs and our food supplies thrown in every direction, and a big bear stretched out in front of our fire."

They heard the patter of swift footsteps outside, and the three fishing at the lake, who had heard the shot, came in, running.

"It's nothin', boys," said Shif'less Sol carelessly. "A gentleman livin' in these parts, but a stranger to us, came into our house

140

uninvited. He wouldn't go away when we axed him to, most earnest, so we've jest put him to sleep."

Ross pushed the bear with his foot.

"He's fat yet," he said, "an' he ought to be in winter quarters right now. Somethin' must have driv him out uv his hole an' have sent him wanderin' across the lake on the ice an' snow. That's what anybody gits fur not stayin' whar he belongs."

"An' ef Jim Hart had stayed whar he belongs—that is, right here in this house, cookin'—he'd have got that b'ar on his back, an' not me," said Shif'less Sol, rubbing the bruised place.

"That's once I wuz luckier than you wuz, Sol Hyde," said Jim Hart, chuckling.

"We've got a lot of fresh bear steak," said Henry Ware, "but we'll have to clean up all this mess, and rebuild our house, just as soon as we can."

They set to work at once. All, through forest life, had become skillful in such tasks, and it did not take them long to rethatch the roof. But they made it stronger than ever with cross-poles. Ingenious Sol cut up the bear hide, and made of it stout leggings for them all, which would serve in the place of boots for wading in the deep snow.

Then the camp returned to its wonted calm. But a few days later, Shif'less Sol, who had been unusually grave, called Paul aside and asked him to walk with him up the path to the hickory trees. When they arrived there, far out of hearing of the others, Shif'less Sol said:

"Do you know what day this is, Paul?"

"Why, no, Sol," replied Paul. "What does it matter?"

"It matters a heap," said Shif'less Sol, not departing one whit from his grave manner. "I know what day it is. I've kept count. See here!"

He pointed to a hickory tree. Clear and smooth was gash after gash, cut in the bark, one above another, by Sol with his stout knife.

"Every one o' them is a day," said Shif'less Sol, "an' to-day is the 24th of December. Now, what is to-morrow, Paul Cotter?"

"The 25th of December—Christmas Day."

"An' oughtn't we to hev Christmas, too, even ef we are up here in the wild woods, all by ourselves? Don't this look like Christmas?"

Paul looked around at the glittering and magnificent expanse of white wilderness. There was snow, snow everywhere. The trees were robed in it, unstained. It was a world of peace and beauty, and it did look like Christmas. They were preparing for it at Wareville at this very moment—the settlers were a religious people, and from the first they celebrated the great religious festival.

141

"Yes, Sol," he replied, "it does look like Christmas, and we ought to celebrate it, too."

"I'm glad you think ez I do," said Sol, in a tone of relief. "I wanted to hear what you thought o' it, Paul, afore I broached it to the other boys. We've got a lot to be glad about. We're all here, sound an' well, an' though we've been through a power o' dangers, we ain't sufferin' now."

"That's so," said Paul.

"Then we'll tell the boys right now."

They walked back to the cabin, and Shif'less Sol announced the date to the others, who agreed at once that Christmas should be celebrated by them there on their little island in the wilderness. All were touched in a way by the solemnity of the event, and they began to feel how strong was the tie that united them.

"We must have a big Christmas dinner," said Jim Hart, "an' I'll cook it."

"An' I'll help you," said Shif'less Sol.

"And I," added Paul.

That evening they sat around the fire, talking in the mellow glow; but their talk was not of the Indians, nor of the chase, nor of themselves, but of those behind at Wareville. Paul shut his eyes and looked dreamily into the fire. He could see the people at the settlement getting ready for the great festival, preparing little gifts, and the children crawling reluctantly into their homemade trundle, or box beds. He felt at that moment a deep kindness toward all things.

They covered up the ashes after a while, and then, in the darkness, every one in his turn laid out some little gift for the others—a clasp knife, a powderhorn, a prized deerskin, or something else that counted among his possessions. But no one was to look until the morning, and soon all fell asleep.

They were up the next day at the first sight of dawn, and compared their gifts with great rejoicings. Shif'less Sol had presented to Jim Hart a splendid clasp knife, a valuable possession in the wilderness, as a token of his great friendship and exceeding high regard, and Jim was like a child in his delight. In fact, there was something of the child, or rather of the child's simplicity, in all of them.

The Christmas dinner was a signal triumph in Jim Hart's life. Capably assisted by Paul and Shif'less Sol, he labored on it most of the day, and at last they sat down to a magnificent wilderness table of buffalo hump, venison, squirrel, rabbit, fish, wild turkey, and other kinds of game, flanked by bread baked of the Indian meal, and finished off with the nuts Paul had gathered. Forest and lake had yielded bounteously, and they ate long and happily.

"Why anybody wants to live back thar in the East in the towns is more'n I can understand," said Shif'less Sol. "You've got room to breathe here, an' the fat game is runnin' roun' in the woods, jest beggin' you to stick a knife in its back an' eat it."

Paul laughed.

"How about the danger from the Indians, Sol?" asked Paul.

"You don't expect to have a perfect world here below, do you, Paul?" replied Shif'less Sol. "Thar ain't never nothin' without a thorn in it, but our thorn is about ez little a one ez you could think of. The Injuns give us a kind o' excitin' variety, an' don't we always get away from 'em?"

No more work was done that day, and in the evening they went to sleep earlier than usual, and slept very soundly. A moon of pure silver came out, and bathed all the vast wilderness in its light. A huge, yellow panther, lean and fierce with hunger, wandered in the snow across the frozen lake, and put foot upon the island. There the pleasant odor of food came to his nostrils, and he lifted up his ears. As the pleasant odor came again his tawny eyes became more ferocious, and the lips curled back from the rows of cruel, white teeth. He drew his long, lithe body over the snow, and came to one of the paths. He might have turned back because the path was strong with the odor of a strange and perhaps powerful creature; but he was a very hungry, a very large, and a very bold panther, and he went on.

The path led straight to the cabin, and the panther trod it on noiseless pads, his eyes glowing, and hunger attacking him all the more fiercely because, mingled with the strange, new odor now came many odors that he knew, and all pleasant—odor of buffalo and deer and others—and he was very, very hungry.

He went down the path to the door of the cabin, and halted a moment there. A red gleam, a glow from the bed of coals, came through a chink beside the door, and it filled his heart with terror. He shivered, and fear drew a low growl from him.

One of the five sleepers inside stirred and sat up. He listened and heard a heavy breathing at the door. Then he arose, took a brand from the fire, stepped noiselessly to the door, and, opening it, rushed out, waving the burning brand in front of him. The panther, stricken with frightful panic, fled down the path, and then over the lake into the woods on the mainland. Henry Ware, laughing silently, returned to the cabin and lay down to sleep again beside his comrades, who had slept on, undisturbed.

143

CHAPTER XVII
FOOTPRINTS IN THE SNOW

The singular existence of the five in the little hollow in the haunted island endured much longer. The great cold had come early, and it held the earth fast in its grasp. The ice grew thicker on the lake beneath the snow, and winds that would freeze one to the marrow swept over its surface. Fortunately, there was plenty of fallen wood on the island, and they never allowed the fire in Hart's furnace to go out. They never built it up high, but a bed of coals was always smoldering there, sending out grateful light and heat.

Henry and Ross scouted at intervals, but only as a matter of habit rather than necessary precaution. They knew that the danger of an attack at such a time had decreased to the vanishing point. Now Paul became for a while the central figure of what he called their little colony. His mental resources were in great demand, and for the sake of his comrades he drew willingly upon his stores of learning. In the evening, when they were all sitting before the coals, and could just see one another's faces in the faint light, Paul would tell what he had read about other times and other lands. He knew the outlines of ancient history, and the victories of Hannibal, Alexander, and Cæsar suffered nothing at his hands, though Alexander, as before, was condemned by Shif'less Sol and Ross. Paul, moreover, had both the dramatic and poetic sense, and he made these far-away heroes, of whom Jim Hart had never heard before, actually live in the little cabin.

"It 'pears to me," said Shif'less Sol reflectively, "that that feller Hannibal wuz jest about the finest fighter o' them all. Ef, ez you say, Paul, he had to hire all kinds o' strangers an' barbarians, too, like the red Injuns out thar in the woods, an' lead sech a mixed lot up ag'in the Romans, who were no slouches in a fracas, an' whip 'em over an' over ag'in, on thar own groun', too, then I call him about the smartest o' all them old fellers. But he shore had the luck ag'in' him, an' I admire the man who kin stan' up an' fight the odds."

"He has my sympathy," said Paul.

"What did them old-time fellers eat?" asked Jim Hart.

"Mostly vegetables and grain," replied Paul.

"No wonder they're dead," said Jim Hart solemnly. "I can't fight an' I can't march good on anything but buffalo steak an' venison an' things uv that kind. I has to have meat."

144

Then Jim rose gravely, and looked at what he called his kitchen.

"'Nough to last three or four weeks," he said. "We'll shorely get fat an' lazy layin' roun' here an' doin' nothin' but eatin' an' sleepin' an' listenin' to Paul's tales."

"You ought to appreciate your chance, Jim Hart," said Shif'less Sol. "Ef me an' Paul wuz to work on you about a hundred years, maybe we might make you into a sort o' imitation o' a eddicated man. But I reckon we'd have to work all the time."

"You an eddicated man!" said Jim Hart indignantly. "Why, readin' a book is harder work to you than choppin' wood, an' they say you won't chop wood 'less two big, strong men stand by you an' make you."

"Never min'," said Shif'less Sol complacently; "I know I ain't had much chances to become eddicated, but I hev the natur' o' an eddicated man. My mind jest glows at the idea uv learnin', an' I respecks eddication with a deep an' lastin' respeck."

Then both stopped to hear Paul begin the story of Troy for the second time, but when he came to the death of Hector he would have to stop to let Shif'less Sol utter what he called a "few cuss words." Hector, like Hannibal, had the sympathy of everyone, and Sol spoke for them all when he said: "'Twa'n't fair o' that air goddess Minerver hoppin' in an' helpin' A-Killus when Hector might hev a-slew him in a fair battle. Women ain't got no business mixin' in a fight. Whenever they do they allus help the wrong feller. I've no doubt that ef me an' Jim Hart was a-hittin' an' a-wrastlin', an' hevin' the terriblest fight you ever heard on, ef any woman wuz to come along she'd pull me off the ornery, long-legged, knock-kneed, ugly Jim Hart—an' me a handsome man, too."

"I wonder all the ice on the lake don't melt when it sees your face, Sol Hyde," retorted Jim Hart scornfully.

"I don't think much uv them old Greeks an' Trojans," said Tom Ross, who seldom delivered himself at length. "'Pears to me they had pow'ful cur'us ways uv fightin'. Think uv a feller, when he feels like takin' a scalp, comin' out before the hull army an' beatin' a big brass shield till it rattled like a tin pan, an' then, when he got 'em all to lookin' an' listenin', hollerin' at the top uv his voice, 'I'm A-Killus, Defyer uv the Lightnin', Slayer uv the Trojans, the terriblest fighter the world ever seed! I pick up a ship in my right ban', an' throw it, with all the sailors in it, over a hill! When I look at the sun, it goes out, skeered to death! I've made more widders an' orphans than any other ten thousan' men that ever lived.' 'Pears to me them

145

wuz the pow'fullest boasters that ever wuz born. Why, what they said wuz mostly lies. 'Twas bound to be so, an' their ways uv fightin' wuz plumb foolishness. Why, ef A-Killus wuz to come along nowadays, beatin' his brass shield in the face an' hollerin' out his big words, some Shawnee layin' behind a rock would send a bullet through his head, jest ez easy ez knockin' over a rabbit, an' thet would be the end uv Mr. A-Killus, an' a good thing fur all, too."

"But there were no Shawnees and no rifles on the plains of Troy, Tom," said Paul.

"What uv it?" exclaimed Ross in hot indignation. "They didn't fight fair, anyway. It's jest ez Sol sez—whut did all them women goddesses mean by interferin' an' allus sp'ilin' a good stan'-up fight? Now, ez Paul tells it, Ole Jupe, a-settin' up on his golden throne, wuz willin' to tote fair an' let the Greeks an' Trojans fight it out among theirselves, but the women critters, whut had more power than wuz good fur 'em, couldn't keep their hands off. Every one uv 'em hed a fav'rite either among the Greeks or the Trojans, an' she had to go snoopin' 'roun', makin' his enemy see double, or throwin' a cloud over him so he couldn't see at all, or pumpin' all the blood out uv his veins an' fillin' 'em full uv water in the place. Why, there ain't a Shawnee or Miami in all these woods thet would he mean enough to take sech an' advantage ez askin' to be helped out by a squaw thet knowed witchcraft. Ez fur thet Paris feller, he wouldn't a-lived a week down in Kain-tuck-ee!"

"But all this happened a long, long time ago, Tom, when ways were different," said Paul.

Henry always listened with attention to these stories, and the sight of Paul's flushed face and vivid eyes, as he talked, would please him. He understood Paul. He knew that his comrade's mind ranged over not only the wilderness in which they dwelt, but over the whole world, and far into past and future times. Hence he respected Paul with a deep respect.

Presently the cold abated a little—just enough to let the surface of the ice and snow soften a bit, and make walking easier. Then Henry and Ross crossed once more to the mainland, partly to scout and partly to hunt. They easily killed a large deer which was half-imbedded in a snowdrift, and might have taken a fine cow buffalo in the same way; but, as the deer was enough, they spared her. They dressed the body of the deer where it had fallen, and, carrying it between them, started back. With instinctive caution they kept to the thickest part of the forest, wishing to be hidden as much as possible by the tree trunks, and they plodded along in

146

silence, carrying their burden easily, because the two were very, very strong. Near the edge of the lake, but still in dense forest, Henry paused and looked down. Tom Ross also paused and looked down, his glance following Henry's. It was never necessary for these two to say much to each other. They did not talk about things, they saw them.

"Tracks of two Indians and one white," said Henry.

"Yes," said Tom Ross. "White is Braxton Wyatt, uv course. He's still hangin' about the Miami village."

"And perhaps suspecting that we are yet in these parts."

"Uv course. An' maybe thar will be trouble."

They said no more, but each understood. Their own trail would be left in the snow, and the sight of it would confirm all the suspicions of Wyatt and the savages. Some such chance as this they had always expected, and now they prepared to deal with it. They turned back into the forest, carrying with them the body of the deer, as they were resolved not to abandon it. Both had noticed that the slight abatement of the cold was not lasting. In an hour or two it would be as chill as ever, and once more the surface of the snow would be icy.

They stayed several hours in a dense clump of trees and bushes, and then, half walking, half sliding, they resumed their journey, but now they left no trail. Each also had every sense alert, and nothing could come within sound or sight and not be perceived first by these two wonderful trailers, masters of their craft. They reached the edge of the lake in the twilight, and then they sped swiftly over the ice to their island home.

"I'm thinking," said Henry Ware, at a council a little later, "that Braxton Wyatt suspects we're here. He, of course, does not believe in the Indian superstitions, and maybe he'll persuade them to search the island."

"An' since they kin come over the ice, we can't beat 'em off ez easy ez we could ef they came in canoes in the water," said Shif'less Sol. "I see trouble ahead fur a tired man."

Paul had been saying nothing, only sitting in a corner of the hut and listening intently to the others. Now his face flushed and his eyes sparkled with light, as they would always do whenever a great idea suddenly came to him.

"If Braxton Wyatt undertakes to persuade them there are no ghosts," he said, "it is for us to persuade them that there are."

"What do you mean, Paul?" asked Henry.

"We must show the ghosts to them."

147

Silence for a half minute followed. Then Shif'less Sol spoke up.

"Meanin' ourselves?" he said.

"Yes," said Paul.

The others looked at his glowing face, and they were impressed.

"Just how?" said Henry.

"If the Miamis come at all, they will come in the night, and that is when ghosts should appear. I'll be a ghost and Jim Hart will be another. The rest of you can lay hidden, ready to use the rifles if they are needed."

"Well planned!" said Henry Ware. "We'll do it."

CHAPTER XVIII
WHAT THE WARRIORS SAW

A few nights later a strong band of warriors left the Miami village, led by the bold chief, Yellow Panther, and the renegade, Braxton Wyatt. The party was about thirty in number, and it included the most daring spirits among them. They were going against the wishes of the aged Gray Beaver, who foresaw only disaster from such a desecration; but Yellow Panther favored the venture, and Braxton Wyatt had urged it for a long time.

Wyatt was no coward, and he did not believe in spirits. They had seen tracks, white tracks, in the snow, and the sight confirmed him in his suspicion that those whom he hated were hiding on the island in the lake. He burned for revenge upon Henry Ware and his friends, but he had to fight all the influence of Gray Beaver and the power of Indian superstition. He was about to despair of moving them when they saw the tracks—tracks that led almost to the edge of the water. He considered this proof of his theory, and he urged it incessantly. He called attention to the encounter in the woods near the lake, and the later affair with the belt bearers. The latter had particular weight, as enough messengers had now passed between the Miamis and Shawnees to show that both had been the victims of a clever and daring trick. Wyatt, therefore, was reinstated in the good graces of the savages, and his words had meaning to them. At last, with the aid of Yellow Panther and the more daring spirits among the younger warriors, he prevailed, and the expedition started.

It was a really formidable war party, thirty warriors or more, all well armed with rifles and ammunition bought from the Canadian traders, all hideous with paint, and all skilled in the lore and devices of the wilderness. Braxton Wyatt had talked to them so much, he had told them so often that their superstitions were mere moonshine, that they began to believe, and they thrilled, moreover, with the hope of securing white scalps.

The cold was intense, and the frozen surface of the snow was very smooth; but the warriors, in thick moccasins of buffalo hide, with the hair underneath, sped with sure step toward the lake. As Henry and Ross had done, they kept in the thickest of the forest, passing from tree trunk to tree trunk, because the Indian loves a surprise, an easy victory being the greatest of triumphs to him. It was such that they expected now, and the blood of every one of them was inflamed by the logic and eloquence of Braxton Wyatt and Yellow Panther.

They reached the shores of the lake when the twilight had merged into the night and the darkness was deep. They had foreseen that it would be such a night, otherwise they would have waited; but all seemed admirably suited now to their purpose. They paused on the bank, and gathered in a close group. Across the white gleam of the snow they could barely see the dusky outline of the island, and, despite the courageous frame of mind into which they had lashed themselves, despite the boldness of their leaders, they felt a tremor. The savage mind is prone to superstitions, and it is not easy to cure it of them. That dim, dark outline out there in the middle of the lake, now that they beheld it again with their own eyes, still had its unknown and mysterious terrors for them.

But Braxton Wyatt and Yellow Panther knew too well to let them hesitate at the very margin of their great exploit. They urged them forward, and the two themselves led the way, stepping upon the frozen surface of the lake, and advancing directly toward the island. Then the warriors came after them in a close cluster, their fur-shod feet making no sound, and their forms invisible thirty yards away. Before them the black bulk of the island, with its great trees, now loomed more distinctly, and they gathered courage as nothing happened.

All knew that the ancient burying ground was on the north end of the island, and so Braxton Wyatt and Yellow Panther led the way to the south end, intending to make a gradual approach to the other portion.

Braxton Wyatt half expected, as he came near, that he might see a light among the trees. In weather so cold one must have a fire, and, relying upon the ghostly protection, Henry Ware and his band would light it. But he saw nothing, and he began to fear that he might be mistaken. If there was nobody on the island his credit with the Indians would be shaken, and he was anxious to establish his power among his red friends. But he and Yellow Panther pressed boldly on, and they could now see dimly the outlines of individual tree trunks standing up in rows.

The low shores of the island rose before them only thirty yards away, then twenty, then ten, then they were there. But another moment of hesitation came. Not in a generation had a Miami or any other Indian, so far as they knew, set foot upon this haunted island, and the beliefs of many years are not to be swept away in a breath.

It was Braxton Wyatt who took the lead again, and he boldly stepped upon the haunted soil. Then a terrible thing happened. Every warrior all at once saw two white figures perched upon the low bough of an oak. They were shaped like men, but the outlines of arms and legs could not be seen. Rather they were the bodies of warriors completely enclosed in buffalo robes or deerskins for the grave, and these figures, swaying back and forth in the moonlight, and bearing all the aspects of supernatural visitors, filled the superstitious hearts of the Miamis with the terrors of the unknown and invincible. The two shapes showed a ghostly white in the pale rays, and the Miamis, in fancy at least, saw fiery and accusing eyes looking down at the sacrilegious men who had presumed to put foot on the island dedicated to Manitou and the departed.

A gentle wind brought a low groan to the ears of every man among them.

The blood of the warriors chilled quickly in their veins. All their superstitions, all the inherited beliefs of many generations, all the lore of the old squaws, told about innumerable camp fires, came crashing back upon them as those two ghostly white shapes, hovering there in the darkness, continued to transfix them with an accusing gaze. There was an involuntary shudder, a sudden clustering together of the whole party, and then, with a simultaneous cry of horror, they broke and fled in a wild pellmell far out upon the icy surface of the lake, and then on, bearing with them in the rout both Yellow Panther and Braxton Wyatt. Nor did they dare to look back, because they knew that the terrible eyes of the long departed, upon whose territory they had intended to commit sacrilege, were boring into their backs. The island was haunted, and would remain so for many a year, despite all that Braxton Wyatt and Yellow Panther had said.

About the time the Miamis reached the mainland, and darted among the trees in the race for their own village, Paul Cotter and Long Jim Hart leaped lightly from the low bough of the oak, took off the enfolding robes of white tanned deerskin, with holes for the eyes.

"Jehoshaphat!" said Long Jim, as he threw the robes on the ground, "I'm glad that's over. Bein' a ghost jest about a minute is enough fur me. I wuz scared to death lest I didn't groan good an' horrible."

"But you never did a better job in your life, Jim," said Henry, as he came from behind a tree. "You and Paul were the finest ghosts I ever saw, and no Indian will dare to set foot on this island in the next hundred years."

"It shorely was a sight to see them braves run," said Shif'less Sol. "Thar's many a tired man in that lot now. I think some o' 'em didn't hit the ice an' snow more'n twice between here an' the lan'."

"Paul's made the islan' ez safe fur us ez a stone fort ez long ez we want to stay," said Tom Ross.

"It was a great plan, well done," said Henry.

Paul's face shone with the most intense delight. His imagination, leaping forward to meet a crisis, had served them all greatly, and he was happy. He had fought not with rifle and knife, but with the weapon of the intellect.

"Now that this job is over, an' we're the big winners," said Shif'less Sol, "I'm goin' to do what a tired man ought to do: go to sleep, wrapped up in buffalo robes, an' sleep about forty hours."

"We'll all sleep," said Henry. "As Tom says, we're as safe as if we were in a stone fort, and we don't need any guard."

An hour later all of the valiant five were slumbering peacefully within their warm walls, and when they ate a good hot breakfast the next morning, cooked in Jim Hart's best fashion, they laughed heartily and often over the night's great event.

"I guess Mr. Braxton Wyatt will hev to work hard ag'in to prove to them savages that he's real smart," said Shif'less Sol. "This is another time that he's led 'em right out o' the little end o' the horn."

They luxuriated that day, resting most of the time In the hut, but on the following day Henry and Ross went on a longer scouting expedition than usual, this time in the direction of the Shawnee villages. The three who were left behind broke fresh holes in the thick ice, and by the use of much patience succeeded in catching several fine fish, which made a pleasant addition to their daily diet.

Henry and Ross were gone nearly a week, but their comrades did not become alarmed over their long absence. When they returned they brought with them a budget of news from the Shawnee villages. Braxton Wyatt had returned to the Shawnees, much disgusted with his stay among the Miamis, but still resolved to form the great Indian alliance, and send it in the spring against the white settlements in Kentucky.

"It's too late for them to do anything this winter," said Henry, and a little exultation showed in his tone, "we've put that spoke in their wheel; but they mean to hit us a terrible blow on the flank when warm weather comes."

"What do you mean by 'on the flank'?" asked Paul.

"They've learned in some manner, maybe by way of Canada, that a big wagon train is coming up through the Wilderness Road in the spring, to join our settlements. If it gets there it will double our strength, but the Indians mean to make a great curve to the south and east and strike it just as it leaves the mountains."

"They're smart in that," said Shif'less Sol. "They'd be sure to hit them wagons when they ain't expected."

"Yes," said Henry Ware, "if the train is not warned."

Paul looked at him and saw that his eyes were full of meaning.

"Then we are to warn that train," said Paul.

"Yes, when the time comes."

"It's the greatest work that we can do," said Paul, with emphasis, and the others nodded their agreement. It was all that was needed to bind the five together in the mighty task that they had begun.

Nothing more was said upon the subject for days, but Paul's mind was full of it. His comrades and he had impeded the making of the great war trail, and now they were to see that reënforcements safely reached their own. It was a continuing task, and it appealed powerfully to the statesman so strong in Paul.

A very cold winter moved slowly along, and they remained on the island, though Henry and Ross ranged far and wide. On one of these expeditions the two scouts met a wandering trapper, by whom they sent word again to their people in the south that they were safe.

Henry and Ross also learned that Yellow Panther would lead the Miamis, Red Eagle the Shawnees, and there would be detachments of Wyandots and others. They would fall like a thunderbolt upon the wagon train, and destroy it utterly.

"And Braxton Wyatt will be with them?" said Paul indignantly.

"Of course," replied Henry.

"Henry, we've got to save that wagon train, if every one of us dies trying!" exclaimed Paul, with the greatest possible emphasis.

"Of course," said Henry again, quietly, but with the stern determination that meant with him do or die.

"It's a part o' our job," drawled Shif'less Sol, "but it must be nigh a thousand miles to the place whar the Wilderness Road comes out o' the mountains. I see a terrible long journey ahead fur a tired man."

Henry smiled. They all knew that none would be more zealous on the march, none more lion-hearted in battle, than this same Solomon Hyde, nicknamed the shiftless one.

"When do we start?" asked Jim Hart.

"Not before the cold weather passes," replied Henry. "It wouldn't be worth while. The emigrant train won't come through

153

the mountains until spring, and we can do better work here, watching the savages."

So they abode long in the hut on the haunted island, and had food and warmth in plenty. But in the Indian villages there was the stir of preparation for the great war trail in the spring, and also the sense of mystery and oppression. Yellow Panther, the Miami, and Red Eagle, the Shawnee, both felt in some strange, unaccountable way that they were watched. Half-lost tracks of unknown feet were seen in the snow; strange trails that ended nowhere were struck; three warriors, every one at a different time, claimed to have seen a gigantic figure speeding in a pale moonlight through the leafless forest; one of the bravest of the Shawnee warriors was found dead, his head cleft so deep that they knew a mighty hand, one of almost marvelous strength, had wielded the tomahawk. There were signs of a terrible struggle in the snow, but who had attacked and who defended they did not know, and the trail of the survivor was soon lost. A mysterious dread filled both Shawnees and Miamis.

Braxton Wyatt raged at heart in the Shawnee village, and had theories of his own, but he dared not tell them. It was known there that it was he who had led the Miamis into the sacrilegious invasion of the haunted island, and it would take his credit some time to recover from such a blow. To reestablish himself thoroughly he must do valuable work for his red friends on the coming great war trail. So he remained discreetly silent about the haunted island, and told all he knew of the white settlements, the Wilderness Road, and the way to trap the emigrant train. Here he could really be of great assistance to the alliance, and he told the chiefs all about the emigrants, how they marched, and how they would be encumbered with women and children.

Meanwhile, the five never ceased their vigilance. Henry and Ross bought a large quantity of ammunition from a Canadian trader whom they met on a trip far to the north, and however much they used in the winter, they were now assured of an abundance when they started southeast in the spring.

The winter was long and very cold. One snow fell upon another; one freeze after another thickened the ice upon the lake; and when the wind blew, it had the edge of a knife. But this could not last forever. One day the wind shifted around and blew from the south. Paul, who was outside the hut helping Jim Hart, felt a soft, warm breath on his face.

"Why, Jim!" he said, "the cold seems to be going away."

"So it is," said Jim Hart, "or at least it's gittin' ready. Spring ain't far off, an' I'm glad, Paul. I'm tired uv winter, an' I want to be strikin' out on the great war trail."

"So do I," said Paul.

"Wa'al, fur the matter o' that," said Shif'less Sol, "we've been on the great war trail fur three or four months now. There ain't to be no change except in the shiftin' o' the trail."

The warm wind continued to blow for days, the surface of the ice on the lake softened, and the snow began to melt. Still it blew, and the melted snow ran in rivers, the ice broke up into great sheets and chunks, and these, too, rapidly dissolved. Then a warm rain came, pouring for a day and a night, and the ice and snow were swept away entirely. But the whole earth ran water. Lakes stood in the forest, and every brook and creek, rushing in torrents, leaped its banks.

The five had remained in their hut when the rain came down, but two days later Henry and Ross were rowed over in the canoe, and went away to spy out the country. When they returned they said that the great war party of the allied tribes would soon be in motion, and it was time for the five to take their flight.

A warm sun had been shining for days, and the earth had dried again. The turbulent brooks and creeks had withdrawn to their accustomed beds, and faint touches of green were beginning to show in the wilderness.

"We'll leave our house just as we have built it," said Henry.

"Unless a white man should come wandering here, and that isn't likely, it won't be disturbed. It's been a good place for us."

"Yes," said Paul, "it has been a good home to us. I've spent a happy winter here, and I want to see it again."

But they had little time for sentiment. They were making the fast touches of preparation for the second stage of the great war trail—arranging clothing, light supplies of food, and, above all, ammunition. Then they left at night in their canoe. As they approached the mainland, all, as if by involuntary impulse, looked back at the haunted island, looming darkly in the night.

"It was no haunted island for us," said Paul.

"No," said Henry.

They landed, hid the canoe, and then, plunging into the forest, sped far to the south and east on tireless feet.

155

CHAPTER XIX
THE WARNING

Meanwhile war belts were passing through all the forest, from tribe to tribe, to Shawnee, Miami, Ottawa, Wyandot—to every band, large or small. Another great effort would be made to drive back the thin white vanguard that was now entering the finest hunting ground savages had ever known—the vast green wilderness of the Mississippi Valley, where the warriors had roamed and killed game for unknown generations. Northern and southern tribes had often met and fought in Kain-tuck-ee, but always each retreated after the conflict to north or to south, leaving Kain-tuck-ee as it was before—a land of forest and canebrake, inhabited only by the wild beast.

Now, every warrior felt that the coming of the white stream over the mountains, however slender it might be at first, threatened a change, great and disastrous to them, unless checked at once. These white men cut down the forest, built houses that were meant to stay in one place—houses of logs—and plowed up the fields where the forest had been. They felt in some dim, but none the less certain, way that not only their favorite hunting grounds, but they and their own existence, were threatened.

They had failed the year before in a direct attack upon the new settlements, but these little oases in the wilderness must in time perish unless the white stream coming over the mountains still reached them, nourishing them with fresh bone and sinew, and making them grow. A great wagon train was coming, and this they would strike, surprising it in the vast, dark wilderness when it was not dreaming that even a single warrior was near.

A great defeat they had suffered at Wareville the year before still stung, and the spur of revenge was added to the spur of need. What they felt they ought to do was exactly what they wanted to do, and they were full of hope. They did not know that the stream flowing over the mountains, now so small, was propelled by a tremendous force behind it, the great white race always moving onward, and they expected nothing less than a complete triumph.

Active warriors passed through the deep woods, bearing belts and messages. Their faces were eager, and always they urged war. A long journey lay before them, but the blow would be a master stroke. They were received everywhere with joy and approval. The tomahawks were dug up, the war dances were danced, the war songs sung, and the men began to paint their faces and bodies for battle. A hum and a murmur ran through the northwestern forests, the hum and murmur of preparation and hope. Only the five, on their little island in the lake, yet heard this hum and murmur, so ominous to the border, but they were ready to carry the message through the wilderness to those to whom the warning meant the most.

The largest wagon train that had yet crossed the mountains into Kain-tuck-ee toiled slowly along the Wilderness Road among the foothills, bearing steadily toward the Northwest. The line of canvas covers stretched away more than a hundred in number, and contained five hundred souls, of whom, perhaps, half were men and boys capable of bearing arms, the rest women and children.

They looked upon mountain, hill and forest, river and brook, with much the same eyes as those with which Henry and Paul had beheld them not so very long before, but they were not seeking at random in the wilderness as the Wareville people had done. No, they moved forward now to a certain mark. They were to join their brethren at Wareville and Marlowe, and double the strength of the settlements. Word had come to them over the mountains that the little outposts in the vast wilderness lived and flourished, and the country was good. Moreover, they and their strength were needed. Wareville and Marlowe looked for them as eagerly as they looked for Wareville and Marlowe.

Spring was deepening, and already had drawn its robe of green over all the earth, but Daniel Poe, the commander of the wagon train, paid little attention to its beauty. He was nearly sixty years of age, but in the very prime of his strength—a great, square-shouldered man, his head and face covered with thick, black beard. His eyes had their habitual look of watchful care. They had seen no Indian sign as they crossed the mountains, but he knew now that they were on the Dark and Bloody Ground, and the lives of five hundred human beings were a heavy responsibility.

"You are sure the country is entirely safe?" he said to Dick Salter, one of his guides.

"I don't know no reason to doubt it," replied Salter. "The savages don't often get down here. The villages uv the northwestern tribes must be close on to a thousand miles from here, an' besides they were beat off last year, an' beat badly, when they tried to rush Wareville."

"That is so," said Daniel Poe thoughtfully; "we had word of it.

But, Dick, we can't afford to take all these people into danger here in the woods. Look at the women and children."

They had just begun to stop for the night, and to draw the wagons into a circle in a convenient, slightly hollowed, open place. The women and children were trooping about upon the grass, and the air was filled with the sound of merry voices. All were browned by the sun, but they were healthy and joyous, and they looked forward with keen delight to meeting kin who had gone on before at Wareville. They had no fear of the mighty forests, when more than two hundred pairs of strong arms fenced them about.

"That is shorely a pleasant sight," said Dick Salter. "I've seed the same many evenin's, an' I hope to see it many more evenin's. We'll get 'em through, Mr. Poe, we'll get 'em through!"

"I hope so," said Daniel Poe earnestly.

They had begun to light the evening fires, and in the west a great red sun blazed just above the hills. Daniel Poe suddenly put his hand upon Dick Salter's arm.

"Dick, what is that?" he said, pointing with a long forefinger.

A black silhouette had appeared on the crest of a hill in the very eye of the sun, and Dick Salter, shading his brow with his hand, gazed long and anxiously.

"It's a man," he said at last, "an' ef I'm any judge uv a human bein' it's about the finest specimen uv a man that ever trod green grass. Look, Mr. Poe!"

The figure, outlined against its brilliant background, seemed to grow and come nearer. Others had seen now, and the whole wagon train gazed with intent and curious eyes. They saw in the blazing light every detail of an erect and splendid figure, evidently that of a youth, but tall beyond the average of men. He was clad in forest garb—fringed hunting shirt and leggings and raccoon-skin cap. He stood erect, but easily, holding by the muzzle a long, slender-barreled rifle, which rested, stock upon the ground. Seen there in all the gorgeous redness of the evening sunlight, there was something majestic, something perhaps weird and unreal, in the grand and silent figure.

"He's white, that's shore!" said Dick Salter.

"He looks like a wilderness god," murmured Daniel Poe, in his beard.

"Look!" exclaimed Dick Salter. "There's another!"

A second figure appeared suddenly beside the first, that of a youth, also, not so tall as the first; but he, too, stood erect, silent and motionless, gazing at the wagon train.

"And a third!" exclaimed Daniel Poe.

"And a fourth and fifth!" added Dick Salter. "See, there are five uv 'em!"

Three other figures had appeared, seeming to arise in the sunlight as if by Arabian magic; and now all five stood there in a row, side by side, everyone silent and motionless, and everyone holding by the muzzle a long, slender-barreled rifle, its stock upon the ground, as he gazed at the train.

A deep breath ran through the crowd of emigrants, and all—men, women, and children—moved forward for a better look. There was something mysterious and uncanny in this sudden apparition of the five there in the blazing light of the setting sun, which outlined their figures in every detail and raised them to gigantic proportions. On those hills only was light; everywhere else the mighty curving wilderness, full of unknown terrors, was already dark with the coming night.

"It is our omen of danger. I feel it, I feel it In every bone of me," murmured Daniel Poe into his great black beard.

"We must find out what this means, that's shore," said Dick Salter.

But as he spoke, the first figure, that of the great, splendid youth, stepped right out of the eye of the sun, and he was followed in single file by the four others, all stepping in unison. They came down the hill, and directly toward the travelers. Again that deep breath ran through the crowd of emigrants, and the chief note of it was admiration, mingled with an intense curiosity.

All the five figures were strange and wild, sinewy, powerful, almost as dark as Indians, their eyes watchful and wary and roving from side to side, their clothing wholly of skins and furs, singular and picturesque. They seemed almost to have come from another world. But Daniel Poe was never lacking either in the qualities of hospitality or leadership.

"Friends," he said, "as white men—for such I take you to be—you are welcome to our camp."

The first of the five, the great, tall youth with the magnificent shoulders, smiled, and it seemed to Daniel Poe that the smile was wonderfully frank and winning.

"Yes, we are white, though we may not look it," he said in a clear, deep voice, "and we have come near a thousand miles to meet you."

"To meet us?" repeated Daniel Poe, in surprise, while Dick Salter, beside him, was saying to himself, as he looked at one of the five: "Ef that ain't Tom Ross, then I'll eat my cap."

159

"Yes," repeated Henry Ware, with the most convincing emphasis, "it's you that we've come to meet. We belong at Wareville, although we've been far in the North throughout the winter. My name is Henry Ware, this is Paul Cotter, and these are Tom Ross, Sol Hyde, and Jim Hart. We must have a word with you at once, where the others cannot hear."

Tom Ross and Dick Salter, old friends, were already shaking hands. Henry Ware glanced at the emigrants pressing forward in a great crowd, and sympathy and tenderness showed in his eyes as he looked at the eager, childish faces so numerous among them.

"Will you keep them back?" he said to Daniel Poe. "I must speak to you where none of those can hear."

Daniel Poe waved away the crowd, and then took a step forward.

"We have come," said Henry Ware, in low, intense tones, "to warn you that you are going to be attacked by a great force of warriors, furnished by the league of the northwestern tribes. They mean that you shall never reach Wareville or Marlowe, to double the strength of those settlements. They would have laid an ambush for you, but we have been among them and we know their plans."

A shiver ran through the stalwart frame of Daniel Poe—a shiver of apprehension, not for himself, but for the five hundred human lives intrusted to his care. Then he steadied himself.

"We can fight," he said, "and I thank you for your warning; I cannot doubt its truth."

"We will stay with you," said Henry Ware. "We know the signs of the forest, and we can help in the battle that is sure to come, and also before and after."

His voice was full of confidence and courage, and it sent an electric thrill through the veins of Daniel Poe. Henry Ware was one of those extraordinary human beings whose very presence seems to communicate strength to others.

"We'll beat 'em off," said Daniel Poe sanguinely.

"Yes, we'll beat 'em off," said Henry Ware. Then he continued: "You must tell all the men, and of course the women and children will hear of if, but it's best to let the news spread gradually."

Daniel Poe went back with the messengers to the wagons, and soon it was known to everybody that the Indians were laying an ambush for them all. Some wails broke forth from the women, but they were quickly suppressed, and all labored together to put the camp in posture of defense. The strangers were among them, cheering them, and predicting victory if battle should come. Paul, in

160

particular, quickly endeared himself to them. He was so hearty, so full of jests, and he quoted all sorts of scraps of old history bearing particularly upon their case, and showing that they must win if attacked.

"There was a race of very valiant people living a very long, long time ago," he said, "who always made their armies intrench at night. Nobody could take a Roman camp, and we've got to imitate those old fellows."

Under the guidance of Paul and his friends, the Roman principle was followed, at least in part. The wagons were drawn up in a great circle in an open space, where they could not be reached by a rifle shot from the trees, and then more than two hundred men, using pick and spade, speedily threw up an earthwork three feet high that inclosed the wagons. Henry Ware regarded it with the greatest satisfaction.

"I don't know any Indian force," he said, "that will rush such a barrier in the face of two or three hundred rifles. Now, Mr. Poe, you post guards at convenient intervals, and the rest of you can take it easy inside."

The guards were stationed, but inside the ring of wagons many fires burned brightly, and around them was a crowd that talked much, but talked low. The women could not sleep, nor could the children, whose curiosity was intensely aroused by the coming of these extraordinary-looking strangers. The larger of the children understood the danger, but the smaller did not, and their spirits were not dampened at all.

The night came down, a great blanket of darkness, in the center of which the camp fires were now fused together into a cone of light. A few stars came out in the dusky heavens, and twinkled feebly. The spring wind sighed gently among the new leaves of the forest. The voices of women and children gradually died. Some slept in blankets before the fires, and others in the wagons, whose stout oak sides would turn any bullet.

Daniel Poe walked just outside the circle of the wagons, and his heart was heavy with care. Yet he was upborne by the magnetic personality of Henry Ware, who walked beside him.

"How far from us do you think they are now?" he asked.

"Fifty miles, perhaps, and they are at least a thousand strong. It was their object to fall suddenly upon you in the dark, but when their scouts find that you fortify every night, they will wait to ambush you on the day's march."

"Undoubtedly," said Daniel Poe, "and we've got to guard against it as best we can."

161

"But my comrades and I and Dick Salter will be your eyes," said Henry. "We'll be around you in the woods, watching all the time."

"Thank God that you have come," said Daniel Poe devoutly. "I think that Providence must have sent you and your friends to save us. Think what might have happened if you had not come."

He shuddered. Before him came a swift vision of red slaughter—women and children massacred in the darkness. Then his brave heart swelled to meet the coming danger. The night passed without alarm, but Henry, Ross, and Shif'less Sol, roaming far in the forest, saw signs that told them infallibly where warriors had passed.

"The attack will come," said Henry.

"As sure as night follows day," said Ross, "an' it's our business to know when it's about to come."

Henry nodded, and the three sped on in their great circle about the camp, not coming in until a little before day, when they slept briefly before one of the fires. When the people arose and found that nothing had happened, they were light-hearted. Nothing had happened, so nothing would happen, they said to themselves; they were too strong for the danger that had threatened, and it would pass them by. Day was so much more cheerful than night.

They ate breakfast, their appetites brisk in the crisp morning air, and resumed the march. But they advanced slowly, the wagons in a close, triple file, with riflemen on either side. But Daniel Poe knew that their chief reliance now was the eyes of the five strangers, who were in the forest on either side and in front. They had made a deep impression upon him, as they had upon every other person with whom they came into contact. He had the most implicit confidence in their courage, skill, and faith.

The wagons went slowly on through the virgin wilderness, Daniel Poe and Dick Salter at their head, the riflemen all along the flanks.

"We'll strike a river some time to-morrow," said Salter. "It's narrow and deep, and the ford will be hard."

"I wish we were safely on the other side," said Daniel Poe.

"So do I," said Dick Salter, and his tone was full of meaning.

Yet the day passed as the night had passed, and nothing happened. They had safely crossed the mountains, and before them were gentle, rolling hills and open forest. The country steadily grew more fertile, and often game sprang up from the way, showing that man trod there but little. The day was of unrivaled beauty, a cloudless blue sky overhead, green grass under foot, and a warm, gentle wind always blowing from the south. How could danger be threatening under such a smiling guise? But the "eyes" of the train, which nothing escaped, the five who watched on every side, saw the Indian sign again and again, and always their faces were grave.

"The train carries many brave men," said Henry, "but it will need every one of them."

"Yes," said Tom Ross; "an' ef the women, too, kin shoot, so much the better."

That night they encamped again in one of the openings so numerous throughout the country, and, as before, they fortified; but the women and children were getting over their fear. They were too strong. The Indians would not dare to attack a train defended by three hundred marksmen—two hundred and fifty men and at least fifty women who could and would shoot well. So their voices were no longer subdued, and jest and laughter passed within the circle of the wagons.

Paul remained by one of the fires, Henry and Shif'less Sol suggesting that he do so because he was already a huge favorite with everybody. He was sitting comfortably before the coals, leaning against a wagon wheel, and at least a score of little boys and girls were gathered about him. They wanted to know about the great wilderness, and the fights of himself and his comrades with the red warriors. Paul, though modest, had the gift of vivid narrative. He described Wareville, that snug nest there in the forest, and the great battle before its wooden walls; how the women, led by a girl, had gone forth for water; how the savages had been beaten off, and the dreadful combat afterward in the forest through the darkness and the rain. He told how he had been struck down by a bullet, only to be carried off and saved by his comrade, Henry Ware—the bravest, the most skillful, and the strongest hunter, scout, and warrior in all the West. Then he told them something of their life in the winter just closed, although he kept the secret of the haunted island, which was to remain the property of his comrades and himself.

The children hung upon his words. They liked this boy with the brilliant eyes, the vivid imagination, and the wonderful gift of narrative, that could make everything he told pass before their very eyes.

"And now that's enough," said Paul at last. "You must all go to sleep, as you are to start on your journey again early in the morning. Now, off with you, every one of you!"

He rose, despite their protests, this prince of story tellers, and, bidding them good-night, strolled with affected carelessness outside the circle of wagons. The night was dark, like the one preceding, but the riflemen were on guard within the shadows of the wagons.

"Do you see anything?" Paul asked of one.

"Nothing but the forest," he replied.

Paul strolled farther, and saw a dark figure among the trees. As he approached he recognized Shif'less Sol.

"Any news, Sol?" he asked.

"Yes," replied the shiftless one, "we've crossed trails of bands three times, but the main force ain't come up yet. I guess it means to wait a little, Paul. I'm awful glad we've come to help out these poor women an' children."

"So am I," said Paul, glancing at the black forest. "They've got to go through a terrible thing, Sol."

"Yes, an' it's comin' fast," said the shiftless one.

But nothing happened that night, at least so far as the camp was concerned. The sentinels walked up and down outside, and were not disturbed. The women and children slept peacefully in the wagons, or in their blankets before the fires, and the clear dawn came, silver at first and then gold under a sky of blue.

The "eyes" of the train had come in as before, and taken their nap, and now were up and watching once more. Breakfast over, the drivers swung their whips, called cheerfully to their horses, and the wagons, again in three close files, resumed the march.

"We'll strike the ford about noon to-day," said Dick Salter to Daniel Poe.

"I wish we were safely on the other side," said Daniel Poe, in the exact words of the day before.

"So do I," repeated Dick Salter.

The wagons moved forward undisturbed, their wheels rolling easily over the soft turf, and some of the women, forgetting their alarms, softly sang songs of their old homes in the East. The children, eager to see everything in this mighty, unknown land, called to each other; but all the time, as they marched through the pleasant greenwood, danger was coming closer and closer.

CHAPTER XX
THE TERRIBLE FORD

"The ford ain't much more than an hour's march farther on," said Dick Salter to Daniel Poe, "an' the way to it leads over purty smooth groun'."

"And we have not seen anything of the warriors yet, except the trails of small bands," said Daniel Poe hopefully. "It may be that our new friends are mistaken."

Dick Salter shook his head.

"Tom Ross never makes a mistake in matters uv that kind," he said, "an' that boy, Henry Ware, couldn't ef he tried. He's wonderful, Mr. Poe."

"Yes," said Daniel Poe. "Nobody else ever made such an impression upon me. And the one they call Paul is a fine fellow, too. I wish I had a son like that."

"He's the most popular fellow in the train already," said Dick Salter.

Both looked admiringly at Paul, who was walking near the head of the line, a group of lithe, strong-limbed boys and girls surrounding him and begging him for stories of the wilderness. Paul remained with the train by arrangement. It was his business to cheer, invigorate, and hearten for a great task, while his comrades roamed the forest and looked for the danger that they knew would surely come. Never did youth succeed better at his chosen task, as confidence spread from him like a contagion.

Paul presently quickened his steps, and came quite to the head of the line, where Daniel Poe and Dick Salter were walking, both circling the forest ahead of them with anxious eyes. They and Paul at the same time saw a figure emerge from the woods in front. It was Henry, and he was coming on swift foot. In an instant he was before them, and Paul knew by his look that he had news.

"They are waiting?" said Paul.

"Yes," replied Henry. "They are in the thickets at the ford, less than two miles ahead."

Daniel Poe shuddered again—for the five hundred lives in his charge—and then his heart rose. The waiting, the terrible suspense, were over, and it was battle now. The fact contained relief.

"Shall we halt?" he said to Henry. Unconsciously, he, too, was submitting to the generalship of this king of forest runners.

"No," replied Henry; "we've got to go on some time or other, and they can wait as long as we can. We must force the passage of the ford. We can do it."

He spoke with confidence, and courage seemed to leap like sparks from him and set fire to the others.

"Then it's go ahead," said Daniel Poe grimly. "We'll force the passage."

"Put all the little children, and all the women who don't fight, in the wagons, and make them lie down," said Henry. "The men must swarm on either flank. My comrades will remain in the front, watching until we reach the river."

Then a great bustle and the chatter of many voices arose; but it soon died away before stern commands and equally stern preparations, because they were preparing to run as terrible a gantlet as human beings ever face, these dauntless pioneers of the wilderness. The children were quickly loaded in the wagons, and all the weaker of the women; but with the men on the flanks marched at least two-score grim Amazons, rifle in hand.

Then the train resumed its slow march, and nothing was heard but the rolling of the wheels and the low cluck of the drivers to their horses. The way still led through an open, parklike country, and the road was easy. Soon those in front saw a faint streak cutting across the forest. The streak was silvery at first, and then blue, and it curved away to north and south among low hills.

"The river!" said Daniel Poe, and he shut his teeth hard.

All the men and the Amazons drew a long, deep breath, like a sigh; but they said nothing, and continued to march steadily forward. The river broadened, the blue of its waters deepened, and from the high ground on which they marched they could see the low banks on the farther shore, crowned by clustering thickets.

Three men emerged from the undergrowth. They were Tom Ross, Shif'less Sol, and Long Jim Hart. The shiftless one looked lazy and careless, and Jim Hart, stretching himself, looked longer and thinner than ever.

"We found it, Henry," said Ross. "Little more'n a mile to the south, men wadin' to the waist kin cross."

"Good!" said Henry. "We're lucky!"

He began to give rapid, incisive commands, and everyone obeyed as a matter of course, and without jealousy. Daniel Poe was the leader of the wagon train, but Henry Ware, whom they had known but a few days, was its leader in battle.

"Take fifty men," he said to Ross, "the best marksmen and the

166

stanchest fighters, and cross there. Then come silently among the thickets up the bank, to strike them when they strike us."

Paul listened with admiration. He knew Henry's genius for battle, and, like the others, he was inspired by his comrade's confidence. The fifty men were quickly told off behind the wagons, and, headed by Tom Ross and Jim Hart, they disappeared at once in the woods. Shif'less Sol remained with Henry and Paul.

"Now, forward!" said Henry Ware, and the terrible, grim march was begun again. There was the river, growing broader and broader and bluer and bluer as they came closer. The children and women—except the Amazons—saw nothing because they were crouched upon the floors of the wagon beds, but the drivers, every one of whom had a rifle lying upon the seat beside him, were at that moment the bravest of them all, because they faced the greatest danger.

"Slowly!" said Henry, to the leading wagons. "We must give Sol and his men time for their circuit."

He noted with deep joy that the ford was wide. At least five wagons could enter it abreast, and he made them advance in five close lines.

"When you reach the water," he said to the drivers, "lie down behind the front of the wagon beds, and drive any way you can. Now, Sol, you and I and Dick Salter must rouse them from the thickets."

The three crept forward, and looked at the peaceful river under the peaceful sky. So far as the ordinary eye could see, there was no human being on its shores. The bushes waved a little in the gentle wind, and the water broke in brilliant bubbles on the shallows.

But Henry Ware's eyes were not ordinary. There was not a keener pair on the continent, and among the thickets on the farther bank he saw a stir that was not natural. The wind blew north, and now and then a bush would bend a little toward the south. He crept closer, and at last he saw a coppery face here and there, and savage, gleaming eyes staring through the bushes.

"Tell the wagons to come on boldly," he said to Shif'less Sol, and the shiftless one obeyed.

"Now, Sol," he said, when the man returned, "take fifty more riflemen, and hide in that thicket, at the highest part of the bank. Stay there. You will know what else to do."

"I think I will," said the shiftless one, and every trace of indifference or laziness was gone from him. He was the forester,

167

alert and indomitable—a fit second to Henry Ware. Then Henry and Jim Hart alone were left near the river's brink. Henry did not look back.

"Are the wagons coming fast?" he asked.

"Yes," said Jim Hart, "but I'm beckonin' to 'em to come still faster. They'll be in the water in three minutes. Listen! The drivers are whippin' up the horses!"

The loud cracking of whips arose, and the horses advanced at a trot toward the ford. At the same instant Henry Ware raised his rifle, and fired like a flash of lightning at one of the coppery faces in the thicket on the opposite shore. The death cry of the savage rose, but far above it rose the taunting shout of the white youth, louder and more terrible than their own. The savages, surprised, abandoned their ambush. The leading wagons dashed into the water, and down upon them dashed the picked power of the allied western tribes.

In an instant the far edge of the water was swarming with coppery bodies and savage faces, and the war whoop, given again and again, echoed far up and down the stream, and through the thickets and forest. Rifles cracked rapidly, and then blazed into volleys. Bullets sighed as they struck on human flesh or the wood of wagons, and now and then they spattered on the water. Cries of pain or shouts of defiance rose, and the furious conflict between white man and red rapidly thickened and deepened, becoming a confused and terrible medley.

Henry Ware and Jim Hart ran down into the stream by the side of the leading wagons, and loaded and fired swiftly into the dense brown mass before them. Nor did they send a bullet amiss. Henry Ware was conscious at that moment of a fierce desire to see the face of Braxton Wyatt amid the brown horde. He knew he was there, somewhere, and in the rage of conflict he would gladly have sent a bullet through the renegade's black heart. He did not see him, but the dauntless youth pressed steadily forward, continually shouting encouragement and showing the boldest example of them all.

A bank of blue and white smoke arose over the stream, shot through by the flashes of the rifle firing, and out of this bank came the defiant shouts of the combatants. Suddenly, from the high bank, on the shore that they had just left, burst a tremendous volley—fifty rifles fired at once. A yell of pain and rage burst from the savages. Those rifles had mowed a perfect swath of death among them.

"Good old Sol! Good old Sol!" exclaimed Henry, twice through

168

his shut teeth. "On, men, on! Trample them down! Drive the wagons into them!"

A second time the unexpected volley burst from the hill, and a storm of bullets beat upon the packed mass of the savages at the edge of the water. Henry Ware had been a true general that day. Shif'less Sol and his men, from their height and hid among the bushes, poured volley after volley into the savages below, spurred on by their own success and the desperation of the cause.

The front wagons advanced deeper into the water and the smoke bank, and the others came, closely packed behind in a huddle. Unearthly screams arose—the cries of wounded or dying horses, shot by the savages.

"Cut them loose from the gear," cried Henry, "and on! always on!"

Swift and skillful hands obeyed him, and some of the wagons, in the wild energy of the moment, were carried on, partly by a single horse and partly by the weight of those behind them. The shouts of the savages never ceased, but above them rose the cry of the dauntless soul that now led the wagon train. More than one savage fired at the splendid figure, never more splendid than when in battle; but always the circling smoke or the hand of Providence protected him, and he still led on, unhurt. They were now near the middle of the river, and Shif'less Sol and his men never ceased to pour their fire over their heads and into the red ranks.

"Now! Now!" muttered Henry, through his shut teeth. He was praying for Tom Ross and the first fifty, and as he prayed his prayer was answered.

A great burst of fire came from the thickets on their own side of the river, and the savages were smitten on the flanks, as if by a bolt of lightning. It seemed to them at the same moment as if the fire of the men with the wagon train, and of those on the high bluff, doubled. They recoiled. They gave back and they shivered as that terrible fire smote them a second and a third time on the flank. The soul of Shawnee, Miami, and Wyandot alike filled with dread. In vain Yellow Panther and Red Eagle, great war chiefs, raged back and forth, and encouraged their warriors to go on. In vain they risked their lives again and again. The great bulk of the wagons bore steadily down upon them, and they were continually lashed by an unerring fire from three points. Well for the people of the wagon train that a born leader had planned their crossing and had led them that day!

"They give, they give!" shouted Henry Ware. "We win, we win!"

"They give, they give! We win, we win!" shouted the brave riflemen, and they pressed forward more strongly than ever. By their side waded the bold Amazons, fighting with the best.

The wagons themselves offered great shelter for the pioneers. As Henry had foreseen, they were driven forward in a mass, which was carried partly by its own impetus. If the Indians had thought to fire chiefly upon the horses they would have accomplished more, but the few of these that were slain did not check the progress of the others. Meanwhile, the riflemen lurked amid the wheels and behind the wagon beds, incessantly pouring their deadly hail of bullets upon the exposed savages, and the drivers from sheltered places did the same. The train became a moving fort, belching forth fire and death upon its enemies.

The defenders did not advance without loss. Now and then a man sank and died in the stream, many others suffered wounds, and even the women and children did not escape; but through it all, through all the roar and tumult, all the shouting and cries, the train drew steadily closer to the western bank.

"Now, boys," shouted Shif'less Sol to his faithful fifty, "they're about to run! Pour it into 'em!"

At the same time Tom Ross was giving a similar command to his own equally faithful fifty, and they closed up on the flank of the allied tribes, and stung and stung. Henry Ware, through the drifting clouds of smoke and vapor, saw the savages waver again, and, shouting to the boldest to follow, he rushed forward. Then Shawnees, Miamis, and Wyandots, despite the fierce commands of Yellow Panther and Red Eagle, broke and fled from the water to the shore. There Tom Ross stung them more fiercely than ever on the flank, and the fire of Shif'less Sol from the high bluff reached them with deadly aim. They broke again, and, filled with superstitious terror at their awful losses, fled, a panic horde, into the woods.

"On, on!" shouted Henry Ware, in tremendous tones. "They run, they run!"

The whole train seemed to heave forward, as if by one convulsive but triumphant movement. Shif'less Sol and his men came down from the bluff and dashed into the water behind them; Ross and his fifty came forward from the thicket to meet them; and thus, dripping with water, smoke, blood, and sweat, the whole train passed up the western bank. The terrible ford had been won!

CHAPTER XXI
THE FLIGHT OF LONG JIM

Although the terrible ford had been won, Henry Ware knew that the danger was far from over. The savages, caught on the flank and shot down from above, had yielded to momentary panic, but they would come again. To any souls less daring than this band of pioneers, the situation would have been truly appalling. They were in the vast and unknown wilderness, surrounded everywhere by the black forest, with the horde, hungry for slaughter, still hanging upon their flanks; but among them all, scarce one woman or child showed a craven heart.

Led by Henry Ware, the wagons filed into an open space—a plain or little prairie—about a quarter of a mile beyond the ford, and there, still following his instructions, they drew up in a circle. He considered this open space a godsend, as no marksmen hidden in the woods could reach them there with a bullet. As soon as the circle was completed, the women and children poured forth from the wagons, and began to join the men in fortifying. There was mingled joy for victory and grief for loss. They had left dead behind in the river, and they had brought more with them; of wounds, except those that threatened to be mortal, they took little count. Even as they worked, scattering shots were fired from the forest, but they paid no heed to them, as all the bullets fell short.

Right in the center of the circle, inclosed by the wagons, a half dozen chosen spademen dug a deep hole, and then the dead were brought forth, ready for burial. A minister prayed and the women sang. Overhead, the late sun burned brilliant and red, and from the forest, as a kind of stern chorus, came the pattering rifle shots. But the last ceremony, all the more solemn and impressive because of these sights and sounds, went on unbroken. The dead were buried deep, then covered over, and the ground trodden that none might disturb their rest. Then all turned to the living need.

The five, barring slight scratches suffered by Ross and Shif'less Sol, had escaped unhurt, and now they labored with the others to throw up the wall of earth about the wagons. A spring took its rise in the center of the plain, and flowed down to the river. This spring was within the circle of the wagons, and they were assured of plenty of water.

Henry Ware looked over the crowd, and he rejoiced at their spirits, which had not been dampened by the sight of their dead. They had fought magnificently, and they were ready to fight again. Already fires were burning within the circle of the wagons, and the women were cooking supper. The pleasant odor of food arose, and men began to eat. Daniel Poe, as usual, turned to Henry.

"You are sure that they will make a new attack?" he said.

"Yes," replied Henry. "They have not come so far to retire after one repulse. We outflanked them there at the river, but they think that they will certainly get us, burdened as we are with the women and children. It's still a long road to Wareville."

"We can never repay the debt we owe to you and your comrades," said Daniel Poe.

"Don't think of it. It's the thing that we were bound to do."

Daniel Poe looked at the setting sun, now red like blood. Far over the western forest twilight shadows were coming.

"I wish this night was over," he said.

"If they attack we'll beat them off," said Henry confidently.

"But the cost, the cost!" murmured Daniel Poe.

Paul meanwhile was within the circle of wagons, in his great role of sustainer. He had fought like a paladin in the battle, and now he was telling what a great fight they had made, and what a greater one they could make, if need be. High spirits seemed to flow spontaneously from him, and the others caught the infection. More than one Amazon looked at him affectionately, as she would have looked at a son. Shif'less Sol joined him as he stood by one of the fires.

"I've been workin' out thar with a spade more'n an hour," said the shiftless one in a tone of deep disgust, "an' I'm tired plumb to death. I'll lay down before that fire an' sleep till mornin', ef every one uv you will promise not to say a word an' won't disturb me."

A laugh arose.

"Why, Mr. Hyde," exclaimed one of the Amazons, "they say there was not a more industrious man in the battle than you."

"Wa'al," said Shif'less Sol, slowly and reflectively, "a man, ef he's crowded into a corner, will fight ef his life depends on it, but I kin come purty near to livin' without work."

"You deserve your sleep, Mr. Hyde," said the woman. "Just stretch out there before the fire."

"I'll stretch out, but I won't sleep," said the shiftless one.

He was as good as his word, and admiring hands brought him food, which he ate contentedly. Presently he said in a low voice to Paul:

"That's right, Paul, hearten 'em up. They've got a lot to stand yet, an' it's courage that counts."

Paul knew this truth full well, and he went back and forth in the circle, ever performing his chosen task, while Henry outside planned and labored incessantly for the defense against a new attack. Fifty men, sharp of eye and ear, were selected to watch through half the night, when fifty more, also sharp of eye and ear, were to take their places. All the others were to sleep, if they could, in order that they might be strong and fresh for what the next day would bring forth.

The scattering fire from the forest ceased, and everything there became silent. No dusky forms were visible to the defenders. The sun dropped behind the hills, and night, thick and dark, came over the earth. The peace of the world was strange and solemn, and those in the beleaguered camp felt oppressed by the darkness and the mystery. They could not see any enemies or hear any, and after a while they began to argue that since the savages could no longer be seen or heard, they must have gone away. But Henry Ware only laughed as they told him so.

"They have not gone," he said to Daniel Poe, "nor will they go to-night nor to-morrow nor the next night. This train, when it starts in the morning, must be a moving fort."

Daniel Poe sighed. As always, he believed what Henry Ware said, and the prospect did not invite.

The darkness and the silence endured. The keenest of the watchers saw and heard nothing. The moon came out and the earth lightened, then darkened again as clouds rolled across the heavens; the camp fires sank, and, despite their alarms, many slept. The wounded, all of whom had received the rude but effective surgery of the border, were quiet, and the whole camp bore the aspect of peace. Paul slipped from the circle, and joined Henry outside the earthwork.

"Do you see anything, Henry?" he said.

"No, but I've heard," replied Henry, who had just come out of the darkness. "The Shawnees are before us, the Miamis behind us, and the warriors of the smaller tribes on either side. The night may pass without anything happening, or it may not. But we have good watchers."

Paul stayed with him a little while, but, at Henry's urgent request, he went back inside the circle, wrapped himself in a blanket and lay down, his face upturned to the cloudy skies which he did not see. He did not think he could sleep. His brain throbbed with excitement, and his vivid imagination was wide awake. Despite the

173

danger, he rejoiced to be there; rejoiced that he and his comrades should help in the saving of all these people. The spiritual exaltation that he felt at times swept over him. Nevertheless, all the pictures faded, his excited nerves sank to rest, and, with his face still upturned to the cloudy skies, he slept.

Far after midnight a sudden ring of fire burst from the dark forest, and women and children leaped up at the crash of many rifles. Shouting their war whoop, the tribesmen rushed upon the camp; but the fifty sentinels, sheltered by the earthwork, met them with a fire more deadly than their own, and in a moment the fifty became more than two hundred.

Red Eagle and Yellow Panther had hoped for a surprise, but when the unerring volleys met them, they sank back again into the forest, carrying their dead with them.

"You were right," said Daniel Poe to Henry Ware; "they will not leave us."

"Not while they think there is a chance to overpower us. But we've shown 'em they can't count on a surprise."

The camp, except the watchers, went back to sleep, and the night passed away without a second alarm. Dawn came, gray and cloudy, and the people of the train awoke to their needs, which they faced bravely. Breakfast was cooked and eaten, and then the wagons, in a file of four, took up their march, a cloud of keen-eyed and brave skirmishers on every side. The train had truly become what Henry said it must be, a moving fort; and, though the savages opened fire in the woods, they dared not attack in force, so resolute and sure-eyed were the skirmishers and so strong a defense were the heavy wagons.

All day long this terrible march proceeded, the women and children sheltered in the wagons, and the savages, from the shelter of the forest, keeping up an irregular but unceasing fire on the flanks. The white skirmishers replied often with deadly effect, but it grew galling, almost unbearable. The Indians, who were accustomed either to rapid success or rapid retreat, showed an extraordinary persistence, and Henry suspected that Braxton Wyatt was urging them on. As he thought of the effect of these continued attacks upon the train, he grew anxious. The bravest spirit could be worn down by them, and he sought in vain for a remedy.

They camped the second night in an open place, and fortified, as before, with a circular earthwork; but they were harried throughout all the hours of darkness by irregular firing and occasional war whoops. Fewer people slept that night than had slept the night before. Nerves were raw and suffering, and Paul found his chosen task a hard one. But he worked faithfully, going up and down within the fortified circle, cheering, heartening, and predicting a better day for the morrow.

That day came, cloudless and brilliant above, but to the accompaniment of shouts, shots, and alarms below. Once more the terrible march was resumed, and the savages still hung mercilessly on their flanks. Henry, with anxious heart, noticed a waning of spirit, though not of courage, in the train. The raw nerves grew rawer. This incessant marching forward between the very walls of death could not be endured forever. Again he sought a way out. Such a way they must have, and at last he believed that he had found it. But he said nothing at present, and the train, edged on either side with fire and smoke, went on through the woods.

A third time they camped in an open space, a third time they fortified; but now, after the supper was over, Henry called a council of the leaders.

"We cannot go on as we have been going," he said. "The savages hang to us with uncommon tenacity, and there are limits to human endurance."

Daniel Poe shook his head sadly. The awful lacerating process had never ceased. More men were wounded, and the spirits of all grew heavier and heavier. Paul still walked among the fires, seeking to cheer and inspire, but he could do little. Dread oppressed the women and children, and they sat mostly in silence. Outside, an occasional whoop came from the depths of the forest, and now and then a rifle was fired. The night was coming on, thick and ominous. The air had been heavy all the day, and now somber clouds were rolling across the sky. At intervals flashes of lightning flared low down on the black forest. Heavy and somber, like the skies, were the spirits of all the people. A wounded horse neighed shrilly, and in an almost human voice, as he died.

"We must take a new step," said Henry; "things cannot go on this way. It is yet a hundred and fifty miles, perhaps, to Wareville, and if the savages continue to hang on, we can never reach it."

"What do you propose?" asked Daniel Poe.

Henry Ware stood erect. The light of the council fire flared upon his splendid, indomitable face. All relied upon him, and he knew it.

"I have a plan," he said. "To-morrow we can reach an unforested hill that I know of, with a spring flowing out of the side. It is easy to hold, and we shall have plenty of water. We will stop there and make our stand. Meanwhile, we will send to Wareville for help. The messenger must leave to-night. Jim Hart, are you ready?"

Jim Hart had been sitting on a fallen tree, all humped together. Now he unfolded himself and stood up, stretched out to his complete length, six feet four inches of long, slim man, knotted and jointed, but as tough as wire—the swiftest runner in all the West. Long Jim, ugly, honest, and brave, said nothing, but his movement showed that he was ready.

"Jim Hart was made for speed," continued Henry. "At his best he is like the wind, and he can run all the way to Wareville. He'll leave in a half hour, before the moon has a chance to rise."

"He'll never get through!" exclaimed Daniel Poe.

"Oh, yes, he will!" said Henry confidently. "Bring all the men Wareville can spare, Jim, and fall upon them while they are besieging us at the Table Rock."

Little more was said. Had the train afforded paint, they would have stained Jim's face in the Indian way; but the utmost that they could do was to draw up his hair and tie it in a scalp lock, like those of the Shawnees. Fortunately, his hair was dark, and his face was so thoroughly tanned by weather that it might be mistaken in the night for an Indian's. Then Long Jim was ready. He merely shook the hands of his four comrades and of Daniel Poe, and without another word went forth.

The night was at its darkest when Jim Hart slipped under one of the wagons and crept across the open space. The heavy clouds had grown heavier, and now and then low thunder muttered on the horizon. The fitful lightning ceased, and this was occasion for thanks.

Jim Hart crept about twenty yards from the circle of the wagons, and then he lay flat upon the earth. He could see nothing in the surrounding rim of forest, nor could he hear anything. A light hum from the camp behind him was all that came to his ears. He slipped forward again in a stooping position, stopped a moment when he heard a rifle shot from the other side of the camp, and then resumed his shambling, but swift, journey. Now he passed the open space and gained the edge of the woods. Here the danger lay, but the brave soul of Long Jim never faltered.

He plunged into the gloom of the bushes and trees, slipping silently among them. Two warriors glanced curiously at him in the dark, but in a moment he was gone; a third farther on spoke to him, but he shook his head impatiently, as if he bore some message, and only walked the faster. Now his keen eyes saw savages all around him, some talking, others standing or lying down, quite silent. He was sorry now that he was so tall, as his was a figure that would cause remark anywhere; but he stooped over, trying to hide his great height as much as possible. He passed one group, then two, then three, and now he was a full four hundred yards from the camp. His curving flight presently brought him near three men who were talking earnestly together. They noticed Hart at the same time, and one of them beckoned to him. Long Jim pretended not to see, and went on. Then one of them called to him angrily, and Jim recognized the voice of Braxton Wyatt.

Long Jim stopped a moment, uncertain what to do at that critical juncture, and Braxton Wyatt, stepping forward, seized him by the arm. It was dark in the woods, but the renegade, looking up, recognized the face and figure.

"Jim Hart!" he cried.

Long Jim's right hand was grasping the stock of his rifle, but his left suddenly flashed out and smote Braxton Wyatt full in the face. The renegade gasped and went down unconscious, and then Long Jim turned, and ran with all the speed that was in him, leaping over the low bushes and racing among the tree trunks more like a phantom than a human being. A shout arose behind him, and a dozen rifle shots were fired. He felt a sting in his arm, and then blood dripped down; but it was only a flesh wound, and he was spurred to greater speed.

A terrible yell arose, and many warriors, trained runners of the forest, with muscles of steel and a spirit that never tired, darted after him. But Long Jim, bending his head a little lower, raced on through the dark, his strength growing with every leap and his brain on fire with energy. He passed two or three savages—far-flung outposts—but before they could recover from their surprise he was by them and gone. Bullets sang past him, but the long, slim figure cut the air like an arrow in the wind. After him came the savages, but now he was beyond the last outposts, and the footsteps of his pursuers were growing fainter behind. Now he opened his mouth, and emitted a long, quavering, defiant yell—answer to their own. After that he was silent, and sped on, never relaxing, tireless like some powerful machine. The pursuit died away behind him, and though some might hang on his trail, none could ever overtake him.

The low thunder still muttered, and the fitful lightning began to flare again. Now and then there were gusts of rain, swept by the wind; but through all the hours of rain and dark the runner sped on, mile upon mile.

Day dawns and finds him still flitting! But now there is full need of thy speed, Jim Hart! Five hundred lives hang upon it!

Speed ye, Long Jim, speed ye!

177

CHAPTER XXII
THE LAST STAND

Henry Ware and the others, listening at the circle of the wagons, heard the flare of shots, and then, a little later, a lone but long and defiant cry, that seemed to be an answer to the others.

"That's Jim Hart, and he's through!" exclaimed Henry exultantly. "Now he'll fairly eat up the ground between here and Wareville."

That night another attack, or rather feint, was made upon the train; but it was easily beaten off, and then morning came, raw and wet. The woods and grass were dripping with the showers, and a sodden, gray sky chilled and discouraged. The fires were lighted with difficulty and burned weakly. The women and children ate but little, casting fearful glances at the rain-soaked forest that circled about them. But Paul, as usual, with his bright face and brighter words, walked among them, and he told them a good tale. Long Jim Hart, with muscles and a soul of steel, had gone forth that night, and he would bring help. They were to march to a place called the Table Rock, where they would stay until the relief came. Gradually downcast heads were lifted and sunken spirits rose.

The gantlet began in the usual fashion an hour later, and throughout all that long, dismal morning it was a continual skirmish. The savages pressed closer than ever, and all the vigilance and accuracy of the riflemen were needed to drive them off. One man was killed and several were wounded, but the borderers merely shut their teeth down the harder and marched on.

Toward noon they saw a flat-topped hill, with a stony surface, a little stream running down its side, and Henry uttered a cheerful shout.

"The Table Rock!" he said. "Here we can hold off all the savages in the West!"

The train increased its slow gait, and all hearts grew lighter. The savages, as if determined that the wagons should not gain the shelter, pressed forward, but after a short but fierce combat were driven off, and the train circled triumphantly up the slope.

It was indeed all that Henry had claimed for it—an ideal place for a protected camp, easy to defend, difficult to take. Not all the surface was stone, and there was abundant grazing ground for the horses. The spring that gushed from the side of the hill was inside the lines, and neither horse nor man lacked for pure water.

Now they fortified more strongly than ever, throwing up earthworks higher than before and doubling the sentinels. Fallen wood was plentiful, and at Henry's direction the fires were built high and large in order that they might drive away discouragement. Then a semblance of cheerfulness made its appearance, and the women and children began to talk once more.

"Long Jim will go through if any mortal man can," said Henry Ware to Daniel Poe.

"Pray God that he succeeds," said Daniel Poe. "Surely, no wagon train ever before ran the deadly gantlet that ours has run."

Shif'less Sol strolled into the circle of fires, and sat down with Paul.

"Now, this is what I call true comfort fur a tired man," he said. "Here we are with nuthin' to do but set here an' rest, until somebody comes an' takes us to Wareville. Them savages out thar might save theirselves a heap o' trouble by goin' peacefully away. Makes me think o' that siege o' Troy you wuz talkin' about, Paul, only we won't let any wooden horse in."

"Maybe there is some likeness," said Paul.

"Maybe thar is," continued Shif'less Sol, in his cheerful tones; "but Tom Ross wuz right when he said the way them Greeks an' Trojans fought was plumb foolish. Do you think that me, Sol Hyde, is goin' to take a tin pan an' go beatin' on it down thar among the bushes, an' callin' on the biggest boaster o' all the savages to come out an' fight me? No, sir; I wouldn't go fifty yards before I'd tumble over, with a bullet through me."

Most of the people laughed, and the shiftless one continued with random, cheery talk, helping Paul to hearten them. The two succeeded to a great degree. There was mourning for the dead, but it was usually silent. The borderers were too much accustomed to hardship and death to grieve long over the past. They turned themselves to present needs.

The night was rainy, and unusually cold for that time of the year, and Henry Ware rejoiced because of it. The savages in the thickets, despite their hardiness, would suffer more than the emigrants in the shelter of the wagons. Henry himself, although he caught little naps here and there, seemed to the others able to do without sleep. He kept up an incessant watch, and his vigilance defeated two attempts of the warriors to creep up in the darkness and pour a fire into the train.

A second day came, and then a third, and the savages resumed their continuous skirmishing. A single warrior would creep up, fire a shot, and then spring away. They did little damage, but they showed that no one was safe for a moment outside the circle of wagons. If help did not come, they would never leave their rock.

Time wore on, and the beleaguered camp became again a prey to gloom. Women and children fell sick, and the hearts of the men were heavy. The ring of savages drew closer, and more than once bullets fell inside the circle of the wagons. It was hard work now for Paul and Shif'less Sol to keep up the spirits of the women and children, and once, at a council, some one talked of surrender. They might at least get good treatment.

"Never think of such a thing!" said Henry Ware. "All the men would be killed, tortured to death, and all the women and children would be taken away into slavery. Hold on! Jim Hart will surely get through."

But the warriors steadily grew bolder. They seemed to be animated by the certainty of triumph. Often through the day and night they uttered taunting shouts, and now and then, in the day time, they would appear at the edge of the woods and make derisive gestures. Daniel Poe grew gloomy, and sadly shook his head.

"Help must come soon," he said, "or our people will not have spirit to beat back the savages the next time they try to rush the camp."

"It will come, it will surely come!" said Henry confidently.

The worst night of all arrived. More of the women and children fell sick, and they did not have the energy to build up bright fires. It was to Ross and Shif'less Sol that this task fell; but, though they kept the fires high, they accomplished little else. Paul lay down about midnight and slept several hours, but it was a troubled night. The savages did not rest. They were continually flitting about among the trees at the foot of the hill, and firing at the sentinels. Little flashes of flame burst out here and there in the undergrowth, and the crackle of the Indian rifles vexed continually.

Paul rose at the first coming of the dawn, pale, unrested, and anxious. He walked to the earthwork, and saw Henry there, watching as always, seemingly tireless. The sun was just shooting above the hills, and Paul knew that a brilliant day was at hand.

"At any rate, Henry," Paul said, "I prefer the day to the night while we are here."

Henry did not reply. A sudden light had leaped into his eye, and he was bent slightly forward, in the attitude of one who listens intently.

180

"What is it, Henry?" asked Paul.

Henry lifted his hand for silence. His attitude did not change. Every nerve was strained, but the light remained in his eye.

"Paul," he cried, "don't you hear them? Rifle shots, far away and very faint, but they are coming toward us! Long Jim is here, and Wareville with him!"

Then Paul heard it—the faint, distant patter, as welcome sounds as ever reached human ears. He could not mistake it now, as he was too much used to the crackle of rifle shots to take it for anything else. His face was transfigured, his eyes shone with vivid light. He sprang upon the earthwork, and cried in tones that rang through all the camp:

"Up, up, men! Long Jim and the Wareville riflemen are coming!"

The train blazed into action. Forth poured the hardy borderers in scores, surcharged now with courage and energy. The firing in front of them had risen into a furious battle, and above the roar and the tumult rose the cheering of white men.

"Long Jim has surprised them, and he is half way through already!" cried Henry exultantly. "Now, men, we'll smite 'em on the flank!"

In a moment the whole force of the train, the Amazons included, were into the very thick of it, while Long Jim and two hundred riflemen, dealing out death on every side, were coming to meet them. The battle was short. Surprised, caught on both flanks, the savages gave way. There was a tremendous firing, a medley of shouts and cries for a few minutes, and then the warriors of the allied tribes fled deep into the woods, not to stop this time until they were on the other side of the Ohio River.

Forth from the smoke and flame burst a tall, gaunt frame.

"Long Jim!" cried Henry, seizing his hand. "It's you that's saved us, Jim!"

After him came a fine, ascetic face—the Reverend Silas Pennypacker—and he fairly threw himself upon his beloved pupil, Paul. And then the brave men from Wareville pressed forward, and some from Marlowe, too, welcoming these new people, whom they needed so badly, and who had needed them. But Daniel Poe said solemnly, in the presence of all:

"It is these who saved us in the first instance!"

He indicated the valiant five—Henry Ware, Paul Cotter, Tom Ross, Shif'less Sol Hyde, and Long Jim Hart. And the whole camp, seeing and hearing him, burst into a roar of applause.

The next morning the train resumed its march in peace and safety.

It was a month later, and spring had fully come. Once more the vast wilderness was in deep green, and little wild flowers sprang up here and there where the sun could reach them. Two youths, unusually alert in face and figure, were loading pack horses with heavy brown sacks filled to bursting.

"This powder has kept dry and good all through the winter," said the larger of the youths.

"Yes, Henry," replied the other, "and we are lucky to come back here and be able to take it into Marlowe, after all."

Henry Ware laughed. It was a low, satisfied laugh.

"We have certainly been through many trials, Paul," he said; "but, with Tom, Sol, and Jim, we bore our part in turning the allied tribes back from the great war trail."

Paul Cotter's face was illumined.

"Kentucky is saved," he said, "and I shall be happy all my life because of the knowledge that we helped."

"It is surely a pleasant thought," said Henry.

Then they whistled to their loaded horses, and marched away through the greenwood, this time to reach Marlowe in safety.

THE END